Officially Losing It

Rebecca Anderson

SCHOLASTIC

Published in the UK by Scholastic, 2024
1 London Bridge, London, SE1 9BG
Scholastic Ireland, 89E Lagan Road, Dublin Industrial Estate,
Glasnevin, Dublin, D11 HP5F

SCHOLASTIC and associated logos are trademarks and/or
registered trademarks of Scholastic Inc.

Text © Rebecca Anderson, 2024
Cover illustration and lettering by Jay Roeder © Scholastic, 2024

The right of Rebecca Anderson to be identified
as the author of this work has been asserted by them
under the Copyright, Designs and Patents Act 1988.

ISBN 978 0702 33356 9

A CIP catalogue record for this book
is available from the British Library.

Printed and bound in Great Britain by
Clays Ltd, Elcograf S.p.A.

Paper made from wood grown in sustainable forests
and other controlled sources.

1 3 5 7 9 10 8 6 4 2

www.scholastic.co.uk

To Past Me, for enduring.
To Present Me, for writing the book I needed as a teenager.
To Future Me, who knows this is just the beginning.
And to anyone who sees a part of themselves in these pages.

1

Turns out it's really hard to focus on *Macbeth* when your flaps are on fire. It's never a good idea to dry-shave with a borrowed razor in the sixth-form toilets, but I had no other choice. My own clogged and rusty one betrayed me this morning, leaving me with half my nether regions as bald as Dwayne Johnson and the other half looking like a badly plucked chicken. All I wanted was a DIY Hollywood job and a hair-free bum – is that too much to ask?

Mrs Marston's mouth is moving as she stands at the front of the class, but I'm only catching one word in every five. *Witches. Prophecy. Cawdor.* Bloomin' hell, this burn is unreal. I shift in my seat, trying and failing to get some relief, but even if it wasn't for the fiery flaps I doubt I'd be sitting still. A mix of anxiety and excitement has been swelling inside me over the last week, the flickering spark that ignited after we made The Decision mushrooming to an all-consuming, raging fire as The Moment draws near.

Friday the 3rd of November, 5 p.m. T-minus six hours, thirty minutes.

In case it isn't clear, I, Rose Summers, am having sex with my boyfriend tonight, and I, Rose Summers, am absolutely bricking it. #prayforme

At lunchtime, tucked away in the corner of the common room, Lena and Demi will not stop talking about it. Seeing as I'm the first of us to get this far, they want to know *everything*.

"Did my razor do the trick?" whispers Lena, even though she could have shouted and no one would have heard over the racket of a napping Richard Gomez being tipped head first off a battered sofa by his so-called "friends".

"It's better than it was. Let's leave it at that."

"An asymmetric pube cut is better than contracting life-threatening tetanus from bacteria-riddled blades." Demi snaps shut the politics book she's been sitting with (but not so much as glancing at) and looks at me with intensely green eyes. I'm always in awe of her ability to draw a cat-eye as precise, sharp and beautiful as her personality. "How are you feeling about tonight?"

"I'm excited to see what it's like," I say.

"I bet it will feel pretty darn good if the hype is anything to go by," says Lena, pulling her platinum frizzy hair into two space buns. Her moonstone bracelet clacks, her wrist a merry-go-round of healing crystals for her various ailments. Today she has informed us they are relieving her PMS. "Full moon tonight too. Best time for a shag."

Demi rolls her eyes, thrumming her perfectly manicured red nails against the table. "I'm not convinced. Penetration is only considered the holy grail because men like it. Everyone knows the clit is where it's at. Seventy-five per cent of people with vaginas need that stimulation to orgasm."

Does everyone know this? It does feel good when Joel touches me there, but he's never put his finger inside, so I don't know which is better. I'm still yet to have an orgasm, full stop.

"Holly came the first time she had sex," I point out.

I haven't yet told Holly about my plan to Do It because I wanted to keep it quiet until we'd Done It. She's not part of our core group of three and I worry she's not the most discreet. When I told her I'd given Joel a handjob for the first time, I swear her best mate Monica was looking at me funny in English afterwards.

Demi raises her eyebrows knowingly. "I think she was exaggerating that detail, IMO."

"Don't ruin it for me!" I groan.

"I'm not ruining it for you. I just want you to have realistic expectations."

"I do!"

"Good."

But Demi's still got her know-it-all face on.

"What?" I say.

"How did you know I was going to say something?" Her perfectly groomed eyebrows twist into a look of bemusement.

"You're pulling *that* face," I say.

"You are, to be fair," says Lena.

"OK, you got me. I only want to make sure you're honestly ready, and you're not—"

"I'm one hundred per cent ready," I say. "Joel's perfect and I can't imagine losing it to anyone else. Anyway, I've already promised him now, so—"

"You can change your mind whenever you like, you know," Demi cuts in.

I do know that. But I'm happy with my decision. Yes, I'm scared (understatement), but I'm also excited.

"He's The One," I say. "I *want* to take this next step with him. OK?"

Demi's face softens. "If you're sure. I just wanted to be certain you're doing it for the right reasons."

"Fair," I say, and shuffle to rest my head on her shoulder. "I promise I am."

"I want to be involved in this lovely moment too." Lena scoots over to our side of the bench and rests her head on my shoulder so we form some weird conga line.

I close my eyes and find a moment's respite from my fizzy energy in the fleeting silence. I love my girls, even if Lena hugs trees and Demi is right all the time.

The hellish razor burn continues in Nando's as I try to engage in normal conversation with the love of my life. But not even good chat and peri-peri sauce can quell my rising anticipation about allowing a penis *inside* me. Also, whose stupid idea was it to put on an irritating thong so tiny I could shit and miss it? Oh yeah, it was mine.

"I love the tunes in here." The ginger giant in front of me shimmies his shoulders to the beat. His hair's perfectly tousled in that way where I know he's run his hands through it a million times throughout the day, and happiness radiates off him as he takes a bite of his burger, swaying absent-mindedly to the music. Normally, I'm

5

right there with him, wiggling like an idiot to anything with the hint of a beat (ringtones, doorbells, you name it) but I'm not in the mood. How can Joel be so calm when what we're doing later is massive for both of us? He's a virgin too. He's never really nervous so I wasn't expecting that, but where is the urgency to get me back to his and rip our clothes off?

I turn my attention to my plate of chips, but I can't face eating them and I'm certain the only thing my stomach is capable of right now is rumbling from the anxiety poo I've been brewing since lunchtime. Coming for dinner beforehand seemed like a romantic way to kill time while we waited for Joel's mum, Sonya, to leave for her Pilates class, but on reflection it was a stupid idea. Now my breath probably smells and too much spice gives me awful wind. Oh God, what if I fart?

"Are you nervous?" I whisper.

"Nervous?" Joel stops dancing and frowns. "I'm having sex with the most beautiful girl in Nando's tonight. I'm not sure 'nervous' is the right word." He tugs at his collar and fans himself.

I stare. "What do you mean, *in Nando's?*"

"I obviously mean in the whole world." One eyebrow raises. "Universe?"

I smile. "That's better. I'm a bit nervous, though." *Aka*

my heart is beating so fast I might die before I get a chance to shag you. "Mostly excited?" I don't mean for it to sound like a question.

Joel tilts his head, concern etched on his brow. "What are you worried about?"

"Well, it might hurt a bit. Quite a big thing has to go into something … much smaller." I bite my lip.

"Quite big, you say? Tell me more…" Joel leans in, grinning mischievously.

"Oi! I'm being serious."

Joel reaches for my wrist and strokes it. "Sorry. Don't be nervous. I'll take good care of you. I love you and you love me. It doesn't get more perfect than that."

He meets my gaze, breaking into a grin again. His eyes crease at the corners in the way they do when he's super happy, and freckles are scattered like constellations across his cheeks and nose. He's perfect and he's right. I have nothing to worry about. We just need to get the first time over with, and it won't be long until we're riding the pleasure train to Station Orgasm.

When we get back to Joel's, as expected, there are no cars on the drive. The bright red door of 88 Sylvester Close seems to wink at me, like it knows I'm entering as a virgin and will be exiting as a Person Who's Had Sex.

"I have a request," Joel says, pulling the keys out of his pocket.

"Oh yeah?"

"Can you wait in the living room until I call you?"

"Your wish is my command."

Joel pulls my hand to his lips, kisses it and then leads me through the door.

He disappears upstairs as I kick my shoes off. The laminate floor is cold on my bare feet as I make my way over to the mirror above the sofa.

Will the person looking back at me in an hour be the same person I'm looking at now? I look like normal me, brown hair all done up and make-up a bit extra today. Despite my slightly wide-eyed reflection, I don't look like I'm on the edge of something massive. I turn away and pace the room – nothing good ever comes from staring existentially into a mirror.

When Joel calls for me, my stomach drops so viciously I'm surprised it doesn't fall out of my arse and through the floor. I fumble in my pocket for a mint, chuck it in my mouth and make my way upstairs. It's happening. I'M OFFICIALLY LOSING IT!

I shuffle into the room. Joel's attempted to tidy up for a change, judging by the pile of clothes shoved under the bed (and the lone sock I won't point out draped over the

8

foot of the bed frame). On the windowsill a single candle that looks suspiciously like the one from the bathroom flickers. The room smells like freshly applied aftershave and Listerine mouthwash.

Joel squints from his perch on the bed. "So…" he says expectantly, "is this up to mademoiselle's standards?"

I move towards the bed and sit beside him. "You're an adorable little weirdo, aren't you?" I say affectionately.

"Not sure that's the answer I was looking for, but I heard the word 'adorable' in there, so I'll take that." He pulls me towards him and we lie down, faces centimetres apart.

I smile. "What I mean is, it's not about the candles and stuff. You know I'm not fussy. As long as this is happening with you, that's all that matters."

Joel laughs. "In that case, there's always the alley behind McDonald's if you're game."

For a few minutes we look at each other and smile. Unspoken words hang between us. *What next? Shall we do it now? Who's going to make the first move?*

How can having sex for the first time ever be a natural thing? With all the anxiety coursing through my body, the only physiological response I'm having right now is fight-or-flight. I suspect my food isn't digesting as it should be, so I doubt my vagina is capable of preparing itself for an invasion. But if I don't say anything we might just be smiling and staring at each other like deranged creeps for ever.

"Right, let's do it, shall we?" I bolt upright. Perhaps I should have worded that differently, as it sounds like I'm talking to an execution squad rather than the person who I'm about to have sex with for the first time.

"Romantic," says Joel, but he's smiling like he's Charlie with the Golden Ticket. He's still lying down, and even from my bird's-eye view he's dangerously handsome. The jaw, the chin, the happy eyes and the ginger curls. "Come here then." He reaches for my waist.

I lie back down beside him and we kiss, although my heart is still hammering like mad. Joel runs his fingers through my hair, moving down to stroke the nape of my neck and lower to caress my hips. I try to focus on the gentle tickling sensation as his skin makes contact with mine, but he's not there long before he reaches for the hem of my blouse and pulls it over my head.

"Ooooooh, is this new?" Joel props himself up on one arm and pulls at the strap of my red-lace bra.

"Yep. Bought it especially."

"Shame it's going on the floor in a minute. Saying that, I'd still want to rip your clothes off even if you were wearing granny pants."

10

I want to relax into his touch, but how can I when he's about to be inside me? *Inside* me.

He pulls his own top off and wriggles out of his jeans, then his hands are running up my thighs beneath my skirt. He pulls at my knickers, and I pray I've removed every millimetre of bum hair, as his thumb rests riskily close to that region.

"You … OK?" Joel says between planting kisses on my neck.

"Yeah, really good." It comes out raspy, the words stifled by my dry throat and stunted breaths. I suppose my nerves are doing me a favour in one way because my heavy breathing is coming across like I'm *really* enjoying myself.

He's tugging my knickers off now and they slide down my legs in a second. On cue, Joel's fingers make their way between my legs, but he's only there for a moment before he moves back to my thigh. It's not like usual, when he touches me just to make me feel good. We both know exactly what he's doing; he's seeing if I'm "turned on", like sticking a meat thermometer down there to determine whether I'm ready. Not much is happening, and the more I think about it the drier it feels. *Oh God.* What if he thinks I'm not turned on? *Am* I turned on? I'm not turned *off*, but it's hard to feel especially relaxed or aroused when I'm so hyper-aware of what's coming next.

11

But if he tries to go in while I'm as dry as the Sahara, that's asking for trouble.

"Did you get the lube?" I hope I've said it casually enough.

Nothing in Joel's face suggests he's worried about anything. He leans over to the drawer beside him and pulls out a tube of KY Jelly. It's not the sexiest option, but the bottle says it's the doctor's choice so it's good enough for me. He puts it on the pillow next to me.

"Shall I open it?" I've never used lube before. Do I apply it to myself? Or does Joel?

"Whatever really. Do you want me to?"

"Yes, please." Why do I feel so weird about using lube? Maybe because I feel like I shouldn't need it, because I'm young and in my prime. But I know Demi would tell me that was crap and that lube is for everyone, no matter their age. She's the one who insisted Joel and I buy some before getting down to business.

As I shimmy out of my skirt and snap off my bra, Joel pops the tube open with ease and squirts a gleaming transparent blob on to his finger.

"Shall we?"

"Kiss me first, please," I say, "otherwise it's weird."

Joel shuffles down to my level and kisses me again, his lips finding my neck tenderly. I reach for his hand to guide it. The lube is so cold it squeezes out what little breath I have left.

"Sorry, is that freezing?"

"How could you tell?" I say, but then I relax into Joel's gentle touch.

All too soon, he pulls away. I could ask him to keep going, but I already asked him to kiss me … I don't want to sound too demanding.

"Let me get the condom," he says, leaning across to the bedside table again.

Any pleasure I had started to zone in on ebbs away as Joel pulls a square condom packet from the drawer and flips it over in his hand.

"*Voilà!*" He grins.

"Do you know what you're doing with it?"

"How hard can it be?" Joel tears the packet open with his teeth and lies back on the bed. It's so strange watching him roll the condom down; the image is alien and feels out of place in the relationship I'm usually so familiar with.

"You ready?" he asks.

No. But also…

"Yes."

"Do you want to…?"

"Shall I…?"

"Lie back?"

"Good idea."

We fumble our words and smile, but as I move on to my back and Joel looms over me, I have a sudden desperate urge to wrap my ankles into a protective knot. Joel's warm hands scald my thighs in a less–than–subtle hint for me to open my legs. I look up at the dappled Artex ceiling as I do. It feels like Joel is crushing me, but his chest isn't even touching mine. He shifts into position and leans his hips towards me, his brows knitted as he focuses on what's going where. The unfamiliar feeling of rubber presses up against me and I resist the primal urge to rip myself away.

He looks at me. "All good?"

"Mm-hmm. Yeah, go on."

There's pressure as he pushes and I brace for impact.

Nothing happens.

"Anything?" I say. The wait is excruciating.

"No, it's not giving."

"Keep trying. I'm fine."

He pushes once more, hard.

And then – searing pain.

2

I'm still a virgin.

Despite my "realistic expectations" of first-time sex being a bit awkward or crap, it never crossed my mind I'd leave Joel's without it actually happening at all.

I've been waddling around for the last twenty-four hours because it still stings, and I silently wince every time I sit down, trying to hide my discomfort from my parents and my older sister Sammy.

What happened? I wish I knew the answer.

I know it didn't go in.

I know it hurt like hell.

I know the pain was such a shock I untangled myself, snapped my legs shut and rolled away from Joel to shield myself from his monster penis. I managed to hobble to the bathroom, the throbbing pain growing as the adrenaline faded.

The stinging sensation got worse as I wiped to confirm: a spot of postbox-red blood on the white paper.

I waddled back in and Joel instructed me to lie on the bed so he could inspect the damage. Modesty not being high on my priority list, I did as instructed and I'm trying not to think about what I looked like in that moment because otherwise I might die of shame.

"It looks torn. Don't worry, though, I'm sure it's fine," said Joel, his face saying another thing entirely.

Torn? That wasn't normal, was it? How could it be? This seemed worse than the typical hymen-breaking surely.

"I *am* worried," I said, trying to swallow down the sobs building in my throat.

Joel shifted to the big spoon position and wrapped his arms round me.

"It's OK. I'm sure we aren't the first this has happened to. Next time will be better, I promise." Joel kissed my neck and squeezed me even tighter. He stroked the space just below my ear for the longest time, until Mum was outside to pick me up.

It goes without saying I've already consulted Dr Google but found nothing matching my exact experience. The word "vaginismus" popped up multiple times, so I ended up falling into *that* social media black hole. This one account in particular, MyVagVicki (yes, really), was so horrifyingly open about her vaginismus diagnosis that I was a) worried on her behalf about her dad/grandma/ teachers accidentally stumbling across it, and b) pretty sure I *don't* have that. Vaginismus seems to be more of a muscle spasm thing, where the vagina tightens up on its own to stop anything getting in. Mine seems to be a more external issue.

Now it's been nearly twenty-four hours since the sex fail, I'm coming to the conclusion that the blood *must* have just been from my hymen breaking, so hopefully next time will be better. Although the thought of trying again makes me want to leg it to the nearest convent and join the nuns in their vow of celibacy.

I promised Joel I'd keep him updated with how it's feeling "down there", so I grab my phone and scroll through the notification screen. He's sent me three messages.

Joel: I hope you're doing OK, beautiful. Let me know. I'm worried about you xxxx

Joel: You're amazing xxx

Joel: I love you. U ok? xxxx

Bless him. Unfortunately Joel's lovely messages aren't the only things sitting dormant in my inbox. The girls have been texting *all* day.

Demi: Good morning 😺

Lena: I'm hoping the radio silence is because you two are making luurrrvvve like rabbits

Demi: Oiiiiiiiiiiiiiiiiii

Lena: ?????

Demi: Hey, you can't leave us hanging. Tell us the gossip!!!!!!!

What can I say to that? *Sorry, guys, the only thing I lost last night was my dignity.*

Maybe I can just … not tell them what happened? If I do, there will be millions of questions, especially from Demi, and I don't know how to answer them. *Ugh*, I'll decide tomorrow. I can't cope with thinking any more about it tonight.

★

It's now Sunday and with my mocks coming up fast, revising is a decent excuse for shutting myself in my room. So far I've managed to avoid Sammy too.

Sammy is six years older than me and has this superpower where she just *knows* when something's up with me. I didn't tell her about my plans to shag Joel because I didn't want her lecturing me or talking me out of it — and also she might have told Mum. Mum, being able to successfully make everything in life about uni at the moment, would somehow convince herself the reason I haven't sorted out my UCAS application is because I'm *sexually active*, even though the two aren't mutually exclusive. The truth is I just don't know what subjects to pick or where to do them.

I can't avoid everyone for ever, though, as the sound of our roast dinner being plated up reminds me.

"Why have you got a face like a slapped arse?" Sammy says as soon as I enter the dining room. She's still in her work clothes, which have seen better days, and her hair's pulled back into a messy bun. As usual, she's not got a scrap of make-up on. When it comes to her looks, she has a no-fucks-given attitude. She's unapologetically herself, and I love her for it.

"It's just my face," I say. "Blame Dad." Big thanks to him for my inherited resting-miserable face. "Why have you got snot all over you?"

Sammy's work overalls are always disgusting. I guess that's what happens when you work with small children. Saying this, being a primary teacher is something she's wanted since we were tiny and she *adores* her job. I want that too: to find something I know in my soul is my dream career, even despite my co-workers sneezing – and occasionally pooping – on me. Unfortunately that dream career continues to elude me, much to the annoyance of Miss Starmann, the head of sixth form.

"Oh my God. I don't, do I?"

I nod. "You look like a walking snot rag."

"Back in two." She runs out of the door.

As she goes, I can't help wondering if we have the same vagina. Maybe I should be brave and talk to her, but I can't imagine a way into that conversation. If she did have any issues, wouldn't I know by now?

Sammy strides back in and flops on to her chair. "Better? Are you sure you're all ri—"

"Anyone for a Yorkie?" Dad cuts her off as he enters the room, followed by Mum carrying a gigantic pile of Yorkshire puddings. It's enough to distract us both. It's only Mum – adorned in her standard floral tunic top that always smells like Soap & Glory shower wash – yet I'm overcome with a sudden rush of love for the woman who pushed my *entire being* out of her vagina. Not all heroes wear capes; some wear Bonmarché and George at Asda. I sidle up to her and plant a kiss on her cheek.

"My lovely Rose," she says with a small smile, and for a millisecond I feel a bit lighter.

In my opinion, you're never too old to act like a toddler when your mum's concerned – I'll still be sitting on her lap when I'm thirty.

Please, god of genitals, make sure I won't still be a virgin by then.

3

On the bus on Monday, I'm squished between the window and a grumpy year eleven who smells like BO and smoke. In the minimal space I have, I struggle to take in breaths deep enough to keep me alive – well, that's what it feels like anyway.

I know Lena and Demi are going to be waiting for me to arrive, brimming with questions and fizzing with expectation. I palmed them off with a text saying "I'll tell you about it in great detail on Monday" to get them off my back, but now Monday is here I'm panicking. They'll want to know everything. How can I tell them what happened when I don't even know myself? I'm *so* glad Joel doesn't go to our school. He has one afternoon a week here for a photography class, seeing as our school is the only one in the borough with a dark room, but he's a student at Abbot Academy on the other side of town.

The bus swings round the final corner and through the gates of Mulberry High School, narrowly missing a group of idiotic year nines, which causes the driver to swear under his breath. I spot Lena's unmistakable white-blonde hair in the sea of navy blazers and swallow down the little bit of sick that shoots up and tickles the back of my throat.

As expected, Lena and Demi dive straight in without even a hello.

"Tell us everything," says Demi, linking her arm through mine with Lena following suit.

"How did it go?" says Lena.

"I want all the details, even the gory ones." Demi looks like she's one step away from making notes. But I don't think she has actual blood in mind.

As they march me to our picnic bench at the edge of the field, I take in their expectant faces and run through my options.

"It went … fine."

Decision made. Fabricate the truth.

"Fine? Just fine?" Demi wrinkles her nose and cocks her head. I avoid making eye contact.

"You let a boy put his phallus in your sacred cave three

23

days ago and all you have to say is that it was fine?" Lena's mouth is agape.

Of course they aren't buying it. I know my audience better than to fob them off with a "fine".

"All right, it was better than fine. It was really nice."

I'm no good at this.

"I suppose that's a bit better than 'fine'." Lena pulls out a breakfast bar and munches on it. "What did it feel like?" she says with her mouth full. "Did it hurt?"

Oh, you have no idea.

"No, not really." Why did that lie fall so easily out of my mouth?

"Bet it felt weird, though."

"Yeah, a bit uncomfortable at first."

Wow, the lies keep coming.

Demi seems to have forgiven my lack of enthusiasm and in true Demi style asks all the important questions in quick-fire succession. There's a reason she's doing Law at uni.

"Did he finish?"

"Yeah."

"Did you?"

To say yes to that would be one lie too far.

"What do you think?" I snort. "I'll learn to walk before I learn to run."

Lena nods. "Fair enough."

"No, not fair enough! It's not all about him." Demi hits both fists on the table. "I demand you have an orgasm next time. Do it for me."

Lena and Demi laugh and I attempt to join in, but my gut is heavy. Should I feel bad for spreading fake information and lulling them into a false sense of security? But then surely my experience isn't the norm. If it is, then the women in my life have a lot of explaining to do.

"Maybe try some tantra next time." Lena's eyes are wide and faraway-looking. I don't know what planet she's on most of the time, but it seems pretty bloody great. "Ooooh. Mum's running a body–mind connection yoga session on Sunday at the centre. You both fancy it? Might help you relax into the whole sex thing too."

"Can't, I'm afraid," says Demi. "Helping Mum out on the market that morning."

I nod. "Sure, sign me up." Lena's mum, Lola, is the manager of a wellness centre called Authentic Soul, which runs exercise and meditation classes. I haven't been since I threw up and fainted during a hot yoga session, but I'm willing to try anything at this point.

Lena looks like she's ready to impart some further wisdom, but I'm done with talking about non-existent sex for today.

"To summarize, it was good, it happened and I'll be sure to butt-dial you guys next time so you can listen in. Now please leave it – Holly's coming." Holly is getting dangerously close so I blurt out the next bit. "Oh, and don't say anything to Joel when he's here on Thursday – I don't want to embarrass him."

Demi grins. "Surely he knows we talk in great detail about his penis."

"MOVING ON," I say. "Oh, hi, Holly."

"'Ellooo. Have I missed anything?" Holly chucks her bag on the bench and scoots in beside Demi.

"Nope," I say quickly. "I've got a meeting with Miss Starmann this morning, though. Wish me luck."

Demi shakes her head. "So your UCAS application is still a shitshow?"

"Oi!" I swat at her. "Shitshow is … harsh."

Holly grimaces. "Ouch."

"Am I wrong, though?"

"Well, no." I shake my head. "I'm no closer to a decision – shock horror."

Demi scowls. "Balls."

Phew, it seems like we are moving into safer territory. Well, ish. The UCAS deadline is at the end of January, which sounds far away, but if you factor in Christmas and my mocks, I'm stressing big time.

I'm hoping Miss Starmann will say some magic words and I'll leave the meeting with a finalized personal statement and a firm, unwavering choice. And pigs might fly.

"Let's do some prep before your meeting." Demi reaches into her bag and pulls out a notepad and pen with a flourish. Here we go.

Lena catches my eye sympathetically. Holly is clearly uninterested, frowning at her phone and texting away. It's probably her ex, Robert. She's pretty fresh from their break-up, and things have been far from amicable. One minute they're enemies and the next they're texting like nothing's happened. None of us can keep up.

"OK, so you're pretty sure you want to do something Biology-related, yeah?" says Demi as she scribbles on the pad. "So, if you want options, you could do Marine Biology, Human Biology, Molecular Biology, Life Sciences, Anatomy, Microbiology…"

"Oh my God, stop listing them! Biology is interesting but I'm not sure I want to base my whole career around one class I like." We've been over this before.

There's also another thing in the mix – Joel. He's doing a Ceramic and Glass degree at the University of Sunderland. There's a Biomedical Science course there, and despite the fact that I'm not sold on it, I'm debating putting it down as an option. After all, Joel is literally the only thing I'm one hundred per cent certain about. Also, now I'm having an awful thought – what if Joel and I don't have sex by the time we leave for uni and he decides on a drunken night out that he can't be arsed to wait for me and loses his V with a beautiful sexually experienced girl? I know I'm being ridiculous, but it feels like even more of an incentive to go with him.

Demi taps the pen on the table, bringing me out of one nightmare and into another. "Oi," she says, "are you listening to me?"

"Yes!" I say more forcefully than intended.

Lena coughs. "I say do what you enjoy and screw worrying about a career at this stage."

That's easy for her to say. She's found a course that has basically been made for her – Spirituality and Transpersonal Psychology – whatever the hell that is. "Just pick something. Future Rose will thank you for sure."

"How do you know that? Future Rose might hate me. What if I change my mind in the future and wish I'd done Maths?" I'm dangerously close to wailing.

"Do you want to do Maths?" asks Demi.

"No, I hate it."

"Stop chatting shit then."

Lena, always the peacekeeper, butts in. "Even if you pick the wrong course, it will be the right one."

Demi and I look at her like she's just grown a bum on her forehead.

I'm confused. "That makes no sense."

Lena looks at us as if saying *Duh*. "It does. It's either going to set you up for your future career, or you can learn a karmic lesson from it and then do something else."

"But then I'll be three years behind and have to start all over again! And think of the student loans!"

"You don't want that," agrees Demi.

Lena crosses her arms. "Trust the universe will present to you exactly what you need, when you need it. Bish, bash, bosh. Job's a good 'un. Thanks, Universe." She looks towards the heavens, which look dangerously close to dropping their load of torrential rain on our heads.

"You don't *have* to go to uni, you know. Do a college course like me," says Holly, reminding us she's still here and is actually listening, despite still not looking up from her phone.

I have considered this option – kind of. Maybe I could take a year out? But Lena, Demi and Joel are all going to uni. I'd be stuck at home. Holly will be too busy on her flight-attendant course making new friends and jet-setting to hang out with me. I'd need to get a temp job to save money – and what if I got stuck doing that for ever?

"It's the same problem. I don't know what I want to be when I grow up."

"Says the person who's going to be eighteen on her next birthday," Demi says dryly.

I nudge her. "I'm an August baby! Cut me some slack."

Holly stands, finally putting her phone in her pocket. "Right, I'm off to find Monica. Laters."

She leaves the three of us sitting in silence.

"I'm still thinking of applying to Sunderland," I blurt out.

Lena and Demi exchange a look. I had a feeling they might make this a Big Deal. Let interrogation number two commence.

"I'm not sure you should base your choices on Joel..." Lena starts picking her nails.

I prickle. "I thought you said whatever choice I make now is the right one?"

"Lena's right – Joel is not a reason to pick a uni. My cousin went with her boyfriend and it didn't end well. Do you even like any of the courses at Sunderland?"

I suck a breath in through my teeth and exhale.

Lena gets there first. "Look, it's your choice at the end of the day, Rose. Trust your gut. You know what to do." She smiles and I can see she means it.

"Mmmm," says Demi without the same enthusiasm.

"I will," I say confidently, but inwardly I'm screaming

at my gut for its inability to give me any clear signals aside from sheer terror or the need to fart.

In Miss Starmann's office she surveys me over a pile of folders and three empty mugs. We've just talked in circles again about my A level subjects: English, Biology and Psychology.

"I'm assuming, seeing as we've got this far in the process, you do actually want to go to university?" she says.

Of course I want to go to uni. Sammy's always banging on about how her years at Warwick were the best of her life. I can't miss out on the best years of my life now, can I?

"I definitely want to go." I notice a ladder in my tights that wasn't there this morning.

"You're in an advantageous position. You're an intelligent girl and you will excel at whatever you choose. It would be a huge shame for you to not grab this opportunity with both hands."

She literally sounds exactly like Mum.

I know she's right, so now I feel confused and ungrateful. Such a first-world problem – I can be anything I like and do anything I want; woe is me. But when there are so many paths to take, how do you choose the right one?

"It is tough having to make these decisions at your age. I get it. A lot of people don't know what they want to do until well into their thirties. Sometimes never!"

Thirties? Never? Oh, man.

"But you need to put something down." Miss Starmann shifts forward in her seat. "What about Biology *and* Psychology for now?"

I didn't realize putting two courses was an option. The cogs in my mind start whirring.

"Could I apply to two different courses at the same uni?" I ask.

"Yes, nothing's stopping you from doing that. Then you can decide in June. We'd have to work on your statement because you can only submit one for all applications, but I can help with that. Let's talk again in a couple of weeks, yes?"

Miss Starmann smiles weakly and hands me some papers, as if they'll magically steer me on to the perfect life path.

Fat chance of that.

4

It's Saturday and Joel and I are wandering hand in hand around the Galaxy shopping centre. It's a bit of a shithole, but in Dad's words: it's *our* shit'ole. As always, it's full of harried families dragging bored children around Primark and elderly couples on their weekly trip to M&S.

But today feels different. I keep looking at the people around me and wondering how their sex life is and how it compares to mine (or lack thereof). I wouldn't be surprised if even the old lady who just shuffled past me in Superdrug has a more exciting time in the bedroom, and I'm sure I saw her husband pat her bum by the laxative section.

It's been a week since our failed attempt and I can't stop thinking about it.

I'm also hyper-aware of all the young, attractive women

here, which I'm never usually bothered by. When I spot one, I find myself glancing at Joel to see if he's clocked them too, though he seems oblivious. Ugh. The last thing I want to do is to turn into some insecure monster.

One thing that hasn't changed is that we've hardly done any shopping; we mostly come to town just to get out of the house and mooch around. Today, wandering around Superdrug, I've taken the opportunity to update Joel on my lack of future plans.

"Forget what anyone else thinks and come to Sunderland then," Joel says while chucking Haribos in his mouth.

Like it's that easy.

"What if something happens between us? Then I'll look like an idiot."

I'm not completely naive. Joel and I breaking up doesn't seem likely, but it's possible. I strongly believe we're soulmates – I think he's my One – but what if I'm wrong?

"I'm offended you'd even think we'd break up." He offers me the bag of sweets and I shake my head.

"Of course I don't think we would; it's just…" My voice trails off. Lines of exotic lube and colourful multipacks of condoms leer down at me from the shelves. Of all the aisles we could end up in, it's contraception and pregnancy. "I'm not sold on the Biomed course at Sunderland." I look at the floor and up my pace.

"Are you sold on *any* courses, though?" Joel's eyes linger on the overfilled shelves.

"No."

"Well, there you go. May as well do a course you're not sold on near *me*."

He's got a point.

We reach the end of the offending aisle and find ourselves surrounded by shampoo and conditioner. My muscles soften. I slide my arm round Joel's waist and lean into him. He kisses my head and we let out the collective breath we've been holding.

"Look," says Joel, "I'm not forcing you to do anything. I want you to go where you'll be happy, but wouldn't it be great to get a flat in the second year together, like proper adults?"

"And halls in the first year?" I say, imagining introducing ourselves to future friends as a united pair. I turn away and examine some toothpaste. For some reason, I can't look at Joel while we talk about this.

"Yeah, defo halls in first year – get the proper fresher experience."

"Mmmm," I say. "It does sound fun."

I want to say screw it. I want to follow my heart and

35

not my head for a change. But if I do, what if I end up regretting it?

"Turn round."

I take a deep breath and spin round to see Joel on one knee, holding out a red-and-yellow Haribo ring and grinning like the Cheshire Cat. "Will you go to uni with me?" he says.

"Get up, you wally!" I reach for his hand and pull, but he stays rooted to the floor. I giggle. "People might see."

"Will you go to uni with me?" Joel repeats, pulling me down to his level. His eyes are sparkling with sincerity. He really wants this. I do too.

"Yes." I hold my finger out for him to slide the ring on and check again to make sure no one's watching. "Now can we get up? My legs hurt." I can't stop myself from smiling.

"*Your* legs are hurting? I'll be surprised if I still have a kneecap by the time I get up!"

I stand and heave Joel to his feet. "You are such a soppy bollock," I say, before leaning into him and pecking him on the nose.

"I'll be anything to make you happy, both soppy and a bollock," says Joel, beaming. He pulls my hand towards him and admires the ring. "It'll be real one day," he says softly. "I've already thought about different ways I could ask you."

My stomach flips and my whole body tingles. "Have you?"

"Yep. Not soon, obviously – we're too young. But one day. I've never been surer of anything in my life."

I grin. "Aww, me neither. You're the one and only bollock I can see myself marrying."

"Is it because I'm the total package?"

"I see what you did there."

Joel laughs. "Enough of the testicle puns. Now let's get back to my place because all this teasing is driving me *nuts*."

Back at Joel's, I'm sitting on his bed while he's rummaging around in the wardrobe.

"I've got a present for you," he says, fiddling with something in front of him.

"Let me guess, you've got your dong out already?"

Joel turns round with his flies firmly done up, holding a small package wrapped in lilac crêpe paper.

"How dare you!"

We both laugh.

"What's the occasion?" I say.

"No occasion, just you being you. Last weekend was pretty crappy for you. I want to make it better."

I don't know what to say.

Joel moves to sit beside me, donning his signature smile with its adorable lopsided squint, and, just like that, my heart is back to feeling so full it might explode.

"Here."

The crêpe paper crunches as I turn the parcel over in my hands. It's much heavier than I expect.

My cheeks flush. "Don't watch me. I'm feeling self-conscious."

Joel turns away. "As you wish. Can't be having madam feeling shy now, can we?" He peeks briefly back over his shoulder, killing me yet again with *that* smile.

I rip off the paper and admire the solid, smooth object. It's made of clay – no surprise there, given ninety per cent of Joel's gifts to me are made by his fair hands. I wouldn't have it any other way.

I found out he liked to sculpt on our first official date, two days after we met, almost eleven whole months ago. When I asked, *What are your hobbies?* (a first date prompt I found on Google), he replied with many seventeen-year-old boy clichés like playing Xbox. In fairness, if he'd said he liked opera singing and fox hunting, my chicken wings and I would've left Nando's immediately. I'd kept pushing. *Come on, you must have a hobby. Everyone has one, right?* said I, a girl with no hobbies. He'd finally told me he was a potter. *Not to be confused with a pothead – I'm not into smoking weed*, he'd said with a laugh. He is, however, into ceramics so much he's got his heart set on going to Sunderland University next year to study it. It's both amazing to have a boyfriend who enjoys doing more than browsing Pornhub and hanging out with "the lads", and also massively crap seeing as the uni is three hundred miles away.

I turn this latest creation over several times, but I can't work out what it is. It's a flat dish with a small erect sausage of clay sticking up from the middle.

"Have you opened it yet?"

"Yes, it's … interesting," I say. "What is it?"

Joel turns round and uncovers his eyes. "Guess."

"A 'to scale' artistic impression of your nob?"

"To scale? Right, give it back." Joel lunges for it and I throw myself back on to the pillow, laughing, dish still in hand. Then he's on top of me, the tip of his nose touching mine. He holds me down by my wrists, his touch gentle.

"I'm sorry," I say. "I love it. What is it, though?"

His warm breath tickles my lips before he draws back.

"It's a ring holder. I remember you said you didn't have anywhere to keep your rings."

A warm feeling rises within me. Until I met Joel, I thought this type of person only existed as the main character in a romcom, not as a lead character in my actual real life.

Joel loosens his grip and I sit up enough to put the ring holder on the bedside table. "Thank you," I say. "I'm very lucky."

"I'm the lucky one," Joel says with a shrug. "Now about this 'to scale' business. Need I remind you your measurements are way off…?" His hands find my wrists again and he wrestles me back down on to the pillow. We're nose to nose again and his eyes glint before his lips meet mine.

I want to relax into the kiss, but my muscles stiffen. I'm back to that moment just before our painful encounter – back in that space where Joel's kisses are solely part of the warm-up.

"Just kisses and naked cuddles?" I say.

Joel nods and kisses my forehead. "Just kisses and naked cuddles."

My whole body melts into the mattress. Any worries about university and another painful sex attempt speedily disappear along with Joel's swiftly removed T-shirt.

5

Lena's waiting for me outside the yoga centre as we pull up in the car. Mum and Dad gave me a lift because the centre is literally a bunch of converted barns in the arse end of nowhere. I hop out and wave to them as they head off for brunch somewhere in town and are entrusting Lena's brother River to drop me home in one piece after the class.

Lena grins, instantly brightening up the grey November day. Alongside the damp mist, the scent of incense hangs in the air, hinting at the serenity on the other side of the doors.

I'm feeling more confident than last time, knowing this class is not going to be conducted in desert-worthy temperatures.

"Fancy seeing you here," I say, pulling Lena into a hug. I can tell she's already been inside because she smells like lemongrass and sage. She's probably been helping her mum set up for the class.

"Are you ready to fully align your body and mind?" she asks.

"I thought you were going to say 'chakras', for a minute," I say, and laugh.

Lena laughs too. "Well, that's just a given. Shall we go in? My chakras are freezing their tits off out here."

I follow Lena in to the front desk, where a guy around our age is typing away on a computer. He has tanned skin and curly black hair and is rather attractive.

"Two here for yoga," announces Lena, gesturing at me. "Lena and Rose."

The boy smiles and looks perplexed at the same time. "You know you don't have to check in. I know who you are."

"Just making sure you're doing your job properly – keeping you on your toes," quips Lena.

Despite this being Lena's "year of dating myself" – she's one of those naturally charismatic people, flirty and friendly. Perhaps lovely auras and aligned chakras are more useful than they sound.

"As always," the boy says, and grins. He pretends to

type on the keyboard and nods. "You're all checked in." His smile is very charming.

Lena shakes her head fondly. "You're a muppet."

"You're welcome. Have a good sesh!" he calls after us.

I follow Lena out of reception and through the courtyard to the main yoga barn. "Who's that?"

"Omar. He's an absolute babe."

"He seems nice."

"He is. Not bad-looking either." Lena gives me the cheeky side-eye.

"Could he make you change your mind about dating yourself this year?" I tease.

"Nope. I'm not interested in him in that way."

I can tell she means it. Lena really is one in a million.

We shuffle into the main hall, where the walls are painted in calming pastels and what sounds like whale noises are playing in the background. Lena and I grab mats and set up in a cosy corner. I always like to be at the back in case I look funny in the positions, need a rest halfway through or – God forbid – let one rip. Lena says it happens all the time and that the sound of a queef or two is as commonplace as meditation chants and whale song.

Mummy Lola, with her flowing hair the same colour as Lena's and a serene smile, glides past. There's a warmth in her eyes that makes me feel instantly at home.

43

Lena moves to lie on her stomach and props herself up with her elbows. "Hopefully this class will help you connect to your body more," she says. Then adds in a whisper: "Get that orgasm."

Ah yes – my elusive orgasm. If I haven't managed to give myself one, I doubt that Joel will be able to. But I guess learning how to be more zen will be helpful anyway and might actually mean I'm relaxed enough for Joel to gain entry.

"I know it will happen one day," I say confidently, moving to lie next to her.

She frowns. "How can you be so sure?"

"I guess it's just one of those things that happens for everyone. It's natural." *Yeah, but so is sex, and you're not yet able to do that…* "I've felt close to something big before, but then I lose it. I either get in my own head or Joel moves away from the spot."

"Why do you think you get in your own head? Do you think you're scared?"

"Maybe. The idea of being so out of control is pretty scary, not knowing what to expect or how I might act. What if I make weird noises or pull stupid faces?"

"Everyone does."

"Do you?"

"Dunno," says Lena. "I—"

"Good morning, everyone." Lola's voice floats across the room, firm and gentle at the same time. Lena and I shift into a cross-legged position.

As we've been chatting, the rest of the class has trickled in, and to my relief it's a small group. I know what's coming next.

"We will start the class with a quick introduction to who we are and why we're here, before going into a brief meditation. Find out who we're sharing our sacred space with."

I stifle a giggle. *Sacred space* totally sounds like a euphemism.

As we go round the room, I learn that I'm sharing my sacred space with a lawyer, a teacher, a stay-at-home mum and a counsellor.

The counsellor's name is Jacqui and she has the type of presence that feels calm and authoritative at the same time. She says she needs to look after herself in order to serve her clients. My stomach pings as I imagine going up to her and asking if she's ever had a client with a problem like mine.

Everyone adds something profound about why they're here, like *I'm here to honour my body* and *I'm here to access my body's wisdom*, and when it's my turn I freeze. What do I say? *Hello, my name is Rose and I'm here because my friend thinks I want to learn how to orgasm during sex, but, in actual fact, when I tried to have sex it didn't even work, so I'm as far away from that outcome as I am from Mars.*

Obviously I don't say that. I just mutter something about needing to relax.

The class begins. Mummy Lola leads us through a guided meditation before we get into poses. I follow Lena's lead, trying to mimic her movements at the same time as trying to feel my way into my body, with a *mindset of curiosity and open attention*, as instructed.

"This," says Mummy Lola, "is about mind–body connection. What are they saying to each other?"

It's far less peaceful than I had envisaged because the only thing my mind is saying to my body is, *WHAT THE HELL IS WRONG WITH YOU? WHY CAN'T YOU HAVE SEX?* Except for when we move into downward dog, when it says, *Don't fart, don't fart, don't fart.* I don't, luckily. How's that for mind–body connection?

6

Over the last two weeks, my vagina has healed and is back to her original self. Note I didn't say *normal* self because whether or not she's normal remains to be seen. I'm still terrified about letting Joel anywhere near it, but I need to move forward. I don't really want to stay a virgin for ever, tempting though the nun idea is. And it doesn't feel fair to make Joel wait much longer than he already has. The other day he mentioned how his mate Tom slept with two girls on the same night. Although Joel didn't say much else about it, I still feel like I need to get a shift on. I'd hate to think he's feeling like he's getting a bum deal stuck with frigid old me.

This weekend Sonya is away for a Pilates retreat. Before we realized my vagina saw itself as Area 51 (strictly no entry), Joel and I had plans to shag all over the house – plans well and truly ruined. However, I have an idea of how we can still use this free time to our advantage.

Rose: This weekend … maybe instead of going straight for full P in V again, we could try to build up to it step by step. Thoughts?

Joel: Whatever feels most comfortable for you, boo x

Rose: It's a plan. Can we give it a name so it doesn't sound so weird?

Joel: Excellent idea

Rose: Quest 4 Sex? Fanny Business?

Joel: Mission Quimpossible?

Rose: Ewww. Hahaha. Quim? WTF

Joel: Don't google that. OMG. Noooo, I've got it!

Rose: ??

Joel: Operation Penetration

Rose: Perfect!! See you later for our first mission xxxx

Pre sex fail, we'd probably have gone to the Rexwood cinema before making our way home slowly, teasing each other with cheeky kisses and wandering hands. Instead, I'm sitting on Joel's bed, cross-legged and butt naked beneath the duvet. I've wrapped myself in it like a weird shawl, tugging it tightly over my shoulders and desperate to disappear into its warm grasp. My nude body is obviously nothing Joel hasn't seen before, but with all the lights on and not being in the heat of the moment, being the only one in the buff feels wrong.

"Ready?" Joel's standing by the door after coming back from the bathroom. He looks at me in a way that makes me want to shrink even further into the duvet and abort this mission completely.

"I feel shy," I mutter.

"Oh no. I don't want you to feel shy. What can I do to make you feel better?" Joel sinks down on to the bed beside me, crosses his legs too and looks at me with concern. It makes me feel worse.

"Dunno."

"Hmm." He sits very still for a second before he jumps up. "I've got an idea." He strides out of the door.

"Erm, OK?" I say to the empty room.

I trace the lines on the duvet with my finger, following their warped paths in a bid to distract myself.

"Close your eyes," Joel calls from the hallway.

"Come in and put me out of my misery." I'm grateful he's trying to make me feel better, but can't we just get this over with?

"Fine… Ta–da!"

It takes me a few seconds to compute what I'm seeing. Joel. Starkers. Swinging free with zero embarrassment. Wearing just socks and a straw hat. Lube in hand.

"What the…?" I splutter.

"Do you like it?"

What a question.

"Why are you naked? Why have you got socks on?" As I take in the ridiculous sight, I can't help but laugh. I allow the duvet to inch a bit further down my shoulders.

"I want to make you feel better. There's now no denying the only ridiculous thing in this room right now is me."

"I can't argue with that." I drop the duvet down a little further so it sits round my waist. Although my entire chest is bare, Joel's eyes don't leave mine.

He sits back down next to me. "You still OK with doing this?"

I think for a minute. Yes. I want to have sex with him and I want to fix this.

"I'd rather not *have* to do it, but I definitely want to." I take a deep breath and lift up the duvet to invite Joel under it before I change my mind. "Let's do it."

"Yes, Captain," says Joel, chucking the lube into the air with a spin and getting into position next to me. We roll to face each other.

"Do you want me to kiss you or anything?" Joel suddenly looks nervous.

"Not with you looking like that." I move on to my back and look up at him. His straw hat looms over me and I burst out laughing again.

"I think I look rather fetching."

"Like a fecking idiot more like…"

"OK, I'll do you a deal. I'll lose the hat but keep the socks. Agreed?"

"Agreed."

Joel chucks the hat off like a Frisbee and it flies out of the open door.

"Good shot."

"Thanks," says Joel before he plants a kiss on my forehead. "So one finger in. Yes to kissing and touching or no?"

I think for a second. Logically, kissing and foreplay

makes sense, because I know how important relaxing is. However, I know that no matter how much Joel kisses me, or how much I try to breathe in for seven and out for eleven, I'm not going to chill. "Nah, let's just get on with it. I appreciate you asking, though."

Joel nods and I close my eyes. Hear the unsexy squelch of the lube being decanted. Brace for the cold goo. Wait for the pain.

I wince. "Ouch."

"Sorry," Joel mumbles.

I sigh. "Not your fault. Perhaps if we wait a second, my body will get used to it."

"Sure. I'll follow your lead."

Silence. I try to think of something to say, but I'm too sore to think. And then—

"Vagina says no," Joel says, totally deadpan and thawing the awkwardness in an instant.

"Don't make me laugh," I beg, desperately trying to hold a giggle in. I'm afraid to laugh in case it makes the fiery sting worse.

"I can't help that I am naturally hilarious."

"I can't imagine this is a normal rite of passage to losing your virginity, can you?"

"Normal is overrated." Joel rubs my shoulder with the palm of his free hand.

"We'll laugh about this one day," I say, as much to reassure myself as anything else.

"I'll make a note for the wedding speech."

"Don't you dare." It's a throwaway comment but his mention of marriage again soothes the part of me that needs to know he's in this for the long haul. "Promise you'll never tell anyone about this."

"Of course I wouldn't!" Outrage is palpable in Joel's voice, but I need more.

"Promise."

"I promise. Boys don't talk about the sort of stuff girls do, not in so much detail anyway."

"Tom does."

"Tom's full of crap."

Reassured, I turn my attention back to Joel's fingertip.

"How does it feel?" I ask.

"Tight. Really tight." He removes himself from me.

I slide away from him and lie back on the bed. He shuffles closer beside me and puts his head in the crook of my neck so his curls tickle my chin. I let out a huge sigh – a mix of relief from no longer being attached to Joel's finger and also frustration that progress seems near impossible.

Operation Penetration is a failure so far.

"I've got an idea," he says, climbing out of bed and making his way across the room. "Can you put my headphones on and stay here so you can't hear or see what I'm doing? Also, put this on." Joel grabs the dressing gown from the hook on the back of his door and hands it to me.

"Please don't come back in with that hat on again."

"I won't. Now headphones on." Joel pulls his knock-off Beats over my ears and fiddles with his phone. "I know just the song."

I squint at him for a moment before the sound of OMC's "How Bizarre" blares into my ears. It's not exactly a love song, but it was playing during our first kiss at Holly's and it feels oddly appropriate now. I can't help but smile.

Joel gives me a thumbs up and mouths something – presumably "Can you hear me?" – before his bare arse walks out of the room.

I reach for my phone and scroll. There's a video of a pig using buttons to communicate to his owner. Cute. Scroll. A dog video. A cat video. Scroll. A video skit of a couple titled *Are you lovers or roommates? Five reasons why sex is important in a relationship*. Really, algorithm? One more scroll. An influencer's photo captioned *Love my eyes in this pic* while facing away from the camera wearing dental floss for underwear. I zoom. How is her arse that flawless?

"Boo." The headphones are yanked off my ears. I lock my phone quickly, hoping Joel didn't see the screen.

"Come with me." He grins and moves behind me to cover my eyes. I sink back into the safety of his chest and let his weight gently guide me forward. We stop about five steps from his bedroom.

"*Voilà*," he says, uncovering my eyes.

We're in the bathroom, candles dotting the edge of the bath and their flickering flames reflecting and distorting in the still, steaming water.

"I know this was one of the things we had planned for the weekend," says Joel, scratching his head and smiling. "It can still be special."

"I… You… I love it. I love you," I say. "What a gent you are."

I step towards him and wrap my arms round his waist, kissing under his jawbone.

"I love you too," he says. He pulls at the dressing-gown tie. "May I?"

I nod and the gown drops to the floor. Joel takes my hand and guides me to the edge of the bath.

"In you get. You can have the side without the taps too. How's that for gentlemanly?"

7

Here we go again. I find Lena and Demi sitting at our bench ten minutes before form time. Their faces are eager and their heads are cocked with intrigue the minute they spy me.

"How was your weekend of sex and depravity then?" says Demi in her usual delicate way.

Every time I've seen Joel in the last two weeks, they've asked me whether we've done it again yet, and I've answered that with an honest no. I've told them that Sonya's been around or I've been on my period. But I'd been talking about this weekend for ages and Demi has a memory like an elephant.

I hate lying to them, but I don't want to admit the truth either. I know I can say the right things; it's just whether

I'll look the part. What does someone look like if they've had a solid three days of wonderful sex? Is their hair more luscious? Do they have a glint in their eye that I'm missing? What will give me away as a fraud?

"It was as filthy as planned," I say, hearing the words come out of my mouth and wanting to stuff them back in.

Demi whoops. "Yes, girl!" She grabs my elbow and squeezes. "Tell all."

"Please and thank you." Lena shuffles towards me so I'm now sandwiched between the two of them.

"Are you sure about that?" I say to buy time.

"Positive." They're fizzing with expectation.

And so the lies must continue.

"OK, so, when I got there I thought we'd watch a film and then, well, you know what happens when we 'watch a film'…" I let the girls fill that part in. "But the minute I walked through the door we started kissing and one thing led to another and then we … had sex." I stop.

"I need to know more, I'm afraid," says Demi.

"Mmm," says Lena, her eyes narrowing. "Me too."

Is she not buying it?

"Between the hallway and the living room all clothes came off. Then we did all sorts of positions we've never done before, pretty much everything you can think of except me being flipped upside down."

Have I gone too far now? I glance at Lena, but her eyes are wide in awe.

"How magical," she says.

"You sex goddess!" Demi is proud of fantasy me. She slaps me hard on the back.

They're definitely buying it – all I can see in their faces is joy and a hint of jealousy.

"After that, we had a bath together, candles and everything. Then we ordered pizza." At least that's true. "Then it was time to go to bed … and we did it again, obviously." I'm getting into this now.

"Twice in less than eight hours." Demi holds up two fingers. "Not bad."

"Yep. And again when we woke up."

"Three." Lena holds up three fingers to join the tally.

Why am I getting so carried away? Maybe because I've dreamt of this weekend a thousand times before my fantasy was well and truly crushed by reality. I'm going to enjoy my moment because, damn it, I deserve it.

"We went to town on Saturday, but I won't bore you with that because it gets really interesting when we come home to cook and I end up sitting on the kitchen counter with my knickers round my ankles. Let's just say dinner was well and truly forgotten."

"I don't know whether to be disgusted, proud or

turned on," says Demi. "Certainly making up for the last two weeks by the sounds of things." I've never seen her so impressed before. It feels as good as it feels absolutely awful.

"Tell me you wiped the counters down afterwards," says Lena. "Anything else?"

I open my mouth to continue the charade, but the bell rings, stopping me mid-flow, and I fall back down to earth with a great big virginal bump.

After school, I'm back on MyVagVicki's account, scrolling her feed endlessly when I should be asleep or revising for my imminent mock exams. It's this or choose to replay my horribly dishonest conversation with Demi and Lena over and over in my annoying brain.

After watching almost all Vicki's videos, I'm still ninety-nine per cent sure I don't have vaginismus like her, but it's weirdly comforting to know I'm not a total anomaly. I can see endless comments from others saying they also have issues when it comes to sex.

One in particular catches my eye.

Moongirlxoxo: For anyone interested I'm setting up an online group to talk about stuff like this. DM me x

There's something tempting about being able to connect with other people in a similar boat, with the added bonus of anonymity. I can't exactly talk to my best friends, given that I've told them everything is dandy in that department.

I probably won't need it. Joel and I are sure to get somewhere with Operation Penetration eventually.

But I screenshot the comment anyway just in case.

8

Dad's bumbling around the kitchen prepping dinner after just getting home from his job as a window cleaner. He's still wearing his work cargo trousers and his polo shirt adorned with a little embroidered water droplet logo Sammy designed in GCSE graphics years ago. It's a miracle he's still wearing anything on his top half to be fair because he usually strips off the second he comes in and subjects us all to his hairy moobs.

"How did your exam go today?" he says with his head in a cupboard.

"I'm pretty sure I bombed the last Psychology paper," I say.

"She's being humble," says Joel, who's sitting at the table beside me, stroking my knee. I put my hand over his to stop him — the flutters it gives me down below don't feel at all appropriate for a family dinner.

Dad chuckles, now busying himself with the fridge. "I'm sure she is. What makes you say that, Rose?"

"I missed the entire back page because I didn't see it, and everything except what I revised for was in the paper. And I'm sure Patrick Stillwater was farting the whole time."

"God. That's evil," says Joel. "Don't you have to sit behind him? Alphabetical, right?"

"Yep. Pure filth." I shuffle my chair closer to his and start to rub his knee.

"Everyone does rubbish on their mocks — it's pretty much a fact of life," Sammy states, charging in and plonking herself at the head of the table.

I snap my hand away from Joel.

"I'm not sure that's true," says Dad. "Rose has worked very—"

"It is true. When I did them, the whole Maths class failed the first time round."

"Well, Rose has never failed at anything in her life."

Apart from at having sex with my boyfriend. I look at Joel, but he gives me a warm smile.

Sammy smiles too. "Didn't you fail that ballet exam once? Remember when you—"

"Enough." Dad rolls his eyes. "Anyway, that's what mocks are for. Keep at it and you'll have the grades you need for university in no time."

Ugh, university. I'll add that to the ever-expanding *things that make Rose feel guilty* list, alongside *sex* and *lying to her best friends*.

"Did someone say 'university'?" Mum strides in now, like a dog who's just heard the word "walkies". Her wrap top and flowy maxi skirt, the unofficial uniform for her shifts at the village library, swing with her enthusiasm.

"Noooo," I wail. "This is not an excuse for you to nag at me." I don't know why she's so preoccupied with my application. She didn't even go to uni, so she can hardly rag on me for taking extra time to apply to the right ones.

Mum raises her eyebrows and blinks. "I don't need an *excuse to nag*. I'm your mother."

Sammy snorts. I wish I could find it funny.

"Please don't." I must smell of desperation because Mum's face softens.

"I'll let you off today because of your mocks," she says. "But I'm not going to forget. You've worked too hard to throw it all away."

"I'm hardly throwing anything away."

"But you haven't sent your applications off yet."

63

"Why do people keep telling me things I already know?"

"Don't be so dramatic. We just want the best for you. We—"

My phone rings, cutting Mum off. It's Holly. She doesn't often call unless she has some juicy gossip to share.

"I need to take this. Two seconds," I say, leaving the room. "Hello?"

Holly gets straight down to business. "Do you think Robert wanking to porn every night of our relationship counts as cheating? I know we aren't together any more, but it's been playing on my mind."

I hightail it up the last few stairs and into the privacy of my room. The last thing I want is Mum hearing I've chosen to talk about wanking instead of sorting out my future.

"I don't think it's necessarily cheating, but I wouldn't like it either." I flop on to my bed.

Holly goes silent for a second. "It's not the wanking I have an issue with. Sometimes I wasn't in the mood so I was pleased he could sort himself out. It's the porn stuff I hate."

I sit up. "Yeah?"

There's a pause. "I think it was one of the reasons he broke it off with me." Holly's voice breaks. "He wanted me to do certain … stuff."

"Oh." I want to say something more comforting, but I'm not sure how. I don't know what *stuff* even means, but I absolutely *want* to know. I can store it in my mind alongside all the sex intel I've started gathering from socials. "What sort of stuff are we talking about, just so we're on the same wavelength…?"

"How do you find it so easy to say no to things you don't want to do? You've still not had sex with Joel and he seems fine with it. Does he just never ask you to do anything you aren't comfortable with? Or are you just insanely good at saying no?"

I'm not sure whether to take what she's saying as an insult or compliment.

"Joel doesn't pressure me." I leave out that I put pressure on myself. Why else would I lie about having sex in the first place, and feel guilty that I can't actually do it? "I hate giving head – tried it once and said never again. He hasn't asked me since."

"So nothing you don't want to do then?"

I want Holly to feel that she can always come to me for reassurance and an honest chat. But at the same time I'm out of my depth.

"Honestly, no. But it sounds like Robert has?"

"Mmm," says Holly, but she doesn't offer up anything else.

"You should never do anything you aren't comfortable doing, end of. And pressuring you to is really not cool."

"You're right."

"Are you two on again? What's the deal?" I ask gently, so she knows I'm not judging her.

"God no," Holly says a little too quickly.

"OK. Well, by the sounds of it, you're much better off without him."

"I know that deep down. It helps to talk about it, though."

A swell of pride radiates in my stomach. Holly spends most of her time with Monica and will always chat with someone like her friend Reggie to show off or get sex tips, but today, when she wanted a real heart-to-heart, she turned to me. It feels good to be that person for someone.

"Always here for you," I say.

There's a brief pause before Holly changes the subject. "Did I tell you I've applied for my cabin-crew training?"

"That's amazing!"

"I know, I'm well excited for it. Anyway, gotta go. Thanks for the chat, hun."

"My pleasure."

I wander back downstairs.

"Rose, just in time," Mum says. She's smiling, but it's a bit wonky – the sort she does when she's not sure about something but is trying to be polite.

"For what?"

"Joel's been showing us his latest masterpiece."

I look at Joel, who is proudly holding up a clay bust of what looks like an older man who's been hit in the face with a frying pan. "Guess who."

"Erm…"

Mum widens her eyes at me and shakes her head.

"I give up," I say. "Who?"

He beams. "You, of course! The assessment was to create a piece to honour the one we love."

I don't look like that, do I? Sammy's not even trying to hide her horror, Dad's shuffling his cutlery around and Mum's smile is so wonky now it's almost vertical.

"Joking." Joel laughs and drops the wet clay monstrosity into the carrier bag by his feet. "I was working on a nice little bust of David Attenborough but dropped it on the way to the kiln."

"Oh, thank goodness for that! Not that you dropped it, of course…" Mum babbles. "I didn't want to say anything but it does look a bit like Trump."

"But with arseholes for eyes."

"Sammy!"

"She's not wrong," mumbles Dad, pushing his chair out to attend to the bleeping oven timer.

"Mum, what do you mean *you didn't want to say*

anything?" snorts Sammy. "Your face said plenty. You'd be awful at poker."

"Since when did you play poker?" Mum puts on her best disapproving expression.

"Uni. Strip poker, obviously."

Joel shakes his head. "Classic."

"Sammy! I raised you to be better than that."

"Clearly you didn't do a good job." Sammy leans over to Mum and pulls her into a hug.

Mum rolls her eyes, but doesn't fight it. "Right, who's for cottage pie?"

9

Over the next two weeks, Joel and I don't try again with Operation Penetration. We don't even talk about it. We just go back to hanging out like before, as if the sex fail never happened. I know it's been on both of our minds, though, and every time we've been in bed together part of me has been braced for him to suggest it again. With Christmas looming I decide I should make an appointment to see a doctor.

I text Joel to let him know, then head to the bus stop so I can make the call in private. I pray the receptionist doesn't ask for details. What would I say? My vagina is broken? Gynaecological issues? I'm about to tap "call" when my phone vibrates.

Joel: I dunno if the doctor is necessary. Isn't it just a bit tight?

Well, that's not helpful. A supportive "good luck" would have sufficed.

Rose: It's not normal

Joel: You can do what you like

A fresh wave of frustration hits me.

Rose: Thanks for the permission 👍

I'm so close to chucking my phone back into my bag and putting the whole thing off but something stops me. Joel might want to downplay it, but it's no use pretending this problem is going to miraculously fix itself. I need to take charge. My body, my rules. I press "call".

I pace the pavement, listening to the irritating trill of the hold music. What if they try to give me a male doctor? I'm about to wimp out when the receptionist picks up and asks how they can help.

"I'd like to book an appointment, please, after school hours if possible. My name is Rose Summers."

"Monday at five with Doctor Capewell?"

Shit, that's in three days. My thumb twitches by the hang-up button.

"Is that a female doctor?"

"It is. Can I have a brief explanation as to why you're coming in to see her?"

The dreaded question. Why do they always ask that? It's none of their business.

"Are you still there?"

"Women's problems," I say like an utter moron. Why am I talking like a thirteen-year-old boy?

"Great, that's all booked."

I text Joel telling him it's done, but he doesn't reply.

10

The first thought I had this morning was: *I have to get my vagina out for a woman I've never met and she might try to put one of those speculum things in.* Also, I'm strongly regretting my choice to shave last night. It feels weird to have shaved for a doctor, but falling short of sticking my pubes back on with eyelash glue, I'll have to let it go.

The only nice thing about this morning was waking up to a message from Joel.

Joel: Good luck later. Sorry I was a bell end. You going to the doctor's makes it seem like something serious and I don't want that to be the case xxx

He didn't offer to come with me but I'd rather go alone anyway. If someone we know sees us sitting in the waiting room together, I'm sure their first assumption would be I'm up the duff – ironic given my vagina is basically its own chastity device.

In the waiting room, I stare at the open book on my lap, but I'm reading the same line over and over and keep shuffling in my seat to the point where I'm convinced everyone is looking at me. I wonder if I'm on the cusp of a massive heart attack? Good job I'm in a doctor's surgery.

Finally, thirty-four minutes later than my appointment time, the screen makes a buzzing sound and my name appears.

Rose Summers – Dr Capewell, Consulting Room 4

I gather my things in a hurried mess. Dr Capewell, I hope you're ready for this.

At the door of Consulting Room 4, I collect myself and knock. I poke my head in and I'm greeted by the doctor, who gestures for me to sit in the chair opposite her. She's middle-aged and, although she smiles when I come in, she's not the most friendly-looking woman I've ever seen.

After keeping me waiting for so long, she's brisk. "What can I help you with today, Rose?"

"I-I can't have sex," I stutter. *Eloquent, Rose, so eloquently put*. It sounds dramatic, but there's no other way to put it without beating around the bush (pun most definitely intended).

Dr Capewell doesn't even twitch. "OK, and what is it about intercourse that you're finding difficult?"

I babble my reply. "My boyfriend and I tried to do it for the first time recently and it wouldn't go in and it hurt and I bled."

Dr Capewell still has no discernible emotion. "You know it's common for some people to feel discomfort and bleed during their first time?"

My muscles tense. Would I be sitting in a surgery asking her to look at my vagina if I thought this was *normal*? I grind my teeth and suck in a breath.

"Yes, I know, but this didn't feel normal. My skin ripped. Fingers hurt too."

"I see. Are you happy for me to examine you?"

I nod and follow her to the couch in the corner, where she pulls down a sheet of protective paper from a roll above the bed. She hands me a square.

"You can use that to cover yourself up," she says. "Take off everything below your waist, sit on the couch and call me in when you're ready." She pulls the curtain round me.

OK. She's a doctor. She's seen way worse than this in her

time. She probably sees old-man bumholes on the reg. If I want to have sex with Joel, then I need to get this over with. *Before he gets bored of waiting*, a little voice in my head adds.

My hands shake as I pull off my leggings and fiddle with the elastic of my knickers. Do I take my socks off?

I rip my knickers off in one swoop before I can change my mind. I tug at the hem of my shirt in a bid to cover myself. I'm still wearing my blazer. Would I feel less exposed if I removed everything? Please, God, don't let the fire alarm go off.

I balance on the couch; the paper is scratchy and wrinkles with every movement I make. The paltry square of it flapping limply in my hand is a pathetic excuse for modesty. What's the point in covering up my pubic bone when the doctor is literally going to be eye to eye with my front bottom?

"Come in," I say, but what leaves my mouth is a dry whisper. *Come on, Rose. Slightly louder.* "OK, ready." Even though I never will be.

I'm bolt upright, legs fused shut.

"I'll need you to lie back and open your knees with your ankles together."

I do as I'm told, the mantra *my body, my rules* very much out of the window. The muscles in my legs quiver, knees hovering at an awkward angle.

"Can you relax them open a little more, please? Just let your knees drop to the couch," Dr Capewell says, looking between my legs as she pulls on a pair of latex gloves and squirts some medical-grade lube on to her finger. I move my knees the final few centimetres and wave goodbye to my last shred of dignity.

Dr Capewell turns on a spotlight and moves it into position. I can't believe this is happening. Why me? Holly didn't end up in this situation in order to have sex with Robert. Nor has anyone else I know.

Dr Capewell snaps me out of my thoughts. "Please can you relax your knees?"

I've tensed up again, holding everything rigidly, muscle-shakingly still. Perhaps if I stare at the ceiling I can whisk my mind away to anywhere that isn't here.

Dr Capewell pokes and prods as I shift around uncomfortably. I'm sure she's trying to be gentle, but the lube makes everything down there feel so wet and cold.

"Does that hurt?" she asks.

I nod.

"OK." She steps back and pulls her gloves off with a snap. "Get dressed and we'll chat."

Dr Capewell disappears through the curtain again. My cheeks are burning and I can tell without looking in a mirror I'll resemble a tomato when I do the walk of shame out through the waiting room.

I scrabble for my knickers and hurriedly pull on my socks and trousers, wishing I'd put them in a pile so the poor doctor hadn't had to work her way round my dirty knickers like some sort of manky obstacle course. My head is fuzzy and I have to check multiple times that I have all my clothes on in the right order before I pull the curtain back and sit down.

"Everything looks fairly normal to me," says Dr Capewell, brow furrowed and head nodding.

"Really?" I say, unable to hide my shock. How is that possible?

"I'll refer you to a specialist for a second opinion, but it might just be your partner is larger than average."

Is she saying Joel has a huge penis? I don't have much to compare it to.

"What can we do about it? It really did hurt. Even a finger does."

"With time it should get easier," she says. "There are a few things that might help. Plenty of foreplay and lots of lubrication. I also wonder whether a different angle might help."

"A different angle?"

"From behind with you on your knees might allow for a smoother entry." Dr Capewell turns to the computer and taps the keyboard.

I repress my urge to laugh, but can't stop the smile on my face spreading. Am I really being prescribed doggy style? Surely she's not writing that in my notes? I thought missionary was beginner level and we'd move up to doggy later. Clearly I had it all wrong.

I nod. "I'll try that." I gather my things, desperate to call Joel as soon as I can.

"You should get a letter from the specialist in the next few weeks confirming an appointment." Dr Capewell smiles and I take it as my invitation to leave.

I make my way through the waiting area in a confused haze. What just happened?

If the doctor had said something was wrong with me, I'd have been gutted, but at least it would have made sense of the pain.

Still, this is good news. Everything is fundamentally fine. Joel and I just need to work on the logistics of angles and foreplay. Operation Penetration is heading in the right direction, and with a little patience we'll get there. I wanted a miracle and I'd got one in the form of doggy-style.

11

Joel and I arrange to meet on Thursday. It feels like a lifetime waiting for it to come round – I'm desperate to try out a new position and see if Dr Capewell is right.

We're in Joel's bedroom. We have one hour while Sonya is at Zumba. There's no time for kissing or foreplay, and frankly I'm not in the mood for it. I know Dr Capewell said it would help, but I want this over with.

I move into position, on all fours with Joel behind me. It's wild I turned down an invitation for a film-and-hot-chocolate night with the girls for this. At least Joel's not wearing a straw hat this time.

Joel squirts so much lube on me it drips down my inner thighs like melting ice cream. I turn round to look at him, then bury my head in the pillow in front of me, twitching and shifting because staying still while he pulls the condom on is impossible with the amount of nervous energy running riot through my body.

"Ready?" says Joel, the bed shifting below me as he moves closer.

I take a deep breath and lift my face from the pillow. "Mmm."

Joel grips my hips like a steering wheel in a car going 80 mph. "You'll need to open your legs up a bit more."

I've heard that more times in the past week than I have in my whole life. I suck a breath in and open them way more than is comfortable. That familiar exposed feeling tickles me, the draught from the open window making it ten times worse.

Joel shuffles some more before placing one hand, warm and firm, on the small of my back, the other engaged with the important job of guiding himself into me. He pushes tentatively. No entry. He pushes again.

"Push harder," I say. "Just get it over with."

Joel stops and sits back on the bed. "I can't; it doesn't feel right."

I don't move. If I move, I won't get back into this position again. I turn only my head to look at him. "What do you mean, *it doesn't feel right*?" I growl, temper rising. "How would you know? It's not like you've had sex before. Try again."

My need to fix this, whatever *this* is, temporarily trumps my fear of being split in two again.

"No." Joel shakes his head. "I don't want to hurt you."

I roll into a sitting position with such force the mattress springs whine in protest.

"You're saying no? Fuck this." I swing off the bed, grab Joel's dressing gown from the back of the door and stomp into the bathroom. It's me who has to endure the pain and humiliation of all this. Why is he robbing me of all control or choice?

I blink away the hot angry tears that I can't stop from falling. In the mirror my face is a flushed blur.

There's a knock at the door.

"You don't have to talk to me, but here are your clothes in case Mum comes back soon," Joel says through the door.

I open the door a crack and let him slide a pile of my clothes in. I pull them on, heart pounding in my ears, breaths shallow and chest tight. By the time I slip on my last sock, the anger that throbbed so fiercely shifts as a realization dawns on me.

It's not Joel's fault — it's mine. If he did force it, God knows how that might have felt.

Why is his kindness making me feel worse? At least if he was an arsehole about it, I wouldn't have to feel so guilty.

How could I be stupid enough to believe a different

angle might work? How could I silence that feeling in my heart that knew it couldn't possibly be as simple as just flipping on to my hands and knees? What idiot would believe that? It's me. There's something wrong with me.

When I'm dressed and have spent a stupid amount of time trying and failing to make my face less red and my eyes less wet-looking, I shuffle back into Joel's room. He's lying on his bed, scrolling on his phone. He doesn't look at me when I come in and there's not even a flinch when I sit by his feet.

Words bubbling at the back of my throat choke me as I kick a dust ball on Joel's laminate floor from one foot to the other. I watch it roll back and forth like the jumbled thoughts in my head.

Finally I force something through my voice box. "Sorry," I mumble. "I know you were only being nice…"

Joel continues to stare at his phone. "It's fine."

"Is it?"

"Yep. Shall we pretend it didn't happen? I will if you will."

Even though my throat is still clogged with unexpressed words, I nod. "Sure."

Joel drops his phone on the duvet and holds his hand out to me. I take it and let him pull me on to the pillow beside him. His face warms mine and the look in his eyes melts me further. He raises his finger slowly to the side of my face and follows its contours with a gentle stroke from temple to chin. I fight the urge to pull my undeserving face away from his guilt-inducing touch.

If I go home having left things like this, I won't be able to sleep. Not only have I yet again been unable to give Joel what he wants (which I want too), I shouted at him for doing the right thing. I need to make this better. How?

I lean into his neck and kiss it, his pulse fluttering beneath my lips. Without any hesitation, I snake my hand down his pants. Sonya is due back any minute now so I don't have long but I'm overcome by the urge to make Joel feel good.

He pulls back and frowns. "Are you sure? I don't mind if you don't—"

"I want to." I hear the words come out, but now I'm wondering, *Do I?*

"OK, if you're sure," Joel whispers. He lies back, chin up, eyes closed. With any luck, my failure will soon be the last thing on his mind.

The minute I get home, I cave.

I DM Moongirlxoxo to join her group chat – obviously under an anonymous account – then I scroll back through old messages.

Moongirlxoxo: Welcome, everyone! I wanted to create this chat for anyone who wants to talk about issues they're having with sex and their bodies in general. Introduce yourselves and ask any questions you like. We might not know the answers but talking can be healing. I'll go first. I'm Moongirl and I can't orgasm

It_hurtttsssssss: Hiiiiii. That sucks. Sex doesn't feel good for me at all. It sometimes hurts and other times just feels meh. Also my bf wants to get straight into it most times, no warm-up!!! Help?

Moongirlxoxo: FOREPLAY FOREPLAY FOREPLAY!

TK_1000: I hate the word "foreplay", like it's only there to lead into something else, when for me it's the best bit LOL. Is it OK for me to be part of this group? I don't find sex painful but I do struggle with other people judging me for enjoying it 🙁

Moongirlxoxo: @TK_1000 Everyone is welcome here! Amazing to hear you enjoy sex. That deserves to be celebrated! I'm sorry you feel like people are judging you. We won't here!

It_hurtttsssssss: Even when my bf and I do fool around before, I'm still quite … dry?

TK_1000: I have the opposite problem sometimes and it's a bit embarrassing. Have you tried lube? And thanks **@moongirlxoxo** <3

It_hurtttsssssss: No. I want to but I'm too scared to buy it 😞

Moongirlxoxo: It's nothing to be ashamed of <3 My mum bought me some. I can send some to you if you want

Endo2005: Endometriosis warrior here. My periods are heavy and painful and sex is something I'm dreading. HELP!

Anon_69: The thought of sex or being intimate in any way makes me feel really panicky. I hate my body and the thought of someone seeing me naked horrifies me

As I scroll and scroll, I'm overwhelmed by the number of reasons why people have joined the aptly named *VagWarriors* chat. So many others questioning, like me, whether they're the only ones in the world to feel like they do.

Does it make me feel less alone to see others flailing too? Sort of. Does it make me feel less confused about what's going on for me? No. How can something so natural be so bloody complicated?

I click off the chat without introducing myself – I wouldn't even know where to start.

12

One week after failed attempt number two and Joel and I are wearing Santa hats, the Christmas songs are on and the crumbs of Dad's home-made mince pies are decorating my duvet. It's our Christmas. We aren't spending actual Christmas Day together because Mum, Dad and Sammy have made it clear they want to spend it as a family. I think Sammy's actual words were: "You'd better be watching *Home Alone* with us on Christmas Eve otherwise I'll smother you while you sleep."

Joel has just opened the presents I got him – a new skin and headset for his Xbox and a pottery experience for two. I was chuffed with myself for finding the pottery experience and owe a big thank-you to Mum and Dad for chipping in too.

"Thank you, I love it. Which of my girlfriends shall I take to the pottery experience then?"

"Cheeky."

Joel's fluffy curls peek out of his Santa hat and I just can't help myself. I grab the faux sheepskin blanket that's sitting across our laps and wrap it round him before smothering his face in a million kisses.

"Oiiiiii!" He ducks out of my grasp, cheeks pink from my love attack.

"You'd better watch your back. I'll get my revenge on you soon…"

"Hey, you two." Mum's voice makes us startle as she peers round the door frame. Awkward. "Dad and I are popping out to drop some cards off. We won't be long and Sammy is downstairs." She catches my eye and I heed her telepathic warning. Before leaving, she opens the bedroom door a little wider.

Joel leans down to rifle through the carrier bag at his feet, but stops the second the front door slams. He lets go of what I assume is one of my Christmas presents and looks at me with a sly smile. I know what he's thinking, but the minute I knew we were doing presents here and not at his, I was looking forward to keeping it PG.

"Is it my turn to open presents then?"

"Soon. Plenty of time for that later." Joel moves towards me and reaches to tuck my hair behind my ear.

I stiffen. "They aren't going to be out long if that's what you're hoping for."

"I don't need long."

"Sammy is here." I hope he doesn't remember his birthday when I managed to give him an extra little present with the door open and the whole family downstairs.

"Hasn't stopped us before." The tone of his voice has changed and his smile is replaced with a frown.

"True, but … I just feel like cuddles and presents today if that's OK?"

Why do I feel like I'm doing something horrible? The past few times I've seen him, I've officially become the Queen of the Guilty Handjob, but surely I don't owe him one *every* time?

"OK, fine." He leans back down to the presents at his feet.

"Don't be mad at me," I say, guilt smacking me square in the face as I spy the number of gifts in the bag. Surely a handjob isn't a huge ask.

What's happened to me? I used to want him all the time. I remember once we were at the park with a few friends on a Friday evening and we actually tried to find a bush to get handsy in. When we couldn't, we left early and walked all the way back to his. Can things really have changed that much in a few short months?

At the beginning it was playful. Spontaneous. Now, ever since our sex fail, there's … pressure.

"I'm not mad. Do you want to open your presents then?" Joel holds a white parcel with a blue ribbon towards me.

"You are mad. I'm sorry. I was just worried about Sammy. We could do something quickly?" I stutter, even though the moment's gone.

"Please leave it." He places the parcel on the bed.

"I'm sorry." There's desperation in my voice now. Why did I have to ruin a nice moment?

Joel takes a deep breath. "It's fine. Open your pressie." He smiles and kisses me quickly on the head.

I scrutinize every detail of his face. I can't tell if it's just my own guilt that's making me feel like it's not "fine" or whether he's actually pissed off. I tug at the paper and pull out the present nestled within.

It's a handmade clay Christmas decoration in the shape of a heart. It's perfect.

"I love it." I hold it up and it twirls, its glittery paint catching in my twinkling fairy lights.

"Good."

"Is that all you're going to say?"

"What else do you want me to say?"

"Doesn't matter," I say quietly. "Shall we go downstairs?"

For the rest of the evening we continue with the festivities – watching *The Grinch* with my family and adding my heart decoration to the tree. However, despite what it looks like, the air between us feels heavy and oppressive, even with the trill of "Fairytale of New York" playing in the background and our stupid Santa hats perched on our heads.

The minute I close the front door behind Joel, I'm desperate to talk to someone who will understand how I'm feeling – the guilt, the shame, the anger. I decide it's time to stop being a lurker in the VagWarriors chat and find the nerve to introduce myself.

I have a speedy scroll through to see if there have been any updates since I last looked.

Moongirlxoxo: I tried again to O this morning – if anyone has any tips, pleaseeeeeeee let me know

Endo2005: Showerhead?

It_hurtttsssssss: Thanks for the lube advice

@Moongirlxoxo and **@TK_1000**. It helped massively!! Still hurts a bit at first but way better than before. I'm aiming to ask for more foreplay and to slow down if I'm not ready, but it's not always easy to find my voice!

Moongirlxoxo: Yay!!! So pleased for you xx. And totally easier said than done to speak up 🙁

TK_1000: WE ARE ROOTING FOR YOU.
@Moongirlxoxo I'm 21 and it took me a while to work out what worked for me. You'll get there x

Hurts a bit at first. Is it weird to be jealous of someone else's vagina? I'm happy for It_hurtttsssssss, but I wish lube was the miracle I'm looking for. I type out my own message multiple times, and my heart is beating so fast by the time I press "send" I'm surprised it doesn't give up on me.

Roseycheeks_x: Hi. I dunno what's wrong with me but when I tried to have sex I tore and bled. It didn't feel normal but the doctor told me to try doggy (!) and referred me on. My bf refused to force it the second time and tbh I'm glad. I don't expect anyone to be able to help but want to tell someone that isn't (cringe) my mum

Multiple usernames start typing.

Endo2005: 🙁 feel for you. We might not know the answers but you're in the right place to talk to people who get it

TK_1000: Yep. Always happy to chat

Moongirlxoxo: So sorry to hear this **@Roseycheeks_x**. We're here if you ever need support xxxxx

Why are their comments making my eyes tear up? Their sympathy feels good and bad at the same time. It makes it feel like a big deal, but it's nice to be validated. I close the chat feeling *marginally* better.

13

Christmas comes and goes in a blur of Baileys hot chocolate, furry socks and watching the entire *Home Alone* franchise on repeat. Like most people, I manage to forget what day it is between Boxing Day and New Year's Eve – the time period I fondly refer to as The Gooch.

It's been perfect, but I blinked and all of a sudden it's New Year's Eve and I have to wave goodbye to my PJs and slippers and say hello to my heels and make-up bag. My festive hibernation has absolutely *not* been long enough.

New Year's Eve is a special night for Joel and me because it's the night we met. Last year, I'd gone to Holly's party thinking I'd be entering the new year forever single unless my boobs grew four bra sizes overnight and I suddenly gained the ability to do more than grunt at the opposite sex. Those miracles didn't happen, but an even better one did – and I knew it the minute I saw Joel duck through the front door.

I've always had a thing for freakishly tall, lanky guys – they can have a face like a foot, but you still *would* – and luckily for me this ginger giant's face was far from footish. My body reacted before my mind did, and if I was channelling Lena, I would go as far as to say my soul just *knew*. It simply said: *Yes, him.*

After one too many ciders, Demi got sick of me saying *He's the one. I think I could love him, you know* and shoved me so forcefully in Joel's direction I knocked his beer out of his hand.

"I'm so sorry." I laughed nervously while looking at the floor. I remember thinking, *Bloody hell, he's got huge feet*, and then my mind drifting off to, *If that's big, I wonder what else is.* Oh, naive little Rose. We'd be much happier right now if it was the size of a party sausage.

"I know Foster's is gross, but I've never seen someone have such a visceral reaction to it before," Joel said. I flicked my eyes up from his feet, scanned his ginger hair quickly and looked back at the floor.

Off went my soul again, a feeling of elastic bands snapping under my skin as I realized that not only was he tall and very handsome with big feet, he also wasn't a total dickhead.

"You can thank me later," I said, shocking myself with my obvious attempt at flirting. "Want me to get you another?"

I thought he'd thank me politely and disappear back into the crowd of people, but he didn't.

"I've got more in the kitchen, don't worry," he said. "It's still Foster's, though – aka warm piss. I'm getting you something nice, though. What you drinking?"

"It's OK. I'll come with," I said, following Joel as Demi high-fived Lena in the most unsubtle way ever. Even now, she still calls herself Cupid.

In the kitchen, Joel grabbed a can of beer from a box on the counter and pulled out the Coke and vodka from the array of bottles decorating the table. Our hands touched as I handed him my empty glass, and I know he noticed because he smiled sheepishly, tipped his head forward to hide behind his curls and bit his lip as he twisted the cap off the vodka. I'm surprised my knickers didn't whip him in the face in their hurry to vacate the building.

"Say 'woo'," he said as he started to pour.

"Say what?"

"Woo. As in, to tell me to stop."

"WOO!" I half laughed, half shouted, realizing he'd

already poured enough to knock out a horse. "I've never heard someone use that phrase before."

"Really?" Joel pulled a face. "I'm now wondering whether it's just something weird my family say… Cool, so now I look like a right nob." He turned as red as his hair.

"Noooo, I like it. I think you may be trying to kill me, though."

"Too much?"

"A little."

"I'll put some back in." Joel attempted to pour some of the liquid into the tiny funnel of the bottle it came from, concentrating so much on the task his tongue popped out of his mouth. I remember wishing it would somehow find its way into mine. "The last thing I want to do is kill you."

"That's the most romantic thing someone who's known me for less than ten minutes has ever said to me."

Joel grinned. "I try my best."

And that was that. We spent the whole night together, chatting for four solid hours up until midnight, when the deal was sealed with a magical kiss.

If you asked me now what we spoke about, I couldn't tell you – and, no, it's not because I was drunk. What has stayed with me was how Joel made me *feel*. His way of being didn't make me second-guess whether my front teeth were too big or my boobs were too small or whether

I was too quiet or too loud. He just seemed to enjoy me for merely existing.

Come to think of it, it's *never* been about the ticks on paper for us – it's about the less tangible stuff. It's not the same favourite song, but the way we both dance to anything with a beat. It's not a shared interest in horror films, but the way we can sit in comfortable silence for two hours simply appreciating each other's presence. It's not that we both love Nando's (although we do), but the fact I can eat five chicken wings with my hands while wearing no make-up and my hair in a messy bun and Joel still calls me gorgeous.

We just fit.

Well, apart from the obvious.

So, yeah, New Year's Eve is an important night for the two of us and it would make sense to spend it together. However, this year I'm in a really tricky situation. Usually, Holly hosts a party, but now she's eighteen she can legally hit up the scuzzy clubs in town and all our mates have decided to join her. Lena is eighteen and Demi and I can use our sisters' driving licences if they use their passports, but Joel's still seventeen and can't find anyone to borrow ID from that looks remotely like him. Gingers really are dying out it seems.

So I'm torn between spending the night with Lena and

Demi on what would be our first night out clubbing or spending it with Joel on our unofficial first anniversary (but at a party with a load of his college mates I barely know).

Everyone had something to say about it.

Can't you spend this one year with us instead of him? It's our first time in town!

You see your mates every day at school, and it's basically our anniversary.

So instead of picking one and pissing off the other, I'm doing both. It's the sort of compromise where no one is one hundred per cent happy and I'll be running around like a blue-arsed fly, but at least no side can complain about being ditched. The plan is to go into town with the girls until eleven thirty, Joel will walk to meet me and we'll go back to Tom's party for midnight and the all-important kiss. Lena and Demi will then join us at the party at one-ish. Sorted. Sort of.

Things are pretty wild in town.

Eruption Nightclub is rammed – unsurprisingly, given we've chosen to pop our clubbing cherry on the busiest night of the year. We're wearing the tallest heels in our wardrobes (big mistake) and the only thing keeping us warm while we huddle in the smoking area is the limited alcohol we've consumed and the sweaty heat of drunken bodies around us. None of us smoke, but after a solid hour of dancing and being jostled by other revellers, the fresh night air is a welcome relief.

Opposite me, Demi is subtly swaying her hips to the dull bass still audible from inside and Lena is huddling so close to me her hair tickles my cheek. I'm vibrating from the pumping music and buzzing from adrenaline.

Demi sucks up the last of her vodka and orange and then frowns at me. "Oi, Rose, are you ever close during penetration?" She shouts it so loudly the bald bloke behind her cocks his head.

"Close? To Joel? I mean, he's inside me…" I think I'm whispering, but the bald bloke's head is now shaking with laughter so perhaps not…

"No, you plum, close to orgasm."

"Oh, right." That definitely wasn't the answer of someone who's been having frequent sex for a couple of months.

"That's a no then. Have you still never had one at all?"

"I have had one actually," I snap. Did those words really just come out of my mouth?

"During sex?"

"No, other stuff." What am I saying? I shouldn't have drunk tonight.

"Why didn't you tell us?!" Lena shrieks. She's not

drinking – *her body is her temple* – but she somehow manages to get high on life and the energy of those around her.

"It only just happened."

"SOOOOOOOOO proud of you. Did you moan?"

"Yes." Wow, who knew I was so full of crap? Sometimes I'm closer to yawning than moaning...

"See, penetration can do one," says Demi. "One of the many good things about being attracted to women is that they're way more clit-focused."

I wish I had Demi's confidence. Despite having never been with another person sexually in her entire life, I have no doubt she knows what she's talking about.

"Are they now?" The bald guy spins round and tries to infiltrate our huddle. He smells like BO and stumbles into Lena, knocking her into Demi.

"Excuse me, bell end. Touch my friend again and I'll sort you right out, and not in a good way," she says.

The bald bloke holds his hands up in surrender and mutters something about "feminist bitches" as he turns round and gets lost in the many other jostling bodies.

I take advantage of the distraction and change the subject. "I love you guysssss," I say. "I'm so glad I didn't choose to spend the whole night sitting on a sofa at Tom's surrounded by people I barely know."

"Me too! It wouldn't have been the same without you," Demi says, forgetting instantly about my fantastical orgasm and squeezing my cheek like my grandma used to. She's way softer when she's had a few units.

"Yesssssssss," says Lena, pulling us into a hug. "It's always best when it's the three of us. And now I want to cry because we're all going to be leaving for uni at the end of the year and—"

"Noooooooo." I shake my head. "Don't cry because it happened; smile because it's done. No, no, that's not the phrase – just … cheers to us!"

I go to raise my drink and accidentally knock into Lena's arm as it snakes its way round my shoulders. My drink splashes over us and we giggle. I stagger under her weight. Is it the drink or the shoes causing my unsteadiness? I don't care either way.

Demi joins in the hug, somehow holding us both up, and then raises her head like a meerkat, squinting over my shoulder.

"Is that Monica and Holly over there? And Skye?"

I scan the swaying heads in the pulsating crowd and spot Holly, a smudge of pillar-box red against the canvas of black shirts and dark jeans of leering men. Monica is equally as distinct, with her pink hair so long it must tickle the backs of her knees. Skye looks effortlessly cool (and ironically much warmer than me) in a baggy pair of jeans and a yellow puffer jacket.

"Eff me, I wish I could be as cool as Monica." Demi shakes her head in admiration. "That hair, man. Look at it. It's like a neon waterfall—"

"Let's go and say hi," Lena says, making her way through the crowd.

I turn to follow, but Demi grabs me.

"Two secs. Let me sort my lipstick out first," she says, whipping out her phone to use as a mirror as she smears on more MAC Ruby Woo. "Ready." She pouts, and then we join the others.

We take turns to hug, a tornado of "heyyyyyy", cold hands, perfume and hairspray. We aren't that close to Monica or Skye, but it would be rude to hug Holly and not them and I'm feeling so high on life now I might even hug that sweaty guy slouching in the corner.

Skye grins. "We're celebrating Holly's dumping. Over two months she's been free of that twat Robert."

Holly giggles. "Best months of my life. And I've already got a guy's number. You know what they say: the best way to get over someone is to get under someone else."

Lena, Demi and I exchange looks – one of us will need to look out for her tonight.

"Shots?" says Monica, winking.

"Yesssssss," says Demi, linking arms with her and Lena, Skye joining the chain too. "Come on, bitches." They stagger towards the club's door, a swaying barricade against the wall of partygoers.

"Wee. Need one." Holly grabs my arm and rolls her ankle as we follow the others in. I fumble for my phone and check the time. Twenty past eleven. Just time for a wee and a shot before I go out to meet Joel. I attempt to tap out a message saying I'll meet him in fifteen minutes, but it's impossible with Holly yanking me through the crowd and with fingers so cold they refuse to do what I want them to.

The toilets smell like shitrus – a mix of toilet and perfume – with notes of alcohol, sick and piss. Holly staggers into a cubicle, yanking me in behind her with icy hands that grip my wrist.

"How're you and Joel? The perfect couple!" Holly slides on to the toilet seat and starts doing a wee. It sounds like a horse who's drunk the entire contents of the Thames.

"We're good."

"Good." She nods.

I remember Holly telling us about her first time with twat Robert. She had sounded all aloof and ambiguous, like it was no big deal. But I think back to our phone call – it felt like she was trying to tell me something. Maybe it's because I've had a drink, but I want to know more.

"Er, just a quick one – you know when you had sex for the first time, did you say it hurt? I can't remember."

Holly shakes her head so vigorously she has to grab on to the toilet-roll holder to steady herself. "Nah, it didn't hurt. It was actually all right." She yanks way too much paper out of the dispenser and her eyes widen. "You've done it, haven't you?"

"Yeah." It falls out of my mouth yet again.

"OMG, why didn't you tell me?" She flaps the toilet roll at me.

"Too busy shagging." I can't believe I just said that.

"Aw, I'm so proud of you. Wait, wait." She holds her hand up and tries to look me in the eye, but the amount of blinking she's doing tells me it's a struggle. "Did it hurt?"

"Not much, just wondered that's all. You hear some people say it does." I can hardly tell Holly the truth when I haven't even told Demi and Lena.

"Yeah, I'm sure my cousin said it hurt. A bit sore, nothing awful."

Is what I feel during Operation Penetration "awful" pain? Or is it just a bit sore? I can't help feeling confused. I *know* the pain I'm feeling is real, but if a doctor is telling me I'm fine, then surely I'm fine.

The sound of Holly loudly blowing her nose snaps me from my thoughts. She's crying. She never cries, always one to be strong and give the impression everything's fine, all the time.

"Shit. What's wrong?"

I crouch down in front of her, trying my best not to kneel in a suspicious-looking puddle on the floor.

"I ... can't ... say," Holly says between sniffs.

"Why not? I want to help."

Holly doesn't look at me. "Don't tell anyone. Not even Demi and Lena – they'll hate me."

"They'll never hate you," I say, but my heart is pounding. What could she have possibly done to think that lovely Lena would ever hate her?

"I went back to him."

"Who?" I say, even though I can make a pretty decent guess.

"Rob."

"Ah, OK." I rub Holly's now shivering calf. "Are you back together then or…?"

"No. Just sex. I don't want to go back, but I'm not sure I can stop myself." Her face crumples again.

My heart breaks for her – she loves Rob as much as I love Joel. I'd like to think that if Joel broke my heart I wouldn't go back there, but I can't honestly say I wouldn't.

"Of course I'd never say anything, but they're your friends. Why would they hate you?"

"Because they think I'm better than that."

"Better than what?"

"Going back to someone who treated me so bad." Holly collapses into her knees, her head hanging limply as she sobs. "I just don't want to lose him."

"It's OK. I understand. It must be so hard not to go back."

"Mm-hmm." Holly blows her nose. "Sleeping together makes it feels like old times again. And I know you'll get this now you've joined the club. You know when you're having sex and you just feel like you're the only two people in the world, like you're the only person that matters to them in that moment? It's nice to be his world for those minutes." A black path of mascara snakes its way down Holly's cheek and neck, pooling in her collarbone. I dab at it with tissue.

I *wish* I got it. I wish Joel and I were having moments like that. God, am I a terrible friend? Holly is only telling me this because she thinks I've had sex.

"There's something else." Holly doesn't look at me.

OK, is this what she was trying to talk to me about on the phone that time? "Yeah?" I say gently.

"He wants to do it *the other way*."

I blink at her.

"You know … the bum." Holly whispers the last

part, not that anyone would be able to hear us over the excitement of everything else going on in the women's toilets.

I'm totally out of my depth here, but I want to support Holly regardless.

"How do you feel about that?" I don't want to make her feel judged if it's something she wants to do, even if it's not for me.

"I really don't want to. There's nothing appealing about it to me. If anything, it scares me. But Robert thinks otherwise. He says any hole's a goal." Holly grimaces and shakes her head.

"What a nob." I can't stop myself from saying it. "That's not OK."

"I know. But then why do I feel bad for saying no? He says he's never done it before and only wants to do it with me."

That doesn't sit right with me at all. It all feels very coercive – I think that's the word I've seen people use online for stuff like this. Trying to manipulate her into doing something she doesn't want to. "If you don't want to do it, then you have every right to say no."

"I know you're right. Again." Holly looks up at me and her eyes are still wet with tears.

I desperately want to grab her by the shoulders and

shake her and say, *You're way too good for that piece of shit*. But I know that's not helpful, so instead I say, "It's OK. I get it. You're worth more than how he's treating you, though. You do know that, don't you?"

Holly shakes her head like a dog after a paddle and stands, pulling her knickers up. "Yeah. I'm going to try my best not to be weak again. Ow, my leg's gone proper dead now." She shakes her leg and I grab her shoulder to steady her. "You're a really good listener, by the way. Please don't tell anyone about this."

"I won't – don't worry." I mime locking my lips and throwing away the key. She's already wobbling past me and unlocking the door.

I follow her out of the cubicle and in a split second she's at the mirror, sorting out her make-up. As her lipstick goes on, so does her default veneer of confidence and charisma – and it's as if our conversation never happened.

"Joelyyyyyyy." I throw my arms round his neck and lean into him. It feels good to take the weight off my throbbing feet as I let him hold me up. "I missed you."

He smells like beer and Joel and fruity shampoo and although I didn't want to leave the girls, especially poor Holly, being in Joel's arms assures me I've made the right choice.

He's stiff beneath my grasp, his hands loose on my back.

"We said eleven thirty," he says gruffly. "It's quarter to."

"Sorry, I needed a wee and there was a queue," I say, not letting go and nuzzling my face into his neck. I smother it with kisses and feel his warmth on the tip of my nose.

He peels me off him. "You're freezing," he says, pulling off his coat and wrapping it round me. It's still hot from his body and I shiver inside its puffy layers.

"Thanks." I take a step and my heel goes into a crack in the pavement. My ankle rolls and Joel grabs my arm.

"Are you really drunk?"

"Not *really* drunk, no. That was my shoes."

"How much have you had?"

"A glass of wine, a vodka and Coke and a shot of something just now." I think that's everything?

Joel looks me up and down. "You can't even stand up straight."

I shift from one foot to the other. "I told you, my shoes are killing me. Want to give me a piggyback to Tom's?" I poke his belly playfully.

"Doubt we'll make it back in time for midnight now."

"It's only a ten-minute walk." I slide my arm in his.

"Let's go then." Joel nods towards the road and starts walking. I have to stagger to keep up.

"Is Tom all right? Was the party messy when you left?"

"Yeah," Joel grunts.

"Yeah he's all right or yeah it was messy?"

"Both."

"Who's there? Anyone I know?"

"Dunno."

"Any girls?"

"Didn't notice."

Ugh, why is he being like this? I stop and force Joel to stop too. "Are you OK?" I ask, searching his face for clues.

His hard eyes soften as a smile forms on his lips. "I'm OK. Sorry. I just missed you at Tom's and was worried we were going to be late for the fireworks."

There's my Joely – I knew he was in there somewhere.

"No, *I'm* sorry," I say. "I shouldn't have been late." It might be nice to see some fireworks on the way there, even if we don't make it. As long as we have our kiss, I'll be happy. I pull him in closer to me and rub my freezing cold nose on his.

He grins. "Fancy that piggyback?"

It's five to twelve by the time we get to Tom's house. Everyone is outside with the patio doors open and the TV on max volume, ready for Big Ben to chime. Joel ushers me to the garden without introducing me to anyone, and those who I do recognize look too sloshed to string a sentence together.

Joel helps himself to a beer from a cooler and offers me a cider. I decline because I've had enough for tonight, but he chugs his entire drink in a few minutes flat. Then the sound of a howling unselfconscious laugh pierces the air.

Joel and I both look in its direction and see Reggie striding out of the back door, arm in arm with Justine. According to Holly, neither of them could get ID so I don't know why I'm surprised to see them here. They stop less than a metre away from us on two plastic garden chairs on the patio. Reggie looks great in a very low-cut dress that enhances her enormous boobs. It takes every ounce of control not to look to see if Joel's noticed. All the boys in our year, and many of the girls too, fancy the pants off her. Joel's never given me any indication he's one of them, but for some reason I can't stop my mind from flitting there.

Justine leans into Reggie. "And then what?" she says loudly.

Reggie grins slyly. "I waited for him in the bedroom wearing nothing but my heels – you know, the red ones."

"We can hear you, you know," a random person I've never seen before calls from the open back door.

Justine snaps her head at them. "So? Stop earwigging then."

"We're not earwigging; we just happen to have ears." The door slams shut.

Reggie shrugs. "Doesn't bother me." She *wants* people to hear, but I don't want Joel listening. She turns back to Justine. "He pretty much fell to his knees when he saw me."

I look at Joel and he pulls his phone out of his pocket to look at it. Is he redder than usual?

I stand, frozen, as Reggie continues to practically shout, listing off sex positions like a shopping list. It sounds so effortless for her. Where did she get all this confidence from? Is it something that comes the more you do it? Perhaps if I managed to have sex once, it would unleash confident sexual energy in me, and I'd be slick and effortless and provocative, jumping Joel like Reggie does her boyfriend. Jealousy and a feeling of total inadequacy twist in my gut.

Joel is still pretending to look at his phone, acting as if he's not hanging off Reggie's every word.

Thankfully, everyone is distracted as the countdown to midnight begins.

"Ten, nine, eight," everyone else in the garden chants.

"Seven, six," I join in, snaking my arm round Joel's waist, desperately shoving the jealousy away. He loosens beneath my grip.

"Five, four, three," Joel joins in now, smiling and looking towards the sky.

113

"Two, one."

The fireworks on the TV go off, and at the same time the sky lights up with explosions of colour and shrieks from the display in the adjoining field.

I pull Joel towards me and kiss him, but his lips resist anything more than a peck. I'm not sure why he's feeling shy all of a sudden.

"You're going to have to do better than that," I say.

There's no way I'm letting this moment slip past me. Not after everything.

I look directly into his eyes. They reflect the rainbow of glittering fireworks making a canopy above our heads. My determination pays off as Joel's eyes glimmer and he leans back in.

But before our lips meet again, Tom staggers into us. He knocks Joel's beer can flying, drenching my legs and feet and making me squeal. Oblivious, Tom slaps Joel on the shoulder and pulls me into a sweaty hug.

"I guess now we're even." I can't help but chuckle. This might not be the romantic kiss I was hoping for, but the repetition of the beer spillage incident of last year is rather serendipitous – a sign from the universe that everything is happening for a reason and Joel and I are still destined to be together for ever.

Joel's face is blank. "Huh?"

"You know – getting me back for last year, when I spilled beer on you?"

"You did?"

Tom looks at Joel and then to me, slurring, "Rose, do you mind if I borrow your bloke for a minute?" Before I'm able to reply, he yanks Joel away.

Joel looks towards me and shrugs. He's mouthing something as he's whisked into a mass of drunk guys in the centre of the lawn. They all jump up and down to a song I don't recognize while I stand alone, shivering and stinking of stale beer and disappointment.

When I'm in bed that night (more like morning because it's almost 2 a.m.) my mind is on what Holly said earlier. About how Rob wants to try sex *the other way*.

I've never been interested, but I'm now briefly wondering whether the other entrance is a viable option. Maybe that one works and might keep Joel happy. My rational voice pops in, reassuring me that I shouldn't have to do something I don't want to do, as I was preaching to Holly. So why am I even considering it?

Sometimes the irrational voice is louder. It's saying stuff like, *Don't you dare lose him. Do whatever it takes to keep him happy.*

Thankfully, this time the rational voice wins. It's a no

115

from me – there's lots I'd do for love, but in the words of Meat Loaf, I won't do that. But it doesn't stop me worrying. Rob dumped Holly after all. Joel isn't an arse like Robert, but still. What if he gets bored of waiting?

What if?

What if?

What if?

Oh, eff off.

14

Nothing between Joel and me has changed.

Ever since New Year, we've been rolling along pretty much as before, if you add in the fact that we see each other even more evenings a week now than ever, both of us aware that next year might look very different and wanting to make the most of the time we can spend together. Every free evening I have at the moment when I'm not doing schoolwork I'm with him or we're on a video call for hours at a time. He still kisses me on the nose every time he says goodbye, we still laugh like lunatics at stupid videos online, and we still end up naked with each other most evenings when we've got the house to ourselves. Operation Penetration hasn't been mentioned again, and instead we're back to exploring each other's bodies and making each other feel good. Well, these days it's more about me making him feel good. I let him touch me back, but I don't enjoy it like I used to. I'm sick of being poked down there and knowing there's more to come. But for some reason the fact nothing's changed feels like we've stalled somehow. Things *should* have changed, so we're sort of … stuck.

The one thing that feels like it's moving forward is my UCAS application, which I have managed to send off, just four days before the 31st January deadline. With Miss Starmann's help on my personal statement – which is now a Frankenstein mash-up between Biology and Psychology – I've applied for Biological Science at the University of Hertfordshire, Biology at the University of Bath, Psychology at Winchester and both Biomed and Psychology at Sunderland. It's a win–win. I have choices in both Psychology and Biology, and the option to be with Joel or not with Joel. Boom, that's how you totally boss UCAS.

Back on the subject of my vagina, the referral letter for the gynae specialist arrived this morning. I've been checking the post obsessively for the last few weeks because I didn't trust Mum and Sammy not to intercept it, the nosy cows. My appointment is in two weeks' time, which feels ages away and too soon at the same time.

I debated getting the bus or a taxi to the appointment but, knowing my family, if they find out I'm not in school or at Lena's/Demi's/Joel's, the police will be called before I'm even able to get my vag out. This means I need to tell Mum ASAP as I'll need to leave school early that day and she'll have to come with me so will need to book the afternoon off work.

I've put off telling her for obvious reasons. Firstly it will confirm to her I'm – the dreaded term – sexually active, and secondly I thought this issue would resolve on its own. I also don't want to say the words "vagina", "penis" or "sex" out loud to her, so I've decided to text her. It will be like the time I got my first period and messaged her about how I was "now a woman" because I didn't want to say the word "period".

Mum has left for work this morning so now's a good time to send her a message so she can't sidle into my room awkwardly before I'm able to mentally prepare for the discussion. Despite this, I'm lying on my bed, scrolling Instagram instead of composing the grand essay.

I groan, heave myself up into a sitting position and click on the notes app on my phone. It's an excellent place to write out a risky text because there's no way you'll accidentally press "send" too soon. I bet there are some right crackers hidden in here – if anyone stole my phone,

I'd rather they saw photos of my boobs than read some of them. The last entry says *five chicken wings and medium peri chips x 2* and I'm now wistfully thinking how I'd rather be typing out the entirety of the Nando's menu than writing to my mum about sex.

I sigh and start tapping.

I type.

I edit.

I delete.

I type.

I edit.

I delete.

I mull over every word until I'm satisfied. Well, I'm not sure if "satisfied" is the right word, but it will do. It *has* to do.

Hi Mum. Wanted to drop you a message because I have something to tell you. No, I'm not pregnant before you start to panic. That would truly be a divine miracle. I have an appointment with a consultant and I need someone to take me and give me moral support. Things aren't working down there if you catch my drift and it hurts a lot. Please don't ask too many questions. It's too cringey and I don't wanna talk about it. Love you x

I've managed to successfully avoid the words "sex", "vagina" and "penis", but I'm hoping my jokes about pregnancy and the Virgin Mary will give her enough context to know what I'm talking about.

I copy the message into WhatsApp and check multiple times I'm sending it to just Mum. The thought of sending this message to the family group or anyone else fills me with the sort of horror that says I'd be better off dead. I also attach a photo of the referral letter for further detail so I don't have to give it, and press "send" before I can change my mind.

I knew Mum would be home by the time I got back from school, so I'm now at the front door, palms sweaty, sick halfway up my oesophagus, rehearsing the many outcomes of this inevitably awkward conversation.

I open the door and shuffle in. After closing the door in slow motion, I slide my shoes off without so much of a breath and tiptoe down the hall. I'm almost at the stairs; if I can make it to the bathroom, I'll have five more blissful minutes of not having to face this.

"Hey, love, I've made you a cup of tea," Mum calls from the kitchen. She must have been waiting for me and I've clearly inherited Dad's inability to do anything quietly. I wonder if Mum's been watching the clock as anxiously as I have.

I close my eyes and steel myself before crossing the threshold to the kitchen.

"Thanks," I say, trying to channel as much of my normal self as possible. I attempt a grin, but my mouth is so dry my top lip gets caught on my teeth. I catch sight of myself in the mirror and cringe.

I sit opposite Mum at the breakfast bar and lose myself in the mug of tea she hands me. She sips hers slowly, as if she's working out how to say something.

"School OK?"

"Yeah, same old. Demi fell head first out of the Music cupboard after getting her foot caught on a violin case." I force a laugh that sounds like a dying goose and it hangs in the air like a bad fart.

"I got your message."

Cool, so we're skipping the small talk.

"That's good." I sip my tea, not looking at her.

Mum shuffles in her chair. "We can talk about it now if you like? I—"

"There's nothing to say, really. I just wanted you to know."

Mum closes her eyes and does a nod so small it might have been a twitch. It's clearly taking all her strength not to press me further.

"Well, you know where I am if you want to talk. I've

booked the day of your appointment off work and told school."

"Ta," I say, downing as much of my tea as possible and blinking back the hot sensation that pricks my eyes. This may be excruciatingly awkward, but I'm so blessed to have a mum who gets shit sorted. I don't know what I'd do without her.

"Love you." I give Mum a tight smile and march out of the room before she can see my face crumple.

15

My appointment is at 2.45 p.m. on a Thursday, which sucks.

Usually Thursday is my favourite day, because I have Biology and Psychology, my top classes. But I can't concentrate on anything with this hanging over me. I've barely taken in a word about gene mutations and Bowlby's Theory of Attachment.

I also usually look forward to Thursday afternoons because the minibus drops Joel off for his photography class just before lunchtime and then we get the bus home together, but today I'll be poked by a doctor while I wear no knickers instead. Sad times.

Still, at least lunch is fun. Sixth-formers enjoy the luxury of being allowed to leave school during lunch and hitting up

Fish Palace instead of having to eat something that looks like it belongs in a Bushtucker Trial in the skanky old canteen.

A load of us are taking a slow meander back up the mammoth hill that leads to school, beautifully salty chips in hand and delicious gossip on our tongues. The current topic of conversation is the house party we all went to at the weekend. Holly knew Robert was going to be there with another girl, so she got absolutely smashed to cope. Unfortunately she got *so* smashed that Joel ended up carrying her to her mum's car before ten o'clock, but not before she chundered on his feet.

"Guys, I owe you all an apology for the other night…" says Holly, scrunching up her nose.

Joel grins back. "I don't know what you mean." He plucks a chip from the paper packet I'm holding.

Demi laughs. "Bollocks. You had a front-row seat. How're the trainers now?"

Joel shakes his head, but he's still grinning. "In the bin."

Holly wails. "Oh, God, kill me now. I bet I won't ever be invited to another party again."

"Are you kidding? It was a roaring success." Joel's glinting eyes catch mine. I love how seamlessly he fits into my friendship group. "Right, I have to get a shift on. I need to grab a camera off Mr Michaels before the bell. See you tomorrow, yeah?"

"Oh yeah, your romantic Valentine's plans." Demi mimes gagging.

"Jealous?" Joel and I both say at the same time.

Demi shakes her head vigorously. "Ha. Not a chance in hell. *Despite* Rose choosing you over the Galentine's invite to mine."

I squeeze Joel's hand. "Enjoy your lesson."

He pecks me on the cheek. "Love you." He sprints away.

"I'd better shoot as well. Phone call to make." Then Holly charges off at lightning speed. Robert, no doubt.

"So tell us again why you're leaving us this afternoon," says Demi, spinning to face me. Ugh, why can't we just keep talking about sicky trainers? Thankfully I came prepared.

"Yeah, where are you going?" asks Lena. "I need you with me in form this afternoon. I don't want to suffer Mr Lomax alone." She curls her bottom lip. "And you're still coming to mine tonight for dinner, yeah? Just you and me because someone" – Lena elbows Demi gently in the ribs – "is too busy killing it with her LNAT prep."

I hold the chips towards her while I run through my fake alibi one more time.

"You two are right nosy cows, you know that?" I say, hoping my trademark wit gives off the impression that I'm *chill* and not completely scrabbling in the abyss for my made-up excuse.

"What are you hiding?" says Demi, her coy smile telling me her question is innocent, but my guilty conscience doing the opposite. The pavement is icy and dangerously shiny under my feet as I avoid looking at either of them.

"I'm going to the dentist. Usually I'd just have an after-school appointment but they only work until three on Thursdays. And, yes, Lena, I'm still coming to yours."

Yes, I've got it out. Do the excess details about the fictional dentist's timetable make it more obvious it's a lie? Why are my palms so sweaty?

I look up from the pavement and I'm now lagging a couple of steps behind. Did Lena and Demi just exchange a look? I up my pace to join them, chin high in mock confidence.

"What was that look about?" I'm daring them to keep digging and pull me up on my lie.

They definitely look at each other this time. Lena is biting her lip and Demi is frowning.

Lena takes a deep breath. "We were just wondering … is everything all right?"

"What do you mean?" My words come out louder than intended.

"You've seemed a bit off recently." Lena crumples the empty chip paper into a ball and rolls it between her hands.

"I'm fine." *Have* I seemed off? I thought I was acting

127

totally normal. "Genuinely don't know what you're talking about."

It's Demi who answers. "You've been busier with Joel recently, seeing us less. Apart from the party this weekend, we've barely seen you outside school since New Year's Eve." Demi doesn't look like she's quite finished her list of how I've been failing as a friend, but Lena butts in.

"For me it's your energy. Your vibe just feels ... different."

"My vibe is fine."

"OK." Lena's face squashes into thought and she looks like she's having an internal conversation with herself. "I'm usually good at picking up on these things, though."

"We've known you long enough to know when you're acting weird." Demi catches the chip packet Lena throws at her and bounces it into the nearest bin.

OK. If I get mad or upset, the jig is up. I need to shut this conversation down before I crumble. "I'm really fine."

Demi huffs. "If you say so. You know where we are when you want to talk."

I hate the fact she says *when* I want to talk not *if*, like she thinks she knows me better than I know myself. Like she knows that something is definitely up.

"Do I need to say it again?"

"Nope." She shakes her head. "I hope your molars are OK."

"Me too," says Lena, "but don't ever leave me to suffer form time on my own ever again."

"Promise I won't."

Oh, if only Lena knew what I'm doing this afternoon, then she'd really know the meaning of the word "suffer".

Mum flicks through one of the grimy magazines from one of the sticky stacks on the table in the waiting room while I shuffle in my seat and scroll mindlessly on my phone.

"Have you decided if you want me to come in with you yet?" Mum continues to look through the pages of *Woman's Weekly*, feigning nonchalance.

"I dunno." The thought of her knowing such intimate knowledge about *everything* makes me want to combust from cringe, but there's still a part of me who wants to sit on her lap and look at her to answer all the difficult questions. Also, if I do go in alone, I'll have to repeat all the information back to her anyway, which would be even worse than having the doctor say it.

"Rose Summers," a voice calls from across the waiting room.

I look up and see a smiling female doctor holding a clipboard.

I stand up and Mum looks at me expectantly, already reaching for her stuff.

"Come on," I say, making a beeline for the lady. I keep my eyes locked to the floor as Mum hurries behind me with her rustling winter coat and three bags.

In the consulting room, the doctor introduces herself as Dr Andrews and immediately begins to read through my notes and relay her understanding of my issues. I cringe at the words "intercourse" and "tearing" and pick my fingernails when she asks whether it's only a problem with a penis or whether I struggle with inserting other things like fingers and tampons. I tell her I tried a while ago to use a tampon and failed, but just assumed I hadn't been brave enough with it and went back to pads because it was easier. I don't look at Mum the entire time and as each second passes my face grows hotter and I'm certain I'm the colour of a baboon's butt.

I'm strangely relieved when Dr Andrews says she will examine me in the other room because I can have a few moments without being under the scrutiny of Mum. When I follow her into the examination room, I can finally breathe.

The relief doesn't last long.

The room has two doors on the opposite wall to the entrance we just came through. Why does one room need THREE doors? They'd better all be locked before I take my knickers off. In the centre of the floor there's a large reclined chair like the one you see at the dentist, but with the hideous addition of leg stirrups at the arse end. My mouth is dry, imagining how ridiculous I'm going to look when I grace this awful throne.

"If you take off your clothes on your lower half and pop yourself on the chair, I can take a look," says Dr Andrews. There's no curtain for her to pull round me and she busies herself rifling through drawers. I look at the doors, pray to the god of locks they're secure and reluctantly pull my trousers and knickers off. Learning from my previous appointment, I make sure my discarded clothes are in a neat pile as far away from the chair as possible and do a cursory and totally unnecessary check for skid marks.

I then climb on to the chair. The paper towel scratches my bum as I shuffle down and settle into the stirrups. It's even worse than the last appointment where I could at least snap my legs shut in a second. What if someone walks in and I'm stuck like this?

Dr Andrews leans in and probes around. I writhe from the sudden wet and cold sensation and my body stiffens from the assumption of inevitable pain. I can't tell if I can feel her hot breath on me or whether it's the heat from the lamp she's using.

"Hmmm," she says as she walks back to the drawers and shuffles through them, the sound of plastic hitting plastic echoing around the room. She turns round with a clear speculum in one hand and looks at it intently. "You know what, I'm not going to attempt to pop this in right now," she says gently. She places it down on the side and walks over to the bin in the corner.

I swallow. That can't be a good sign. If the doctor isn't confident enough to put a speculum inside me, there must be something properly wrong.

"Nothing's going in there," she mutters to herself as she pulls off her gloves and drops them into the pedal bin with a clang.

Did I hear her right? I can't have. Joel will fit in there. He *has* to. My heart starts pounding so fast I feel like I'm vibrating.

I force my breath to slow.

In. Out. In. Out.

This will be over soon. Everything will be fine. Joel is just large in the penis department, like the last doctor said. There's nothing wrong with me. We can fix it. Together.

Dr Andrews returns to me and lowers the stirrups. "You've done really well, Rose. Pop your clothes on when you're ready." Then she disappears through the door.

I step off the chair and teeter my way to the pile of clothes in the corner. My eyes dribble hot tears down my already scalding cheeks. I swat them away. I don't need to cry before I even hear what the doctor has to say. If I go back into the room crying, Mum will try to comfort me and I don't want her to worry.

I pull my clothes on slowly and go back into the consulting room.

I can tell Mum is looking at me, but I don't look back and instead focus on Dr Andrews.

She looks sympathetic, which worries me.

"OK, Rose, now the first thing I want to say is that you were absolutely right to get this checked out. Trying to have sex must have been very painful for you. It seems the structure of the vaginal opening has been altered, possibly due to a skin condition you might have had at some point in your life, perhaps as a baby, so you may not even remember it. My guess would be lichen sclerosus, although there is no active condition at present. But scar tissue doesn't stretch well, you see. It also looks to have affected the vulva by eroding and fusing your labia minora, making it pretty much non-existent. The clitoral hood looks fairly tight and small also. This would explain why you felt this pain when attempting intercourse…"

Eroded? Altered structure? It's confirmed: I'm not normal and there is something wrong.

Dr Andrews is still talking, but I zone out.

How am I going to tell Joel? Perhaps I should be

133

thinking about myself and how I feel. But all I can think about is that he definitely won't stick around now. Why would he?

"Rose, how are you feeling about all this?"

I'm pulled against my will back into this nightmare. Mum and Dr Andrews stare at me.

How do I feel? Don't know. There's only one answer I need right now.

"What's next?" It comes out as a whisper.

"The structural damage can only be reversed with surgery."

My stomach plummets and the dizziness returns to swallow me whole.

"Surgery?" Mum and I say in unison.

"I understand this is a shock, but it's very minor surgery, just a little trim to cut away scar tissue, and it has an excellent success rate. It's the only thing I'm confident will allow you to have penetrative sex."

The chips I ate for lunch threaten to make an appearance as I grapple for a breath. "I–I don't want to have an operation," I stammer. Why should I have to be put to sleep and have my bits cut with a scalpel to do something that's meant to be as natural as breathing? No one else in the VW chat has ever mentioned surgery – trust me to stand out among a group of individuals who already stand out.

"There are other options you can explore first while you're on the waiting list for surgery, if you'd like? There's likely to be a three- to four-month wait."

Options? Yes please.

"I'd do anything to avoid having surgery," I whisper. It's already been three months since Joel and I first tried to have sex. I can't wait three to four months more. That's a lifetime.

Dr Andrews starts tapping something into her computer. "I understand that. As I said, surgery is the most effective option—"

"I still want to try." I'll make the alternatives work.

Doctor Andrews nods and continues to move her mouth, but I hope Mum's listening because I can't take in anything else.

16

So, at the age of seventeen, I have an impenetrable vagina. When I should be focusing on my A levels, the prom, shagging my boyfriend and the last few months before heading off to uni, instead I'm dealing with a vaginal hell I never knew existed.

I pull out my phone and update the VagWarriors. I need to get everything out of my head because currently words like "scar tissue" and "erosion" are bouncing around my skull with nowhere to go.

Roseycheeks_x: So there is something medically wrong with me. I might need an operation and I've been prescribed a vibrator and plastic vaginal dilators – and that's not even the worst part. I'm being referred for pelvic floor physiotherapy 😢 😢 😢

Endo2005: How does any sort of physiotherapy exist for that omg??!!

Moongirlxoxo: I'm googling pelvic floor physio now <3 xxxx

Anon_69: same

Of course that was the first thing I did when I got back. Yeah, I *really* wish I hadn't.

Your physical therapist may assist you with inserting progressively sized dilators to stretch and desensitize your vagina…

That's right – I'll be watched doing things I'm not comfortable doing in my own bedroom. When Dr Andrews first mentioned physiotherapy, I really wanted to believe I'd be coached through a curtain, but, of course, that would be too dignified. If my stomach fell out of my arse after reading that first part, it dropped through the crust of the Earth and into its molten core when I read the next bit:

> *Your physical therapist will also use manual therapy such as intravaginal massage (soft-tissue massage inside your vagina) using their own fingers...*

Inside. Your. Vagina.

Surely it's not OK to let a stranger – doctor or otherwise – insert their fingers inside me, like properly in and wiggling around? Doesn't that mean I'll be leaving the session having been fingered by the physiotherapist?

Kill me now.

Endo2005: OMG NO

Moongirlxoxo: Oh gosh, that doesn't sound ideal :/

Anon_69: MORTIFYING

It_hurtttsssssss: Sounds crap but better than an op surely?

TK_1000: It sounds horrendous

Roseycheeks_x: The dilators have to work. Not gonna even think about an op yet. The waiting list is months anyway

Anon_69: When is your first session?

Roseycheeks_x: 7th March 😕 We're giving the dilators and physio two months

I glance at the time. I'm due at Lena's in twenty minutes. I lock my phone and drop it on to my bed. I'm absolutely not in the mood to go anywhere right now, apart from the kitchen for some commiseration chocolate or the bathroom to wash off the remnants of lube sticking my butt cheeks together. But I'm going anyway because she's already suspicious and I need to continue acting as normal as possible – whatever the hell that even looks like any more.

I should have stayed at home. The minute Lena and I get into her bedroom she shoves a tarot deck into my hands and tugs me down to the floor.

"Shuffle the deck." She drops to her knees opposite me. She takes the Tarot very seriously, so I do as I'm told then hand the shuffled deck back to her. The sooner I can switch her out of witch mode the better. I feel vulnerable enough as it is. I just want to watch telly in her bed, not have her looking into my soul.

She lays the cards out in some intricate spread and does that thing where she frowns and her tongue pops out. I wait for her brow to soften, but it doesn't. She shakes her head.

"I knew it."

I laugh nervously. "Don't tell me it says I'm going to die."

"Nope. And we've been over this. Even if you did get the death card, it doesn't mean you'll die. The death card is more about—"

"What do my cards say? You've made me nervous now." I don't even believe in this stuff.

Lena bites her lip. "The cards say you are going through a life change and have battled or will be battling hardship."

Balls. Perhaps it's not total rubbish after all. "That could mean anything. Uni?"

Lena's mouth scrunches and she shakes her head again. "That's not what I'm getting. I'm getting…" She closes her eyes. Her moon-shaped clock *tick tick tick*s as the seconds pass.

"What? This is stupid. Put them away."

"I'm getting feminine energies. I'm getting sexuality. I'm getting secrets." Her eyes open and she looks at me with such intensity I feel like she's stripped me bare.

"Well, you're wrong." I move to get up, but she grabs my wrist.

"The cards are never wrong. Please tell me what's going on. I love you – I want to help."

I desperately blink away the tears that are assaulting me, pull away from Lena's grip and flop on to her bed. "Those stupid cards." I bury my head into her pillow.

I sense Lena moving to lie next to me. She sighs. "Sorry. My vibe is never off. Never."

"Clearly." I sit and wipe my eyes with her bedcovers. The jig is up. "I have a lot to explain."

"We have time."

I take a deep breath. "Joel and I haven't had sex." I say it before I can talk myself out of it.

"What?" Lena's face crumples in such confusion I'd be inclined to laugh if I wasn't so disgustingly ashamed.

"Ever? But … you said you had. Lots of times. I mean … how come?"

"It's complicated."

Lena nods slowly. "It usually is."

"Basically we tried and it didn't work. Saw a doctor who told me to try doggy. Still didn't happen. Saw a specialist this afternoon who told me I was broken. That's it in a nutshell."

It feels scarily real to say it out loud.

Lena frowns. "Hang on a sec." She reaches for her phone and fiddles with it for a few seconds. Is now really the time to be texting?!

My phone pings. I reach into my pocket and look at it. One new notification in the VagWarriors chat.

Moongirlxoxo: Testing my Wi-Fi...

"Hang on a minute," I say. "Are you—"

"Moongirl! Are you Roseycheeks by any chance?" Lena's eyes widen.

I stare at her and nod.

Lena shakes her head in disbelief. "Is this actually happening? How did you find the group?"

"Through MyVagVicki."

"Ohhh. I'm a bit obsessed with her, I must admit. She's great, isn't she? So open."

"Very open. I could never." I shake my head, still in total shock that Lena has been in the VagWarriors this whole time. "I can't believe you're Moongirlxoxo."

"The universe works in mysterious ways." Lena has that faraway look in her eyes again. "I'm so glad our souls chose to reincarnate again together in this life as well as our previous ones. So we can at least go through this together."

"You think we've shared past lives together then?"

"Absolutely. We both have very old souls. Mine is ancient. Been on this Earth in many different guises before. I reckon in a previous life I was your mum."

I laugh. "What did I do in a past life to deserve a best friend like you, eh?"

Lena grins. "Perhaps you were a really good daughter to me … or maybe an excellent lover."

"Well, whatever the hell it is, I'm eternally grateful."

Her face drops from a smile to an expression of horror. "Oh my God. But that means … you're the poor soul who might need yoni physio?"

"That's me. I'm terrified about the whole thing – the physio, the op…"

"My poor lil Rose. Come here." Lena pulls me into a hug and squeezes. I suck in a breath and pull at the ears of her childhood toy Runey Rabbit that's lying on the bed. "How's Joel been about it?"

"I haven't actually told him yet that it's proper serious. He's been OK about not having sex, but I still feel guilty."

Lena bites her lip. "I'm glad he's not pushing you, but I hate that you feel guilty. Remember, you don't owe him this. Sex is way more than the phallus entering the yonic space."

"Mmmm." I know she's trying to make me feel better, but what if I *want* Joel's phallus to enter my yonic space? I'm ready for that. I chose that. But, in Joel's words, my vagina said no.

"Hold up," I say. "Enough about me. You have your own issues, right?"

Lena's watery blue eyes meet mine quickly before dropping to the duvet we're sitting on. She twirls her pendant necklace in one hand and bites the nails of the other. "Mmm. I'm worried I might have anorgasmia."

"When you can't orgasm, right?" Our chat at the yoga session a while back pings in my mind. Now I understand why Lena was so curious about my non-orgasm. "Why do you think you've got that?"

"My mum has it. Ever since she mentioned it, I've been so worried I have the same thing." She moves to rest her chin on her knee.

"You spoke to your mum about that?"

Lena chuckles. "You know what she's like. She's been talking about the power of my sacred cave since I could talk."

I nod. "Wow, anorgasmia must suck."

"Mum *hated* it for a long time, but she's at peace with it now and still enjoys sex – unfortunately." Lena mimes being sick. "It was worse when she was younger. Men would see her as a challenge, like they thought they could do a better job than those before, and even Mum herself!"

I roll my eyes. "Oh, to have the confidence of a man."

"Yep. Now Mum focuses on the nice sensations rather than aiming for the end goal. And tantra … The less I say about that the better." Lena pulls a face.

"So do you think you have it?"

"Dunno. I'm going to try a few more things out. Mum says the worst thing I can do is stress about it because your head's gotta be in the right place for it to happen. Maybe I'm psyching myself out."

"We're a right pair, aren't we?" I lean into Lena's shoulder and rest my head in her curls. They smell like coconut. I hate that she's having her own issues, but I can't deny my relief that I'm not alone in all this.

"Yep. So weird we're both VagWarriors. Our little exclusive club." She tips her head on to mine and squeezes me in the space between her ear and shoulder.

"One I'd rather not be a member of." I laugh. "Good name, though."

"Has a nice ring to it." Lena lifts her head and finds my eyes. "Are you going to tell Demi? I assume you haven't."

I hadn't even thought of that. I really don't want to tell anyone else. Demi will have so much to say, and I don't know if I can face any more questions.

"You assume correctly. I haven't yet. You're the only person who knows, apart from Joel and Mum."

Lena's eyebrows rise. It's as close as she'll ever get to judging me. "You've not even told Sammy? Why not?"

"The fewer people who know the better. It makes me feel so … abnormal and … ugh. This is why I kept it from you guys this whole time. I'll tell Demi soon, though."

"OK." Lena taps me on the nose. "Your secret's safe with me."

17

For twenty-four hours I don't say anything to Joel about my appointment. Once I tell him, it'll make it real. I manage to hold him off with a message that simply says: Yeah, I'm OK. Can explain more tomorrow.

But tomorrow is now, so I'll have to tell him. It was Valentine's Day on Wednesday and tonight is our chance to properly celebrate, which makes having to tell him the news even more shit. I know he's got plans for us, and I don't want to ruin them. But the only other way to put off telling him is to cancel and I'm not going to do that.

So here I am, hopping off the bus, feeling rather sorry for myself and expecting to see Joel at the bus stop as usual. But he's not there.

He's *always* there before me on a Friday.

I pull my phone from my pocket, but have no messages or missed calls from him. That's weird. The bus hisses as it pulls away, and everyone else who got off at my stop disperses, leaving me standing alone, trying to look like I'm not being stood up.

I perch on the narrow metal bench, its coldness seeping through my trousers and making my bum numb. I try Joel's phone, but it goes straight to answerphone. On cue, it starts to rain – not a gentle patter, a zero-to-one-hundred deluge hammering the flimsy plastic shelter.

I fire off multiple messages to Joel in quick succession.

Where are you?

Are you OK?

I'm worried!

Call me!!!!!!

Everything stops at one tick – not delivered. I try to call again, but it still doesn't ring. He'd never stand me up, would he?

"Rose!"

Wet slapping footsteps grow closer and through the rain

and smeared windows of the shelter a tall blur of ginger, grey and red comes into focus.

I stand as he swings round the corner.

Water droplets run down his nose and drip off the tip. His curls are flat and plastered to his forehead, and what I assume are his light grey joggers are three shades darker than normal. He's clutching a bunch of roses to his chest. He thrusts them at me and runs his hands through his fiery hair.

"What a mess! This is not how I planned it." He's out of breath, but he's smiling the biggest smile I've seen from him in weeks. That cheeky glint in his eye is back. I throw my arms round him, roses still in his hand. His neck still smells like him despite his aftershave being washed off by the rain. Freezing-cold water drips down my sleeves and collar and I squeeze him tighter. God, how am I going to tell him what the specialist said?

Joel tries to pull away gently, but I don't loosen my grip. He chuckles. "You OK?"

I nod into his neck. "Yep, just love you."

He chuckles again. "I love you too. It's only been five minutes."

"Seven," I correct him. "I thought you were standing me up." I release him and take the roses, admiring their velvety folds. "Thank you for these."

"You're welcome. And the reality is way less dramatic I'm afraid. There was a queue at Foliage and Florals and my phone's dead."

Silence hangs between us, only interrupted by the odd car splashing past. I stare at the roses again, willing myself to be lost in their hypnotic swirls.

I let out a sigh. "I need to tell you something."

Joel looks at me, eyes creased with concern. "Is everything OK?"

"Yes. No. Ish?" I push Joel on to the bus-stop bench, put the flowers down and stand in front of him, tucked between his legs. I want to look him in the eyes, but I can't, so instead I busy myself fiddling with his collar.

What I want to say is: *Oh my God, I'm so scared and confused. Please cuddle me and tell me everything is OK and that I'm worth sticking around for.* But I can't say that. I don't want to scare him into thinking this is a huge thing.

I finally find my voice. "I need to debrief you on yesterday. Basically, the doctor said that when I was a baby they think I had a skin condition that left scarring. It means the skin down there is tighter and the hole smaller. There are options to fix it, though." I take a short breath, but don't stop long enough for Joel to say anything. "I can try these things called dilators and also a vibrator." I finally meet his eyes.

"A vibrator?"

"Apparently it will help me stretch during physical therapy. The other option is an operation, which I REALLY don't want to do, but I'm on the waiting list. So, yeah, that's the current situation." I stop and take a deep breath. There's no going back now.

Joel's eyes dart all over the place, clearly processing what I've just said. Finally he speaks. "How's a vibrator different to my dick, though?"

Is he serious? That's all he's going to take from that?

"Out of everything I said, you're focusing on that?" I search his face, waiting for it to soften, but it doesn't.

"It's just a bit weird."

"Weird for me or weird for you? I'm not exactly thrilled at the thought of using a vibrator in front of an old lady at a hospital."

His brow creases. "You'll use it in front of her? We've never even done anything like that."

There were many responses I was expecting from him, but this was NOT one of them.

"Do you not fancy asking if I'm OK? Or, you know, saying what a decent boyfriend would say – that you'll support me through this? Is the only thing you're arsed about the fact that I'll own a vibrator?" I pull back from him and cross my arms.

Joel shrugs. "I'm just saying if you can fit a vibrator, then you can definitely fit me."

I'm momentarily lost for words, before too many words come at once.

"It didn't even cross my mind you'd be jealous of that, given it's SO RIDICULOUS. The doctor has literally prescribed it to me. I don't WANT IT. I NEED IT! What's wrong with you? Maybe you're joking? Surely that can only be a joke … SURELY?"

I start pacing the pavement. I don't care if there are other people around – what the hell is wrong with him?

"So are we going to stop trying then?"

My eyesight blurs with furious tears. I blink them away and stare at him.

"WHAT PART OF WHAT I'VE JUST TOLD YOU IS ME NOT TRYING? ALL YOU HAVE TO DO IS SUPPORT ME AND BE PATIENT."

I worried so much about telling him and spent so long choosing exactly the right words so he didn't have to feel as crappy about the whole thing as I do, and he's throwing it back in my face. I dismissed my own feelings, and for what?

"I'm leaving." I spin away from him and start striding away. I have no idea what my plan is. I just walk, despite the downpour.

"Where are you going?" Joel shouts after me. "Rose, wait. You left your flowers."

"Keep them," I shout back, not turning round.

"Please don't go. I'm sorry! Please just stop for a second." Joel's beside me now.

His apology halts me and the tears I was holding back come thick and fast. I stop and stare at the ground, frozen.

"I mean it. I'm really sorry." He cups my head and pulls it into his chest. He kisses my hair and I lean into his firm chest. "I don't know what to say. I feel useless and pushed out and I panicked. Please take this as my pledge to you that I want to fix this with you, whatever that looks like, dildo included."

I feel my soul relax into him even more.

"I forgive you. I'm sorry too," I mumble into his chest, although I'm not sure why I'm apologizing.

"Don't be sorry. You didn't do anything wrong. I was a massive dick."

I choose not to say, *Yes, you were* – anger placated somewhat by his pledge, the comforting scent of his damp, musky chest and the blur of red from the roses squashed between us.

When I get home, I put my roses in a vase and stare at them. I know I'm lucky to have Joel, even if he doesn't always say the right things. No one's perfect and he did make it up to me by taking us to Wagamama's and then snuggling while we watched a film at his after. We didn't do anything sexual because I was all touched out from my examination yesterday and just wanted a cuddle. Thankfully, he didn't complain.

My phone buzzes as I settle into bed.

Holly: Secret intel incoming

Holly: Rob and I are back on. He asked me to be his girlfriend again!!!

Rose: OK. Why do you wanna keep it a secret?

Holly: Rob does. He thinks it will take the pressure off us

Rose: Are you OK with it?

Holly: Yeah! It makes sense tbh. I'm sure Monica and Demi would have plenty of opinions on the matter!!!!!!

I also have opinions on the matter, but I know if I get too vocal about Robert she'll still see him, but deal with it alone rather than having someone to talk to. I'm diplomatic with my reply.

> **Rose**: They only care about you, though, like I do! I'm still worried about you but I trust you've got this. You know where I am if you need me xxxxx

There's also a notification in the chat.

> **Anon_69**: MyVagVicki just posted this – might be useful to you **@Roseycheeks_x**

I click on the link. In the video, Vicki is talking about her dilators and how she's excited for her first physio session. How on earth can she be excited? She then shows them on screen, talking through the different sizes and marvelling at the cute little bag she's bought to keep them in.

"So there are five sizes, starting with the smallest, just larger than a tampon," she says as she waves the little white tube in front of the camera as if she's a beauty influencer showing us her new #gifted lipstick. "And it goes all the way up to the largest."

Bloody hell, the size of it! It's like a large can of deodorant – wide as well as long. Vicki then waves the plastic stick base that the tubes attach to like it's some sort of phallic magic wand.

I watch the video three times and afterwards I can't work out if it's made me feel better or worse. It's nice to know I'm not the only person in the world facing physio, but Vicki seems to be taking it in her stride. She's confident and chill, excited even, all things I am absolutely not. She's here showing the world what I can't even bring myself to share with Demi – one of my best friends – and, as the date of my physio ticks closer every day, all I feel is utterly horrified.

18

My life has ended and this is hell. My mum has bought me a vibrator.

She's holding a discreet black bag over the dining-room table. "Here," she says. "I'll let you do the honours."

"Thanks," I mutter, grabbing it from her and reaching inside. My cheeks are already flaming as her eyes bore into me. How am I supposed to act in this situation? I pull out the box and look at it quickly, ignoring the three bottles of lube rolling around the bottom of the bag. I nod. "Yep, that's what the doctor ordered. Thanks."

Her posture relaxes. "It was rather embarrassing. I couldn't find the one the doctor suggested – Promises it's called – so I had to ask a shop assistant. I'm sure she must have thought I was way too old for such a small sparkly thing." She snorts.

The room falls silent.

"Go on then, crack it open."

Really? Surely it's best for both of us if I go upstairs, hide the damn thing before Dad and Sammy come back and then pretend this never happened.

"I'll look at it later." I check the clock. No one else is due home for over two hours.

"Go on – I'm intrigued!"

"You're so nosy!"

"I'm allowed to be nosy – I bought it. Give it here." Mum takes the box and goes to the drawer to get a pair of scissors.

She attacks the box for a few moments, removing the plastic insert the toy is stuck in before popping it out. It's hot pink and glittery like Mum said, but it certainly isn't *small*. I guess small is only relative to what you've had going in – or out – of there in your lifetime. I can see how it's small for someone who has pushed two heads out, but for someone who struggles with a finger, it will be a miracle if I even get an inch in.

"Right, how does this work then?" Mum gives it a shake. Nothing happens. "They're all different, I swear. Why does it have to be so complicated."

158

Ew, why does she sound like some sort of expert? No. Just no.

Perhaps if I treat it like a new toy at Christmas I can temporarily forget my mum is holding my doctor-prescribed sex toy in her hands.

"Did it come with batteries?" I ask.

Mum tips the box upside down and two wrapped batteries drop out. "Genius," she says.

I watch as she fiddles with it, twisting the end cap off and slotting the batteries in. She turns the toy back up the right way and stares at it. "Now what? There's no button." She drops the vibrator on to the table and it starts buzzing, a loud hum filling the room as it grinds against the wooden table. "Ahhhhhh," she says, flapping, both smiling and grimacing. She's enjoying this.

"Oh my God, really?" I grab the vibrating monster off the table and begin to flap it about myself. "Where's the off switch?"

"I don't know!"

"You turned it on!"

The vibrations course up my arm. I turn the vibrator round in my hands, pushing the end to no avail and then twisting it one way and then the other. The tremors cease.

"Oh, you twist the bottom." I demonstrate just to be

sure. On. Off. I look at Mum, who is biting her lip to prevent herself from smiling. I'm guessing I look the same, but with the addition of a glittery penis in my hand.

We burst out laughing.

"Well, that's enough excitement for one day," I say, diving for the carrier bag and dropping the toy into it.

"Maybe not for you." Mum smirks.

Oh my God, as if she said that. There's something worse about her thinking I'm using a vibrator than knowing I tried to have sex. "Gross. This is for medical use."

"I'm only joking. Now off you pop. Sammy's back in a couple of hours so you might want to make the most of the empty house."

"Noooo," I whine, suddenly regressing to a toddler.

"Right, well, I'm putting my foot down then. Fill the dishwasher or go upstairs and give this a whirl."

I look around at the carnage of last night's dinner: the stacks of plates, bowls, pots and pans everywhere after Dad tried a new experimental recipe for the first time. I groan. "Fine. Don't come upstairs." With the carrier bag swinging on my wrist, I head out of the kitchen.

In my room, I close the door and pull the beige bag of dilators out from their hiding place at the back of the wardrobe – unlike Vicki, I have no plans to treat myself to a new bag to keep them in. They arrived in the post yesterday morning and had a much more discreet arrival than the vibrator.

I upend the bag of dilators on to my duvet with a clatter − a phallic symphony. I tip the vibrator and the lube from their own bag and survey the collection in front of me. It looks so pornographic against my Cath Kidston bedding. I can't believe I have an appointment with these bad boys every night for the foreseeable future.

My phone lights up on the bedside table.

> **Demi**: I'm passing yours on way back from my aunts.
> Mum said she can drop us off at the cafe in village if
> you're around for a quick catch-up?

I look again at the scene in front of me and sigh. She really does pick her moments (unconsciously, obvs). The truth is I'd love to join her, but now is *not* a good time.

> **Rose**: Sorry I can't. Soon though, need more warning
> next time!! Xx

I lock my phone and place it face down so I'm not distracted again.

The first thing I should do is look at my vulva − see what I'm working with to determine which size to try first. Doctor Andrews' words about how I'm *altered* down there have been lurking in the back of my brain ever since she uttered the words "eroded" and "labia minora".

I tiptoe back to my door to listen to Mum downstairs, as I need to be certain she isn't going to be marching past my door every few minutes. But the TV's turned all the way up and the muffle suggests she's got the living-room door shut too. It's safe. Well, as safe as can be.

I put it off for a minute longer by quickly messaging the VW chat – *Dilators here I come* – before finally pulling my trousers and knickers down and quickly getting under the duvet. I grab a mirror with a long handle from my bedside table and take a deep breath, readying myself for what I might see. Lena has helpfully sent me a gallery of lots of different pictures of vulvas for comparison, but stressed to me that *no two yonis are the same*.

At first glance it looks pretty – dare I say it – normal, whatever that means. There's a hole and if the doctor hadn't said anything I would have assumed it was of average size. There is a high bit of skin covering some of it, but I'd have thought that's what a normal perineum looks like. My inner flaps (*labia minora*) are pretty much non-existent, but my clit is definitely there, just not as prominent as some people's. I want to sigh with relief, but there's no relief to be had because it's now time for the dilators.

I'm tempted to try one of the medium-sized ones – fast-track my progress by a few weeks – but a closer look at their size makes me discard them instantly. Who am I kidding? I pick up the smallest one, fix it to the wand with a click and then reach for the lube.

I fumble under the covers, but I can't see a thing. I inch the duvet back, just enough so I can adjust the angle of the wand but not so much that I can't yank the covers over me if someone were to come up the stairs.

I forge ahead, repeating the mantra *Do it for Joel. Do it for Joel* in my head.

I push through the burn until I'm able to get the smallest one in enough to consider it progress.

Relief overwhelms me as I take it out. But it feels like I'll never be able to work my way up to the biggest one, or even the smaller tapered tip of the vibrator. I can see that taking months or even years. Joel would hardly stick around for that long and I wouldn't blame him.

I grab the vibrator and twirl it around in my hand. I hold the tip of it centimetres from my face; it smells like sweet rubber. *Promises*. That's a name full of hope if I ever did hear one.

19

This is the perfect moment for me to tell Demi my secret.

We're in the common room alone together. I'm on my laptop with a million tabs open, displaying all the possible Biology-related careers I could possibly do on this side of the Atlantic. Now I know I'm either doing something linked to Biology or Psychology I'm keen to work out what it is I want to do with my degree once I get it. Demi is balanced on a chair behind me, leaning back with her feet on the desk and scrolling through her phone. Lena is in a meeting with Miss Starmann and Joel's due to arrive soon.

I have to tell Demi. The guilt is getting heavy and she knows something is wrong. Telling her might make me feel more in control because it's on my terms.

Demi huffs and moves to perch on the radiator next to me.

"Won't you get piles sitting on that?"

"I like having a warm bum." She wiggles her hips to labour the point.

"I don't. In Dad's car, the heated seats make you feel like you've just farted—"

"Ooohhhh!" Demi thrusts her phone into my face. "How about a doctor? Doctor Rose?"

"Hmmm. Maybe? I wouldn't want too much responsibility – not life-and-death stuff."

I turn my attention back to my screen. "Doctor Rose" does sound good, but my soul still hasn't reacted in a favourable manner. Also, I'd have to do loads of training after my degree to become one, and if I wanted to do that I should have chosen a medicine undergrad degree.

"Food for thought." Demi shifts back to sit on the radiator again and keeps scrolling. She's frowning and biting her lip. "Total topic change here, but I wanted to talk to you about something—"

"'Ello, 'ello."

She's interrupted by Joel walking through the door and joining us. He wraps his arms round my shoulders and kisses my head. "All right, Demi?"

For a second, I think I catch her eyes roll, but then she

165

slaps on a grin. I must be seeing things. "All good," she says. "Just trying to find a career path for your lovely girlfriend. How d'ya fancy going out with a doctor?"

"Oooh, matron," says Joel in a high-pitched voice.

"Don't get your hopes up," I say.

Joel slides his hand into mine and squeezes.

There's a beat of silence as Demi keeps looking at her phone.

"Oh my God." Demi slaps me on the shoulder. "You could be a gynaecologist."

My stomach flips and Joel's hand stiffens.

"What?" we say in unison.

I avoid looking at Joel, but I'm sure the hot flush of my cheeks is giving me away.

Demi turns back to her screen, none the wiser. "There are doctors for all sorts of things," she says. "How about willies?"

Joel shakes his head. "I'm off. Lesson in five and I need a piss." He heads to the door without his usual kiss on my nose.

Demi's brow creases. "Is he all right?"

"Think he forgot his camera," I lie. I'm not going to make it even more obvious we have a complex about sex. I breathe out, plaster on a smile and shrug. No harm done.

"So no to being a gynae then?"

166

"Definite no." I half laugh. I can't tell her now. The moment is gone. Another time.

"Oooh." Demi flaps her hands at me. "Seventh of March. Put it in your calendar. That new Greta Gerwig film is out in cinemas and I need to go and see it with my girls. Dinner at mine after? I—"

'I already have plans on the seventh of March." It's physio day. I bite my lip and wait for her to ask the inevitable.

'Why? What are you doing?"

"Joel," I babble, scared that if I think too much I'll overcomplicate it or, God forbid, actually tell her the truth.

"You're *doing* Joel? I'm not sure that's a good enough reason to stand me up again." Demi frowns at me.

Stand her up? It wasn't my fault she texted the other day with absolutely no notice whatsoever about hanging out. Just because she was free doesn't mean I needed to drop everything for her. But I'm not arguing about that now. 'Sorry, not *doing* Joel. His mum said she wanted to take us out."

"Why?"

"Because she will have just been paid?" What am I on about?

Demi sighs dramatically and then forces a smile. Clearly she can't be arsed to discuss this any further either. "It's fine. Right. I've got a favour to ask. I was wondering if you'd talk to Skye."

I frown. "About?"

"I'll let her explain it, but basically she wanted to talk to someone about sex."

"Why doesn't she go to Holly or Reggie? Or you? Isn't she your Chemistry chum?" The feeling of panic returns.

"Apparently I'm not good enough for my Chemistry chum because I've not had sex yet, apart from with myself obviously." A timid-looking year twelve looks up from the computer he's at and Demi looks like she's about to growl at him. "And she's tried Holly and Reggie and they weren't helpful. She's heard through the grapevine, and by the grapevine I mean Holly, that you're a fountain of knowledge on the subject."

"She has?"

"Here she is now." Demi nods at the door. Skye wanders in, offering me a shy smile. Demi raises her eyebrows at me and pats me on the bum. "Off you go, sex goddess. Impart your wisdom."

Great.

I shuffle towards Skye and return her smile, not quite meeting her eye.

"Demi said you wanted a chat? Where do you want to—"

"Have you eaten? We could go to McDonald's. I've got my car." Skye's already turning round and walking down the corridor.

"Sure, sounds good." I'm always jealous of the students who have cars – or friends who have them. They nip off to McDonald's, Subway and Starbucks and come back flaunting their wares, making us bus-dwellers sniff the tantalizing scent of their steaming nuggets and pumpkin-spiced lattes. Once George Thurrock came back with an entire cooked chicken from Sainsbury's.

I slide into the passenger seat of Skye's car – a Fiat 500, thankfully without the eyelashes – and busy myself with my seat belt. Skye and I never hang out without other people around so it feels weird and awkward.

She turns on the engine and pulls out of the school car park before I find my voice. Like Holly, Skye's come to me for help. I might not have all the answers, but at the very least I can offer her some reassurance and a listening ear. "So … what do you want to talk about?"

Skye bites her lip and stares straightforward – I'd like to think it's because she's a careful driver, but, given the number of times we've gone airborne over the speed bumps near school, it's more likely because she's too uncomfortable to make eye contact with me.

"How did you know you were ready to shag Joel?"

The dense feeling in my stomach lightens. This is a question I can answer. Yeah, OK, I've not *actually* shagged him, but I did know that I was *ready* to.

My mind flashes back to the moment I decided. Demi, Lena and I were in the common room when Holly appeared out of nowhere.

"Leila told me she and Otis had dry sex," she had stated.

"I thought that was for dogs?" said Lena.

Demi, Lena and I had all agreed the concept was bollocks, to which Holly just shrugged.

"Any developments in that department for you guys?"

Lena had grinned. "Nope. Still focusing on myself this year."

Then Holly had turned to me. "Rose? You've been with Joel for ages now. I'm surprised you haven't yet."

I knew she didn't mean anything by it, but it didn't exactly feel good to hear that. Joel was hardly starved for attention in that department. Anyway, I was waiting for him. I didn't know *why* we hadn't done it yet – sex was the next logical step in our relationship.

Very predictably, I was super anxious before doing *anything* below the waist when we'd first started seeing each other – the idea of being touched by someone else made me feel so … vulnerable and sort of gave me the ick too. But then one night when Sonya was out it just happened, and it felt nice and weird and scary and right all at the same time. I figured that sex would happen in the same way. But time had passed and it hadn't. I'd been waiting for Joel to mention it. But he hadn't. Why not? Did he not want it? Was he scared too? Was it just not as much of a big deal to him?

By the time I'd got into bed that evening, Holly's words still ringing in my ears, I'd got myself so worked up I'd texted Joel just that: Why don't you want to have sex with me?

He called me. "You're a numpty," he'd said. No hello or anything.

"Why?" I'd said sheepishly.

"To think I wouldn't want to have sex with you."

"Well, it hasn't happened yet and I thought it might have by now—"

"I didn't know you wanted to. I'm not a mind-reader." He'd laughed and I'd relaxed a bit.

"I was waiting for you to make the first move."

"I was waiting for *you* to. I didn't want to push you or make you feel like it was moving too fast, ya know."

"What an absolute gent."

"I do try. So do you want to then?"

"I think so."

"You think?"

"I *know*," I'd said.

All that feels like yesterday and an entire lifetime ago at the same time. I look at Skye as she signals into the McDonald's car park. "It just felt right." I shrug. "Like I knew he was the one I wanted to do it with for the first time. I trusted him and I felt comfortable with him to know that I could communicate how I was feeling. I felt … safe."

"So it was a feeling?"

"Yeah, I guess so. Maybe even a deep knowing. In the same way you know your name or that you're hungry."

We pull into the drive-through and order two lots of chicken nuggets and chips. We roll forward to wait in the queue to pay.

"OK. It's just that on paper I *should* be ready to have sex with Tegan. But I'm still not sure I want to." Skye taps her card through the open window and I drop my half of the money into her coin tray. She thanks the cashier and on to the food hatch we roll. She hands me the drinks and the brown bag, its warm grease seeping into my lap as we park up.

"What makes you think you *should* then?"

"Well, we've been seeing each other for over six months, and they're absolutely my person."

"So what aren't you sure about?" I say through a

mouthful of nugget and BBQ sauce. "And it's absolutely OK that you're not sure."

Skye slurps her Fanta, face thoughtful. "I'm not sure I want things to change. I'm happy with all the kissing and cuddling and fooling around. I worry that all the nice stuff like that will stop. Did it change when you and Joel did it? Get more complicated?"

I want to laugh. Did things change and get complicated when Joel and I "did" it? Does a bear shit in the woods? I miss the cuddling we used to do all the time without the thought that I need to do something sexual for Joel hanging over my head, and I continue to earn my self-given title of Queen of the Guilty Handjob most times I see him, whether or not I'm in the mood myself. I *resent* the fact that the dynamic between us has changed because I can't give him what he wants and feel like a failure. I know it's different to what she's asking, but the decision to have sex did change everything – just not in the way I could ever expect.

"The honest answer is yes. But I guess change isn't always bad?" I feel like offering her at least some hope. My experience is clearly not the norm and I guess our problems stem from the lack of sex, rather than an abundance of it.

"True."

"Have you spoken to Tegan about it? Do you know how they feel?"

Skye nods and sighs. "They're ready. So I feel guilty."

Now guilt is something I know *very* well.

"I get that."

"You do?"

"Mmm." I stuff the final wad of chips into my mouth and crumple up the bag. I keep catching sight of the time on the dashboard and it's getting worryingly close to afternoon form time. We need to wrap this up, even though I don't want to. I could sit here and talk to Skye all afternoon. "Look, it sounds to me like you know deep down whether you're ready or not. And if you're not, there's nothing wrong with that. You shouldn't feel pressured to do it and Tegan will get it – it's so obvious they love you. They'll wait."

Pot. Kettle. Black. But I know I'm not the only person not to take my own advice.

"And if they don't? Wait, I mean."

"Then they're not the one for you. But I doubt that very much – Demi's told me about the way you look at each other in Chemistry."

"Thanks, that's actually really helpful."

"It is?"

Skye nods and then switches the engine on. She reverses out of the parking space without looking, grinning at me. "You're a really good listener; has anyone ever told you that?"

Actually they have – more times in the last few weeks than in the rest of my entire life.

"You should be a counsellor," Skye continues.

I look at her and start to laugh – me, the screw-up, a counsellor – but she's smiling at me and totally serious. Something in my tummy flutters.

Gut instinct, is that you?

Could I be … a counsellor? Is *that* my dream job? I suddenly remember that weird ping in my stomach that time during yoga when that lady said that she was one. I thought it was because I wanted her to reassure me, but, oh my God, do I actually want to *be* her?

I don't know. And yet the cogs in my head are turning and there's a flicker of something in my soul that hasn't been there in a long time.

I can't stop thinking about Skye's comment when I get home, and the gut-instinct flutter refuses to settle, so I pull out my laptop and dive on to Google to do some more research into counselling. I should be doing my coursework or my physio, and I've also got three messages from Joel and one from Demi sitting unread in my inbox, but this takes priority.

About an hour later, I call Lena.

"Long time no speak," she jokes as her face pops

up on my phone screen. She's lying on her stomach on her bed, her navy bedroom ceiling with hand-painted constellations visible over her shoulder.

"I have news." I too get comfortable on my stomach, despite the angle doing my weak chin zero favours. I shuffle my phone on to the pillow to look slightly less like a looming thumb.

"Spit it out then."

"I think I've found The One."

"What about Joel?"

"I mean my career."

"Oh my God! I'll do you a drum roll." Lena slaps her hands on the duvet with muffled *fwump*. "And the winner is…"

"Screw Biology, I want to do Psychology!" I say, like I'm a contestant on a game show. "It gives me plenty of options – I could be a counsellor, maybe one who specializes in sex. I could even be a sexologist in the future." As I say it, the flutters in my stomach are so wild I feel ready to take off. "I could help people like me – people who are scared or confused by sexual issues and want someone other than a doctor to talk to."

"Amazing! Listen to that feeling. It's your higher self talking."

I grin. "And the best part is that I applied to both

Biology and Psychology at Sunderland. So I can be with Joel anyway."

Lena flaps her hands together and looks like she might combust. "Oh my God, this is so exciting. Definitely a massive step towards your authentic self. Eeeeeeeee. The future is bright."

I laugh. "Don't get too carried away. The future is certainly *brighter*."

And for the first time in ages it feels like it might be.

20

Nine days later, Lena, Demi and I are sitting in the corner of Costa after Demi called an emergency Saturday meet-up. I debated not coming at such short notice (spontaneity, who is she?) but I can't not go. It's been a while and for once I don't have plans with Joel as he's visiting his grandparents. I'm still seeing him tonight, though.

"I've got a conditional offer from LSE!" Demi bounces up and down in excitement causing the sofa below us to wobble.

"Isn't she clever?" Lena squeals, and a group of yummy mummies and a serious-looking man in a suit stare at us.

"Knew you'd smash it," I say. "What are the conditions?"

"A★, A, A." Demi's lip curls into a look of uncertainty.

"Easy for a genius like you," says Lena.

Demi smiles, chuffed, but never one to get too carried away. She turns to me. "Where are you at with all your offers, Rose?"

"I've heard back from three. Offers from Biological Science at Herts and Psychology at Winchester. Bath didn't want me—"

"Booooo," says Lena, doing a thumbs down and blowing a raspberry.

"I know, right? And I'm still waiting to hear back from Sunderland." I'm not even letting myself consider the fact that they might not offer. They have to. This is my future we're talking about.

Demi and Lena nod. "I'm sure they'll be in touch soon," offers Demi with an expression I can't quite work out.

We go quiet for a few seconds while Lena sips her drink and Demi takes the last bite of her blueberry muffin.

"Lena and I decided we're going to go to town tonight to celebrate," Demi declares with a sultry shimmy of her shoulders. "Thought we'd check out Evolution because apparently it has a revolving dancefloor."

Lena does a *Saturday Night Fever* move that reminds me she's a sixty-year-old in a teenager's body.

Demi and Lena decided? When? My initial excitement disappears instantly. Why am I only just hearing about this now?

"When did you decide that?"

Demi ignores my question. "You have to join. Monica and Holly are coming. Holly got accepted into her cabin-crew training this morning too." She grins.

So even Monica and Holly have been consulted before me. Do they have some WhatsApp group that I'm not in or something? If they'd have included me in the conversation, they'd know I can't do tonight because I'm seeing Joel. Demi won't see that as a legit excuse to not come, though, even if I had plans with him first.

"Dunno. I'm not feeling great to be honest," I say.

"Rose, come on, really? You look fine to me."

"I'm on my period," I lie.

"So? That shouldn't stop you from living your best life."

I want to say something, but I can't find the words. Maybe I'm just being pathetic. But it does feel like I've been totally left out of the whole planning of this.

"It's fine, you don't have to come."

Did Demi just roll her eyes? She's the one who decided to forge ahead with her plans without asking me first.

"Fine, I won't." I swirl the last dregs of my latte round the bottom of my mug.

Instead of saying anything, Demi stands up with her cup and empty muffin wrapper and heads off to the bin.

"We'll miss you, but we'll do a takeaway soon. How about that?" Lena says.

Demi returns and flops back on to the sofa. She's staring at her phone and won't look at me. My stomach clenches. This is absolutely *not* my fault.

After a painful silence, she finally speaks. "It's not because Joel isn't invited, is it? It's not my fault he can't get ID. I'd rather it was just girls anyway."

"No, it's not that," I say, trying to keep the outrage in my voice undetectable, but my hands shake with the effort.

"I'm finding that hard to believe if I'm honest."

Is she for real? She has no idea what I'm trying to juggle right now. It's not just Joel; it's everything.

"Why do you always think you know better than me about my own life?" It comes out as a hiss. "If you'd asked me properly, instead of the two of you making plans behind my back, I—"

"Making plans behind your back? This isn't some kind of conspiracy against you."

"I went round Demi's earlier to drop a book off and it happened to be at the same time she got her offer." Lena's voice is high and wobbly. She hates conflict.

"And why do Monica and Holly know before me? Why am I the last to be invited?"

"Because I wanted to tell you in person. Wish I hadn't

bothered now." Demi's brow is creased, and if looks could kill, I'd be as dead as a dodo.

Oh. That makes sense. Unless she's saying that to make me feel bad? Doubt it – Demi's the most direct person I know. Ugh, so it is me being out of order.

"Sorry." I force it out through my tight throat. "Can we move on?"

"'K," Demi says while staring at the table. That's a no then. Not that I'm surprised. She's one of the most stubborn, bloody-minded people I know, so I'm sure I'll have to do a fair bit more grovelling to get back in her good books. Right now I don't have the energy.

I look at Lena, who's chewing her nails. She raises her eyebrows at me, but I don't know what she's trying to say.

After the whole thing with Demi earlier, I'm not in the mood to have another argument today, but when I meet Joel he's acting ... weird with me. He didn't hug or kiss me at the bus stop and while walking back to his he walked ahead of me and replied to my questions with one-word answers. When we got back, he went straight upstairs while I stood chatting to Sonya for ten minutes.

I've just come upstairs to find him, and he's lying on his bed on his phone and hasn't even looked at me. My mind races, trying to work out what's up. We've not argued for at least a week now, with the roses on my windowsill a slightly sagging reminder of Joel's pledge of support.

I perch on his bed and stare at him, but he still doesn't look up.

"Oi," I say, prodding his side gently, my finger meeting a small layer of doughy flesh before hitting muscle. "You all right?"

"I'm fine."

The dreaded "fine".

"You're acting strange." I wring my hands to do something with the nervous energy that's building. This is beginning to feel like a habit now.

"You're acting strange with me," he snaps.

I genuinely have no idea what he's talking about. "How am I?" My voice wavers.

Joel shifts from his prone position. "You ignored my texts last night for ages and the day before too."

Have I been ignoring him? I think back to last week where I was busy with coursework, doing some career research and speaking to Lena. And the past few evenings recently it's been more schoolwork then physio, physio and more physio. But I always text Joel when I get home and before bed. I relay this to him.

"Exactly. You messaged me maybe twice, three times. You managed to talk to Lena on the phone and do everything else under the sun, but not me? And there's a whole hour when you're doing your 'physio' where you're clearly too busy to let me know how it's going." As he says the word "physio", he uses his fingers as quotation marks.

"What do you mean 'physio'," I reply, copying his gesture. What does he expect me to do? Text with my nose while my hands are busy with Promises? And yeah, OK, maybe I am messaging him a bit less, but that's because I'm trying to juggle a million and one different things. My life can't always revolve round him. First Demi, now Joel. I can't please anyone at the moment. My heartbeat quickens. It seems like his newfound maturity at our Valentine's evening is dying alongside my wilting roses.

"Clearly you were too busy enjoying yourself last night to even think about me." He picks up his phone again and chews his lip so emphatically it turns red.

If only he'd seen the reality of last night. Promises didn't even go in a centimetre. I did turn on the vibrations for about ten seconds, but they did nothing for the pain and I soon freaked out at the buzzing in case Dad or Sammy could hear. I ended up turning her off in a strop and would've thrown her out of the window had I not wanted to risk knocking out the neighbours' cat.

I exhale sharply. "Are you seriously still jealous of a

vibrator? What happened to The Pledge? I'm assuming that was all bull—"

"So you were using it then." He looks away from me.

"What do you mean "using it"? I'm sticking it into MY OWN BODY even though it causes me EXCRUCIATING PAIN. Do you think I WANT to do that? You think I ENJOY doing that? In five days' time I'm going to have to go to my first actual physio appointment and use the fucking thing in front of a complete stranger. And all you're thinking about is yourself." I almost spit the words, but I'm so not done. "Also, even if I was masturbating, what would be wrong with that? You wank all the time, do you not?"

Joel shrugs. "It's different for boys."

"That's a load of crap. You know, I fell out with Demi earlier to be here and I turned down an invite to town to celebrate her getting an offer from LSE!" I suddenly feel like a complete idiot. I turn away from him. I can't stand that self-righteous expression on his face and I'm scared I might throw something at it if I have to keep looking at him. How does he have the cheek to say that the hour I spend every night doing my physio is pleasurable for me?

Joel sighs. "Do you realize it's been ages since you last let me touch you?"

Oh, so that's what it's about. Excuse me for feeling

like I've been touched down there enough to last me a lifetime – and not in a good way.

"A couple of weeks really isn't that long – I was on my period for one of them, and I gave you a handjob last weekend."

"No, you *almost* did but we got interrupted. The last time was over two weeks ago actually," Joel mumbles.

"So you're counting now?"

Joel shakes his head.

We sit beside each other, me huffing and Joel in silence until the tension finally becomes too much even for Joel to bear. He throws his head back, smacks the cushion beside him then buries his face in it.

"Fuck's sake!" he growls, causing my already shaking body to jolt. "What's happening to me? Why am I doing this to you?"

He hurls the cushion to the floor without looking up. He sniffs and a tear falls on to his lap, but he doesn't move, just blinks.

My anger and frustration weaken instantly. I've never seen him cry before and I can't stand it; every inch of my body needs to make it better. My eyes prick too with the stab of hot tears.

I shuffle next to him, as close as I can be without sitting on his lap, and I put my arm round him and squeeze him tight. Instead of his usual unshakable firmness, he's trembling beneath my own quivering grasp.

"What's happening to us?" I whisper.

21

School limps by in a haze of intrusive visions consisting of dildos and old ladies watching me use them. It's 7th March and it's physio day. At 2 p.m. sharp, Mum is picking me up outside the school gates, with Promises tucked away in the footwell, to whisk me off to the hospital.

At break time, Lena sidles up to me, looking sheepish, dangling a vegan chocolate bar in front of my face. "Thought you might want a snack," she says.

"Yeah right. What do you want?" I joke, taking the chocolate from her. "Thanks. Shall we share?"

"Nah, it's OK. I've already had two," she says, settling into a chair beside me where I'm camped out with multiple textbooks.

"So I do actually want a favour. I sort of told Monica

that you were going to be a therapist and she wants to talk to you about something."

My stomach flips again. Excitement or dread? "About what?"

Lena shrugs. "If I knew that, I wouldn't need to ask you. Relationship advice, I think."

I really am getting a name for myself around school at the moment as being the school's unofficial relationship therapist – God knows why.

"When does she want to talk?"

"Dunno. She said she'd text you, but wanted me to give you a heads-up."

"OK, that's fine," I say. I'm much more relaxed over message anyway. I *think* it's excitement I feel at being the Chosen One for these important chats, but it only lasts a few minutes before I realize that in less than two hours I have my physio.

Two p.m. arrives far too quickly. I'm still lacking the enthusiasm that MyVagVicki expressed about her first physio session, and haven't had the nerve to check and see if she's done a new video updating her followers on how it went. If she said it was the best experience of her life I wouldn't believe her, and if she said it was the worst experience of her life I wouldn't be sat here in the waiting room now. Ignorance is bliss – ish. I'm only just getting used to using the dilators and Promises in my own company so I certainly don't feel ready to have an observer – and according to TikTok user SexGoddess216, if I was to have an audience then it should be Joel, because apparently men love watching women *pleasure themselves*. Fantastic. Not.

The waiting room is definitely not how I imagined it would be. Mum and I are sitting on plastic chairs in a room full of people, including an older man with crutches and a younger man with his wrist in a bandage. It seems this wing of the hospital is for people needing actual muscular physiotherapy too. No one else looks like they've got a vibrating sex toy in their Sainsbury's bag for life. My face has been red-hot since the moment I confirmed my appointment at the desk, and the receptionist looked at me like she knew exactly what was in the bag. As is standard nowadays, my stomach is churning so hard I'm on the cusp of being violently sick and shitting myself at the same time.

The room is silent apart from the occasional awkward cough, but Mum insists on whispering at a volume that isn't whispering at all.

"How are you feeling?"

"I'm fine," I whisper back, pulling out my phone to make it clear that this isn't the time for chit-chat.

"I'll be in the cafe downstairs with my book and a coffee while you're in there." Mum shakes her book at me.

I raise my voice slightly. "Is that *Fifty Shades of Grey*, Mother?" I smirk.

Mum turns crimson and I turn my attention back to my phone that's just pinged.

Monica: Lena said you didn't mind me messaging. I don't know who else to talk to about this…

The term "imposter syndrome" is apt right now, but I suppose I *can* keep secrets. I've proven that a lot recently, even if we're talking about my own.

Rose: Always happy to try to help. Don't have all the answers, though!

Always good to put a disclaimer in.

Monica: And promise not to utter a word to anyone. Not even Lena or Demi!

Rose: You have my word

Monica: OK, so I like this girl. I've been with a girl

191

before so that's fine. But she hasn't. I don't know if she likes me that way

Rose: I see how that could be scary. Have you thought about just asking her?

Monica: I want to ask her, so much. But she's a really close friend and I'm worried about ruining it. Do you think I should say something?

It's a tricky one. I've seen on some of my research that the counsellor's job isn't actually to give answers or recommendations – that takes away the client's autonomy. Instead, it's to guide the client to make the right choice for themselves by asking questions and reflecting back what you hear.

Rose: It sounds like you want to ask her but are scared. Can you imagine not telling her? How might that be?

I really nailed that.

Monica: Good point. Seems impossible. I'm not sure I can ignore my feelings for her for ever. They get stronger every day. I have to tell her. Scary

Rose: Scary, but it could be so worth it. You could make it clear you don't want to pressure her or ruin your friendship. You'll be OK. You can always message me again x

Monica: Thanks x

After I close the message, I see I have an email notification. It's UCAS, saying that the status of my application has changed.

My heartbeat quickens. It's got to be Sunderland as that's the only one I'm waiting to hear back from. I navigate to the portal and check, trying my best to keep my breath steady.

Oh my God. Sunderland has offered me a conditional place on their Biomed course. I audibly sigh with relief; the fantasy of doing uni with Joel can now be a reality. I scroll down and –

Shit. Shit. Shit. My application for Psychology has been unsuccessful. My stomach clenches like I've just been punched. If I want to do Psychology, I can't be with Joel. I'll have to choose between doing uni with Joel or the course I know deep down in my heart is the right one for me. How the hell am I going to make that decision?

"Rose Summers?" an older lady calls, having appeared

from round the corner. No time to think about it. Before I can move, Mum answers for me, standing up and waving.

"Yep, she's here. Go on, love." Everyone in the room turns to look at us. "Don't forget your bag." She thrusts it towards me. "I'll meet you back here in an hour. Good luck!"

My cheeks flame as my mind plays out a scenario where the vibrator tumbles out and buzzes across the floor. I snatch the bag and walk as fast as I can away from everyone's prying eyes.

I follow the lady into a room that's white, small like a cupboard, and set up with two facing chairs and an examination couch along one wall. I'm glad there aren't any windows, but everything feels intimate and that's with me still fully dressed.

"Nice to meet you. I'm Dr Joy. Take a seat." Dr Joy gestures to the chair by the door and sits down opposite.

I kick the carrier bag under the chair and drop my coat off my shoulders, the pounding of my heart louder in my ears than my own thoughts.

She tells me everything I already know from my late-night googling sessions and asks if I have any questions. I do, but not ones I'm comfortable asking. For instance, what if my body enjoys it and I have no control over its response to the vibrator? It's been made with the specific purpose of pleasure, so what if I can't help it?

I shake my head. "No questions, thanks."

"If you want to pop yourself on the table and get ready, I'll be back in a minute. I'll knock when I'm back so you can give me the all-clear to come in." Dr Joy quickly disappears out of the room.

If all she needs to do is knock to enter, that means she isn't going to lock it. I can see it now. In the three minutes Dr Joy is out of the room, a lost patient (probably a young and good-looking male, knowing my luck) will accidentally wander in and be confronted with my naked bottom half and a vibrator at my feet.

I peel my socks and school trousers off, the linoleum cold and sticky underfoot, but I'm not going to take my knickers off while that door is still unlocked. I wait for what seems like for ever before there's a knock on the door.

"Yes?" I reply, voice meek and feeble. I hold my breath as the handle twists and pray that it's my doctor and not a random person I've invited in.

My shoulders collapse with my sharp exhale when I spy Dr Joy's white-blonde hair as she slips inside. She locks the door behind her, and only now do I feel safe enough to shimmy out of my knickers.

I'm so glad that I didn't have to go back to school today because there's no way in hell I'd be good for anything after what just happened. Obviously now I'm a pro at having my bits gawked at and talking about how this doesn't fit into that, but this really was on another level. I don't have the words to describe it aside from "wrong". Wrong, wrong, wrong.

Dr Joy was all up in there, prodding and poking. She stopped when I said it was painful, but telling her it hurt was a gross understatement when how it actually felt was that I was mere seconds away from ripping in half. Lena's breathing techniques helped a little, but the only way I could use my breath as effectively as needed would have been to hold it for long enough to pass out completely.

Once the internal massage was over, a glance at the clock confirmed I still had the second half to endure. I thought of Mum in the cafe with a book and a latte and I wanted nothing more than to be sat opposite her with a hot chocolate. Instead, in my little windowless cupboard, it was Promises' time to shine.

"OK, so, for the next half hour I suggest we use the vibrator," said Dr Joy. The word "we" in that sentence almost had me laughing out loud given how ridiculous it sounded, yet it was not some comedic sketch on TV – it was actually happening.

"Do you want to get prepared? Make sure to apply plenty of lubrication to the toy and to yourself." Dr Joy looked at me, encouragement in her eyes, as she gestured at the vibrator's box.

And so, after the torturous preparation that looked pornographic before I even started, off I went. I did what I've been doing every evening since acquiring Promises, trying to inch her in, only this time with an audience. As I flicked on the vibrations – which the doctor claimed could help with the pain – my mouth was dry and every muscle in my body was clenched to the point my whole body was shaking. I forced my focus to drift off yet again to a spot on the corner of the ceiling, towards the door. The door I couldn't wait to walk out of.

When Dr Joy finally looked at the clock and suggested I clean my toys and get my clothes back on, I couldn't get my knickers back on quick enough, but I dragged out the act of washing Promises in the sink and boxing everything up to give my cheeks time to go a little less red. It didn't work and I'm sure that when Mum met me in the waiting room, as I scurried out still sticky with lube and with a dull burn in between my legs, she raised her eyebrows.

I can't believe I have to do it again in two weeks' time. Dr Joy has suggested fortnightly sessions, with me doing my "homework" in the weeks between. That means I have to endure three more humiliating sessions before going back to Dr Andrews to see if it's worked.

I know rationally everything that happened was legal and the doctor was just doing her job, but the feeling of violation runs deep, turning my stomach. I wish I could talk to my girls. Demi would say the right words that would help ease the shame and help me feel like an empowered, strong woman. Lena would just get it too. Without saying any words, she'd look at me in that way only she can, and I'd feel seen and understood, in a way I can't by Joel, or even Mum.

In the car on the way home, I tell Mum about Sunderland.

"How are you feeling about it?"

"I don't know. Obviously happy that I have an offer for Biomed, but I want the option of Psychology." I'm a bit worried about saying it out loud in case I change my mind, but it just slips out.

"Mmm, I see." Mum frowns at me. "But you've still got a Psychology option at Winchester, correct?"

"Well, yeah."

"So if you do want to do Psychology, then Winchester it is. You've still got both subject options available to you."

"Yeah," I say, non-committal.

Mum glances at me. "How long until the deadline?"

"Eighth of June. I've got ages. Like three months."

"But you don't want to leave it that late now you've got all your decisions back."

"I want to make the right choice."

"So you keep saying." She reaches over and squeezes my knee. "It sounds like the right choice might be Winchester, if that's the course you're most drawn to."

I hate how she thinks it's so bloody simple. I wish it was, but it's so not. I pull out my phone, hoping she'll leave it.

Joel: How was physio? Sorry I was a dickhead about the vibrator. Again. I'm just scared I'm going to lose you

Rose: It was OK, thanks for asking ☹ I'm doing it for both of us. PS I've got a conditional offer for Biomed at Sunderland but not Psychology x

Joel: Are you OK with that?

Rose: Yeah :)

I don't want him thinking I'm having second thoughts about going to uni with him. It's not *him* I'm having second thoughts about anyway; it's the course.

Joel: Yay! Can't wait to have you at uni with me (if you choose to come obv). Can't wait to see you tomorrow too xx

I've also got a few notifications in the VW chat.

Moongirlxoxo: **@Roseycheeks_x** I hope it went OK today. Was thinking of you and sending you distance healing in art <3 xx

Endo2005: Yes, let us know if you survived your physio

Roseycheeks_x: It was as awful as expected. No other words right now. Send me some more of that healing, would you?

Moongirlxoxo: ON IT! BTW I was thinking that we should do a thing in the chat where every week we share something positive. Little Wins This Week <3.

Anon_69: OMG cute. I'll go first. I've got a counselling session booked for next week. I'm hoping it will help my anxieties. Not expecting miracles but I want to like what I see in the mirror

Moongirlxoxo: **@Anon_69** That sounds like such a positive step! xxx

Roseycheeks_x: **@Anon_69** LOVE THAT FOR YOU xxx <3

Later that night, after I've shoved my Shame Sack (the new name for my bag of physio apparatus) as far under my bed as I can and have taken the hottest shower my skin can take, the smell of lube still hangs in my nostrils. Alongside the lingering scent, a feeling of disgust and violation sticks to me like glue. It all felt so … clinical.

I know it's a medical thing and that Dr Joy is doing her best to make me feel comfortable, but I see now how important it is to have emotional support alongside all this physical stuff. I wish I had someone – someone trained in this – to talk to. If I were a counsellor, I could give people like me the support I'm in desperate need of right now. Seeing that Anon_69 is also having counselling almost feels like a sign from the universe confirming it's the right choice for me. But then I remember. At Sunderland it won't be an option. That dream feels like it's slipping from my grip before I've even had a chance to grab it.

22

Two weeks later and I'm munching on my after-school Nutella toast when Mum strides in. I'm feeling quite aggy today because I'm still trying to recover from my second physio session earlier in the week. It was even worse than the first. Like last time, I did as I was told, to lie back and drop my knees to the couch, surrendering to the fact that this was apparently what I'd signed up for. The familiar feeling of being exposed accosted me, followed by the probing rubber-gloved finger of the doctor. But as she was touching me, I had this horrible realization. In many ways, the manual physio feels similar to the dilators and Promises – uncomfortable, covered in lube and violating both my privacy and my pain threshold. But it's way easier to distance yourself from a medical instrument. Fingers are a totally different ballgame. Fingers are attached to people with a consciousness and an experience all of their own. When Dr Joy's fingers are inside me, not only can I feel her, she can feel me. That thought makes me feel all kinds of ick and so, like in previous examinations, I sought out my trusty dirty spot on the ceiling, willing my soul to temporarily leave my body and relieve me of the crushing shame that blazed within the core of my being.

I turn my attention back to my toast.

"How was school?" Mum says as she passes me in the kitchen. She sweeps away the crumbs I've left on the side, with a grunt.

"Fine."

It's not a lie. I was busy in lessons all day apart from one free period, which just so happened to be when Demi and Lena were in their Music lesson. At lunchtime, Demi had band practice so Holly, Lena and I just chilled in the common room, testing each other on osteoclasts and osteoblasts, followed by a discussion on Shakespeare's attitude towards women, both topics highly likely to come up in our exams. It was a nice break from obsessively thinking about the fact that my relationship is rocky and my vagina is uninhabitable.

Mum moves to lean on the breakfast bar beside me. "Care to expand?"

"Not really. I'm tired but I feel on top of things, ish." I offer her a weak smile.

She beams back. "That's excellent."

"Ta." I scoff the final bite of my toast and head over to the kettle. I flick it on again; it's still warm from Mum's last cup of tea.

For the next few minutes, the room is quiet except for the furious bubbling of the kettle followed by the tinkling sound of the teaspoon hitting my mug as I stir.

"Help me bring some washing down, will you, darl? While the tea brews."

"Sure."

On the upstairs landing, Mum grabs the lights and I grab the darks. I follow her back down the hallway. "I'll only mention it once, but how's the university app—"

"Can we give the whole uni thing a rest for tonight?" I shut her down.

Why can't I just be left alone and not be interrogated for one night?

"I'm just saying," Mum says, while navigating the stairs and dropping a pair of Dad's dirty pants in her wake.

I bend down to pick up the rogue undies. "Well, don't."

"Now you've heard back from all the unis, you need to confirm your firm and insurance choices."

"I told you, I still have time! Stop rushing me. I don't want to make the wrong choice and mess it up."

"You won't fudge it up. I don't understand what the issue is."

I raise my voice, my patience waning. "I can't choose which course I want to do. I'm torn between Psychology and Biomed. Why is it that hard for you to wrap your head around?"

Mum's eyes narrow. "You said you were leaning towards Psychology."

"I never said that," I say, trying to keep the atmosphere chill, but things seem to be going from chill to frosty so quickly I'm surprised I don't slip on the last step as we reach the ground floor. "Biomed at Sunderland is still in the running. Joel—"

Mum scoffs. "I'm not having you go there because of a boy. It's miles away too."

Oh my God, why can't she just shut up? I want to say, *You don't get it. I'm scared. Scared about everything changing. At least if I went with Joel, I'd feel a tiny bit more secure.*

"It's not *because of a boy.*" It comes out much louder than I intend it to. "But, even if it was, I've been with Joel for ages. It's not like we're going to split up. What's wrong with going to the same uni?"

"Do you like the course?" Mum says it firmly, but doesn't raise her voice to match mine.

"Yes," I lie. "I wouldn't have applied for it if I didn't."

Mum drops the basket on to the floor in front of the washing machine with enough force that its plastic base makes a cracking noise.

"I don't believe you. If you liked it, you'd have accepted it already, regardless of what I have to say on the matter." Mum proceeds to seize handfuls of laundry and punch them into the washing machine.

"This is my choice, no one else's." After being prodded and poked and frowned over, after feeling confused and scared and helpless, why can't she see how important this choice is to me? I crouch down beside her and grab a pair of my jogging bottoms in a bid to distract myself from my quickening pulse. It doesn't work. I'm on my feet now. "I'm a grown-ass adult – don't tell me what to do," I shout. She's so out of order. Yes, Joel wants me in Sunderland, but why is Mum *so* dead set against it?

"I'm not telling you what to do. I'm trying to support you." Mum's shouting now too, voice raised over the tinny clunk of fabric hitting metal.

I clutch the joggers so tightly my knuckles are ghostly white. "Why don't you get off your high horse? You didn't even go to uni." I throw the jogging bottoms on the floor.

"I'm trying my best, for God's sake! Why, whatever choice I make, is it always wrong?" I storm out of the room and thump as hard as I can with each step. I want to feel the floorboards break beneath me. I want her to see how much I'm hurting.

But Mum doesn't shout back, nor does she follow me. Everything is quiet.

And then I hear it: the gentle sound of sniffing. I shuffle back into the kitchen and stare at her.

"You don't know how lucky you are," she whispers, eyes red and shiny. "Go upstairs. Now."

I leave the room as quickly as I can before I cry too.

Fifteen minutes later, my door opens and Sammy strides in. "I'm coming in whether you like it or not," she declares, and then sits on my swivel chair with her arms crossed.

I don't move from my hunched position at the foot of my bed.

"Don't be sad. Uni is something to look forward to, not get worried about." Sammy spins in the chair and looks at the framed photos on my desk – lots of Joel and me, and some of Lena and Demi too.

All I do is snort.

"Mum's annoying sometimes, but she's also *sometimes* right."

"It's not just Mum. Everyone has an opinion," I say through sniffs. "I can't seem to make anyone happy at the moment."

Sammy nods slowly. "You'll hate me for bringing another one into the mix then, but I have to. I'm going to be straight with you. Out of all my school friends and my whole floor in halls – that's about twelve people – only two couples from sixth form made it through the first year. Most of them cheated on their better halves too. It was so awkward having to meet their respective partners when you knew that the night before they were banging Sabrina down the hall."

"Why are you telling me that?" I wail. "That's not helpful."

She moves next to me on the bed. "I don't want to lie to you."

"You're basically saying that the only way Joel and I will last is if we aren't long-distance."

"No! Not at all. The point I'm making is that the people who really wanted to make it work, made it work. They're still together four, five years later, and the people who weren't right for each other moved on. You can't base massive decisions like where you study solely on whether your boyfriend is going with you or not. Your relationship should be strong enough to have your own lives, but still be faithful. Well, if you're both agreed on monogamy anyway…"

"What?"

"You know my mate Anna? She's in an open relationship. She's got one steady partner who she adores, but she's also able to have the excitement of dating other people. She was always a one-person kinda gal at school and uni, but she's making up for that now."

"Not for me," I say bluntly. The thought of opening up my and Joel's relationship makes me feel sick. Disappointing multiple people sexually while Joel is able to see how much better every other girl is at it than me? No thanks.

"Fair enough. Look, if you love the course in Sunderland, I say go for it and make it your firm choice. If not, go for Psychology. If I know Joel well enough – and I hope I do, he'll support you no matter what. If he doesn't, then it's his loss and he's a giant nob who doesn't deserve you. It's your choice at the end of the day. Do what's right for you and only you. Not Joel, not Mum, not Dad, not your friends and not me. You."

I nod. "It's not just the Joel thing. I'm scared. What if no one likes me?"

Sammy nods. "I understand that. I was shitting myself when I first went."

"You seemed fine when we dropped you off."

"The minute I closed the door behind you guys I burst into tears. The only way I found the courage to leave my room was because I got to the point where I was so hungry I had to choose between introducing myself to them all in the kitchen or die of starvation." Sammy is half laughing, but I see vulnerability behind her eyes. She did a really good job of hiding her panic at the time, so it's funny to think that she was actually just as worried as I am about the whole thing.

"You also knew exactly what you wanted to do there. What if I hate it?"

Sammy shrugs. "Then drop out or switch courses. Making friends is way easier than you think, helped massively by the fact that everyone else is also shitting themselves and no one knows what they're doing – and alcohol also tends to break the ice." She grins mischievously and waggles her eyebrows at me.

"I bet."

"You get into your own little routine after, like, two, three days. You make your room all nice, you consult your student cookbook and plan your meals for the week – pasta, pasta and more pasta. You go to bed whenever the hell you like. You can choose to do film and hot choccy nights with your hallmates, stay in your own bed with Netflix or get utterly wankered on a Wednesday night and ride home in a trolley with a traffic cone on your head." Sammy's super animated now, gesticulating as she reminisces on her crazy uni days. Her enthusiasm is infectious.

"It does sound like a laugh."

"Once we take you on an IKEA trip you'll feel more pumped about the whole thing. Nothing like a brand-new colander and your own set of colourful plates to get you in the mood for it."

I nod, feeling a little more optimistic. "It does sound fun. And I do remember feeling insanely jealous about your lime-green colander and bog brush in the shape of a ... I want to say cherry?"

"An apple! Close, though."

"Thanks for the pep talk."

Sammy smiles. "I'm so excited to see what you do in life, whatever that may be." She squeezes my knee and rests her head on my shoulder. "Now, do you wanna watch *Shrek the Musical*?" she says. "It's on Netflix and the soundtrack is a right bop."

23

Holly, Lena and I are crowded by the front of the bus, positioned in a tight gaggle round the luggage rack. It's a rare occurrence that we are all on the same bus, given various school clubs, lifts from parents, etc., but it's nice to have company for once. It's a challenge trying to hold the grimy pole with one hand and cling on to the lukewarm dregs of coffee left over from my free last lesson, but I'm trying to make it look as effortless as possible.

As sixth-formers, legend says that we should rule the back seats and bully any younger students who have the audacity to sit there. However, the reality is that the current year eights lounging across the last two rows, bags and feet across the chairs, are right little scary turds, and I'd rather stand than risk being humiliated by them. Demi, the sly cow, has managed to nab herself a decent seat in the middle of the bus, saved for her by Monica. Holly was outraged, given that it's usually reserved for her, but was quickly told by Demi, *You snooze, you lose.*

"OK, so I've been working on having an orgasm using just my mind." Lena closes her eyes and points to her temples. She wobbles as the bus turns the corner and I have to grab her before she falls.

"What are you on about?" Holly scrunches up her face, unimpressed by Lena's eccentricities.

"There was an experiment back in the nineties where some woman managed to get herself off by imagining her chakras moving up and down her spine."

"And you believe that?"

"They measured her heart rate and everything and it proved she wasn't faking."

"That's ridiculous. You sound like that woman on the news who said she had an alien lover. Rose, back me up here?"

"That one was a bit of a stretch."

"Just *a bit* of a stretch?" Holly says incredulously.

Lena shrugs. "I wouldn't be so quick to write it off. Stranger things have happened—"

"There's zero proof aliens even exist, and even if they did I'm sure they have better things to do than stick their alien chodes into a lonely Karen from Scunthorpe. What about just getting a vibrator? That's the normal way to get yourself off." Holly leans back on the pile of bags behind her and yawns dramatically. A year eleven sitting near us nudges his mate and looks incredibly interested in what Holly has to say. I shift myself to block his view at the same time as my phone starts to ring in my pocket.

Lena's gaze is on me, but I'm not going to look at her in case it makes Holly suspicious. Obviously, Lena knows I've been spending every night with Promises and that it has been far from pleasurable. I'm actively trying *not* to connect to my body in that way because if I let myself enjoy it, even once, my body might decide that it's OK to react to that type of stimulation. If my body thinks that, God knows what it might do in physio. Is it possible to accidentally orgasm? I don't want to find out.

I tip my coffee cup and will the paltry final drops to moisten my drying mouth.

Holly continues, oblivious. "Showerhead's OK, but I'm not always in the shower when the mood strikes, ya know?"

"Also, my mum mentioned the other day that with the rising cost of household bills, not everyone can afford such luxuries," adds Lena.

Holly looks horrified. "You and your mum are so weird," she says before turning to me. "Any suggestions?"

Her eyebrows are arched as if she's judging my words before they even leave my lips. My phone starts ringing again. I pull it out of my pocket.

"Er, Joel t-takes care of it for me," I stutter, looking at my phone screen and confirming that it's him calling. I decline it – I hope I can pass it off as an accident later. I'm only three stops away from mine.

"You could use it together; guys love that stuff."

My cheeks flush hot. There's sniggering behind me and it's a shame I have no coffee left to chuck over those eavesdropping year elevens.

"Go on, get a vibrator with me. Then tell me Joel is all you need." Holly follows up her loud declaration with a howling laugh, which causes funny looks from the driver. If I had Promises with me right now, I'd smack her over the head with it.

"I'm really all right."

"You're boring."

"Fine, I'll come with you to buy one if you want," I say, just to shut her up. How's that for boring?

Holly's so slouched in the luggage rack she may as well be horizontal. She heaves herself to her feet as the bus pulls into her stop.

"Deal," she says. "See you tomorrow." Monica follows her off the bus, smiling at me, oblivious. I wonder if she's confessed her feelings to her friend yet, or whether she's decided against it. Demi comes to join Lena and me. She waves and jokingly blows kisses at Monica and Holly as the bus pulls away.

"What did I miss?" says Demi.

"Nothing," I say.

"If you say so. Look, I have to talk to you about something."

Oh my God, there goes my phone for the third time. Why isn't Joel getting the damn message to wait?

I roll my eyes. "Sorry I have to answer this. It's the third time he's called. Two seconds, then I'm all yours."

"But it's impor—"

I turn away from Demi to face the window and take the call. "Hey, you OK?"

"Yeah, you?"

He'd better not have called three times for a casual chat. "Yeah, fine," I say over the noise of chattering students. I hope he doesn't notice the edge to my voice.

"I'm one hundred per cent going to Sunderland, as in accepted the offer and starting to look at accommodation and finances. Because it's an unconditional offer, they can't take it away from me." Joel chuckles. "How exciting is that?"

I stiffen. He's going to be living in Sunderland, five hours away from home, for the next three years. Why does this feel like a gut-punching shock when I've known the entire time this is the plan? I suppose it's because it's real now and no longer a hypothetical scenario.

"That's amazing!" I force the words out and hold back the selfish bile bubbling in my throat. *You're leaving me behind unless I choose to follow you.* "I'm so proud of you."

And I am both proud and excited for him. This course is all he's wanted since we first met. But alongside that there's panic – panic that the ball is now in my court and all I want to do is chuck it back out.

Someone taps me on the shoulder. I turn round. It's Demi, mouthing something at me.

Joel speaks again. "Thanks. Now all you need to do is accept your offer and we're riding off into the sunset. Well, into Sunderland. But the important thing is that we'll be together. If that's what you want, of course."

My stomach twists as two visions compete in my mind – the two of us having breakfast together in our own flat before lectures versus Joel and me hundreds of miles apart, him getting off his face in the clubs, surrounded by beautiful girls.

"Mmmmm," I mutter. What am I meant to say?

There's another tap. It's Demi again. She's rolling her eyes and tapping her wrist.

"I *really* need to talk to you," she mouths.

We're just round the corner from her and Lena's stop. I nod quickly. "Joel, I have to—"

"The thought of doing long-distance sucks balls, but we'll make it work either way," he says.

"Really?" I say as the bus pulls over and the doors hiss open. I turn round to see the back of Demi's head making its way down the steps, followed by Lena, who looks up at me and shakes her head. I mouth *What?* at her more aggressively than I mean to. I'll text them both later. "That means the world to me to hear that. Love you." I whisper the last bit because the last thing I want is anyone else to hear it.

"Love you too," says Joel. Then he's gone.

When I get home, I have one thing on my mind – to apologize to Mum. She left for work this morning before I woke up and I can't sit with the weight of being a crappy daughter any longer.

I find her in the living room with an Agatha Christie and a cup of tea.

"Hi," I say, sitting on the sofa beside her.

"Hello." She doesn't look up.

I take a deep breath. "Sorry."

Mum sighs and shuts her book. She looks at me, eyebrows raised, lips in an uncertain line. "You're forgiven," she says.

I look down at the vibrant Turkish rug that Mum and Dad got on a holiday pre-kids. I trace the patterns with my toe. "I'm sorry I was nasty to you. I didn't realize you'd get upset."

"I do have feelings, you know. And I'm sorry too. You're right. It's up to you what you do with your life. It's just hard for me to see you have so many choices and not make the most of it."

"I know. I promise I want to make the most of it. I'm just scared. And confused."

"That's because it's scary and confusing. But it's not your fault I didn't get the chance to go to uni."

Oh. It makes sense now. I thought Mum not going to uni *was* a choice. I didn't realize she had wanted to go but didn't have the opportunity.

"Anyway, consider my nose out of it," she continues. "I'll support you and help if you want it, but you're a big girl now and big girls make their own choices."

"I'm not sure I want to be a big girl yet." I stick my bottom lip out in a mock sulk.

"Come here then." She pulls me into a hug and holds me tight. "You'll always be my little girl, even when you're fifty, I'm pushing one hundred and the bum-wiping duties have well and truly switched."

"There's no one else's bum I'd rather wipe than yours."

I grin. "Right, I need to go and sort some school stuff out. Sorry again. I love you."

Mum releases me. "I love you too."

After my chat with Mum, things are clearer. Sammy's words are still on my mind too. I don't want to regret making the wrong choice when it comes to my future. Joel's doing his thing and I need to do mine. I feel more like I could – and should – do uni for myself without Joel. Yes, it's terrifying, but I'm also feeling excited about my future for the first time in ages. He also said we'd make it work long-distance and I need to believe him.

I spend a good portion of the evening watching YouTube videos about counselling and sex therapy, and I'm even more sure it's what I want to do. I decide to take a step to hold myself accountable – I've told Lena about my interest in counselling, but I'm also ready to update the group chat. It seems a lot less scary than telling Mum or Sammy yet.

Roseycheeks_x: I'm thinking of being a sex therapist. Seriously – I might study it at uni. Thoughts?

It_hurtttsssssss: LITTLE WIN THIS WEEK EVEN THO IT AINT LITTLE LOL

Endo2005: YESSSSSS. You can help people like us!!!

TK_1000: Sounds like a dream job!

Roseycheeks_x: Hope so. Already done a shitload of research into the basics lmao! Active listening, reflecting back and empathy. Deffo reckon I could do that – loads of people tell me I'm a good listener. Maybe this is my calling?!!!! x

Demi has also messaged me asking if I'm free this Friday. She knows I see Joel on Fridays so I feel like she's purposely setting me up for failure. I start typing my reply, but my phone rings.

"You should have spoken to Demi on the bus earlier." Lena's face is scrunched in the corner of the screen.

My stomach tenses. "Hello to you too."

"She felt really let down. Like you don't have time for her any more."

"Well, you can tell her the feeling is mutual," I huff. "So have you both been talking about me behind my back then?"

Lena takes a deep breath, not rising to my bait. "You should tell Demi what's been going on. She'd never judge you. She might even be able to help."

"How could she possibly help? No one can help; I just have to deal with it."

Lena sighs. "I know you have a lot on, but do I think it would be better for our little threesome if there weren't any secrets? Yes. Do I think it's better for your friendship to be honest with each other? Also yes. But I know it's not up to me, even though I seem to be in the middle of it all." Lena's face drops for a millisecond, but then she's softly smiling again – her default expression.

I hear what she's saying, but the more she pushes me to tell Demi, the more I don't want to. I've had enough of people telling me what to do. I stand from the bed and busy myself with pulling out my Shame Sack from the bottom drawer.

"Are you listening to me?"

"Yes. I'll think about it." I pause for a second and chuck the Shame Sack on the bed beside an open Biology textbook. I want to change the subject. "How's your Yonic Mission going?"

Lena shakes her head. "No blast-off yet. I've tried all sorts. Tuning in to my mind, electric toothbrush, porn. It feels good, but then it feels too much and it's painful. Exactly like how Mum described it." Lena sticks her bottom lip out.

"You've watched *porn*?" The shock is audible in

my voice despite the fact I whisper it. "I thought only boys watched it." Looks like I have a lot to learn before becoming a sex therapist. No time like the present.

"There's some awful stuff out there, and also some not awful stuff too. Stuff by women, for women. Mum pointed me in the direction of the safe stuff."

"I can't get over the fact you talk to your mum about that."

Do I want to be able to talk to my mum in that way? I'm not sure I do. I think I'm happy pretending she's only ever had sex twice – once to make Sammy and once to make me – rather than for pleasure. Ew.

"It's a blessing and a curse. I see you told the chat about your plans to be a therapist."

"Yeah. I'm surer than I've been in a while that it's the right thing for me."

"Yessssss, higher self. Told you she had your back."

I grin and we sit in comfortable silence. I look between my bag of dilators and textbook, trying to decide which one is going to be lucky enough to be graced with my attention first. I fiddle with the zip on my Shame Sack while Lena applies her nightly moisturizer with her jade face roller.

I could sit here watching her do her entire nightly routine and it would be better than what I've actually got planned, but needs must. "Right, I'd better get going," I say.

"Sure. And you're not boring by the way. You know what Holly's like."

I smile and wave a dilator to camera. "Thanks. Although I think I'd rather be boring than have to sit here with my magical dildo wands."

"Oh, did I interrupt your yoni homework?"

"Almost."

"I'll leave you to it. Don't forget those breathing techniques I showed you."

"Love you," I say. "I'm going to do some more research into anorgasmia soon and will share my findings with you. That'll be my way of giving back to you everything you've given to me!"

"Eeeeeeeeee. Love you too. But you owe me nothing."

I hang up the call, beaming. Future self, here I come.

24

"I know you aren't going to want to hear this, Rose, but our only option now is surgery." Dr Andrews delivers the news gently, but it hits me like a punch in the stomach.

No. This can't be happening. Eight weeks ago, I was sitting here with hope. Hope that the dilators would work and that I'd be fixed and not need an op. I can't have gone through the physio for nothing.

I look at Mum. *Fix this for me, please.*

She's quiet, her lips a thin line, and she's looking back at me, waiting for me to say something. They both are.

I force myself to talk. "But the dilators. They're working, I think? And maybe I could go and see a counsellor in case this is in my head?" My voice cracks. This can't be it. I just need more time.

Dr Andrews offers me a pitying smile and shakes her head. "You've tried really hard with your physio. But I'm afraid it's not enough. We said we'd give it two months and reassess and, by the looks of the progress you've made so far, I don't think there's capacity for your vagina to stretch much more. And you're correct: difficulties with sex *can* often have a mental cause, but not in your case, Rose. Yours is very much physical. Which is great because it can be fixed with a minor op."

And that's it.

Any hope I was clinging on to is gone. All I can do is nod. Mum puts her hand on my shoulder and squeezes.

I blink, sniff and nod. Blink, sniff and nod. The room spins.

Surgery.

"And there really is no other option?" asks Mum.

"You can decline the surgery for now, come off the waiting list. There's no rush, but" – her eyes meet mine – "if you want to be able to have penetrative sex, Rose, then, yes, surgery is the only way for that to happen."

I almost laugh. If. *If* I want to have penetrative sex. Like there's another option. Like Joel wouldn't leave me if I turned round and said, *Sorry, never going to happen, but you'll stay with me, won't you?*

"It's not like I have a choice," I say.

"You do, Rose. There's a lot more to sex than penetration. But if you want to conceive naturally at some point, then penetration does play an important role." Dr Andrews' tone is matter-of-fact, like these are perfectly acceptable words to chuck at a seventeen-year-old virgin.

I'm fully aware that plenty of people don't see penetration as a necessity. Demi is always saying it's overrated. If I was giving advice to someone else, I'd say it too, so I'm aware I'm a hypocrite. But I need this option. *Joel* needs this option.

I can't be in this room much longer. It's too hot. Too airless. I'm going to faint or be sick.

Dr Andrews says something about thinking it over, but we agree I'll stay on the waiting list and that I'll get a letter as soon as an appointment becomes available, which could be any time now. Mum and I leave with a leaflet and a quick goodbye, as any hope I had lies in tatters on the floor.

Just like that, I change my mind about uni. Screw doing it for me and screw the risk of going long-distance with Joel – I'm not willing to take that chance. I know it's the opposite to what I decided the other day, but I need to feel that one thing is certain.

Joel. Joel and me together.

★

It's done. Sent. I've officially accepted Biomedical Science at the University of Sunderland as my firm choice. Fifteen minutes from Joel's campus, five hours from home and a whole lot further from my fledgling dream of being a therapist.

I've just messaged him. I know he's been banging on about me going to Sunderland for ages, but now I'm terrified he'll think I'm clingy. I should tell him about the operation too, but I want to see how the Sunderland news lands first.

My phone's ringing. Joel's face pops up on the lit screen; it's a photo he sent me as a joke where he's purposely given himself three chins and is gurning like an idiot, but even that doesn't do anything to quell the tidal wave of anxiety gushing through me. Do I answer it or let it ring out?

Answer it.

"Hey." I pace the room.

"You put it as your firm then?" No hello.

"Yeah, hope that's all right…"

"Are you kidding? It's more than all right! This means we can start to properly get excited about it."

I perch on my bed, phone wobbling in my shaking hand. "Really? I was worried you'd changed your mind."

"You do worry about stupid things sometimes."

"S'pose I do." I grab a pen from my side table and

scribble black circles on a blank page in the open notebook propped there.

"I'm so pumped you're joining me."

"Me too."

I'm on my feet again and back to pacing. Do I tell him now about the op? I don't want to ruin this nice moment, though.

"You OK? You seem a bit quiet?" Joel's voice snaps me back into the call. "You do think you made the right choice, don't you?"

"Yeah, definitely." I force a little more enthusiasm into my voice.

"Really?"

I sigh. "I promise I'm really excited; it's just—" My voice cracks. Say it. Quick. "I think I'll definitely have to have an operation for the sex thing." I say it all in one go and then gulp in a breath.

Silence.

I've ruined the moment.

"Shit."

"Mmmm." I can imagine what Joel's doing now. Rolling his eyes and thinking, *Crap, no sex for bloody ages then*. I don't blame him.

"Sorry to hear that. I don't know what to say."

"Sorry you'll have to wait longer." My voice breaks again.

"Don't be silly. I know it's scary, but it's for the best. Everything will be OK. You're the priority right now."

I struggle to push words through my closing throat. "Will it be OK?"

"Yes."

"Will *we* be OK?"

"One hundred per cent," Joel says with certainty.

"Only one hundred per cent?" I sniff and half laugh at the same time. I'm glad this isn't a video call because I have to wipe my runny nose with the back of my hand.

"Infinity per cent. Better?"

"Much better." I cough to clear my throat, but it still feels like someone's hand is wrapped round my neck.

"Love you. Wish I could give you a big cuddle."

"Love you." I say it so quietly I wouldn't be surprised if he didn't hear it.

Joel down, Mum to go. I debated not telling her, but she's the one person I cannot lie to. Get me and my feeble attempt at morality. At least I didn't tell her about my dreams to become a counsellor. I know she said she'd leave me to make my own choices, but to have backtracked on it in less than a week would have been a surefire way to disappoint her even more than I have already.

Dad's in the greenhouse and Sammy's having one of

her famously long baths – an hour and a half is her current record. Mum's in the living room and I stand by the door in case I need to make a hasty retreat.

"I made my choices on my UCAS application finally. Biomedical Science in Sunderland is my firm." I lean into the door frame, words partially muffled as I say them to the floor.

I wait for Mum to tell me I've made a huge mistake. "OK," she says, sporting the same face she was wearing when Joel showed her his face-plant clay bust. "Well done for sending it off."

I know it's difficult for her, but she's doing what she said she would – trusting me to make my own choices. I can't help but think, though, that perhaps I shouldn't be trusted.

25

"I'm so bored of this essay I can't look at it any more." I click "save" and click the X in the corner of the computer screen. It's been five days since the op news and I'm pretending it's not happening. But I'm still struggling to concentrate on schoolwork.

We're in the sixth-form computer room. Jack Lee and his gang are playing cards for what looks like a bag of Doritos and a vape, and Reggie and Justine are doing some cringe dance that I have to look away from before I die of embarrassment. Even with my headphones on I'm not surprised I've only managed to write one measly paragraph in the last forty-five minutes. Demi is nowhere to be seen. When I casually asked Lena where she was, Lena gave me a cryptic reply, saying she was with Monica, doing some music-related thing. Perhaps Monica has replaced me as one of her best friends, not that I have the right to be jealous.

"Are you still writing? I've been prom shopping for the last fifteen minutes," says Lena. "There's, like, less than a month to go now. Scary."

I can't believe that prom is coming up so fast, but I suppose my mind has been elsewhere this entire year. Our school always has sixth-form prom before exams rather than after. Our theory is that the head thinks we're less likely to get carried away if it's before and wants to ruin our fun. But it's not going to stop us.

I've not told anyone else about Sunderland because it will only go down like a sack of shit. Also, by not telling anyone, I can pretend that I might not have made the biggest mistake of my life.

Lena squeezes my shoulder, oblivious to my mental turmoil. "Oh my God, I've had an idea. Let's go on holiday. You, me and Demi. It's a rite of passage for eighteen-year-olds to take their first holiday away from Mummy and Daddy. I'm not thinking Shagaluf or Ibiza – screw that. Somewhere more 'us'." Her glimmering eyes are so wide I'm surprised they don't pop out of her head.

A holiday? A break from life? An opportunity to make up for being a rubbish friend to Demi *and* a way to prove to everyone (and myself) that life isn't always planned around Joel? Sign me up.

"Let's do it."

There's a spark in my belly for the first time in a long time. Hope. Excitement. Something to look forward to. But then in comes my rational self and tramples on the embers before they have a chance to catch. Joel. Money.

I don't even have enough for a kebab in my account at the moment.

"Not sure how I'd afford it."

Lena thinks for a moment and then her eyes light up. "Mum's always looking for some extra hands around the centre. She's hiring at the moment, looking for someone to work alongside Omar. How about it? She loves you."

The embers in my belly are back.

"Your mum loves everyone!"

"She loves you the most, though." Lena pats me on the head and squeals.

"Can't hurt to look, even if it's just for fun." *I won't get too excited*, I tell myself.

"How about Venice?" Lena taps on the keyboard and within three seconds the computer screen is filled with beautiful pictures of gondolas, the canals and the colourful houses of a little island called Burano.

By the time the bell rings, we've got an itinerary of all

the places we want to go in Venice and Lena's printed out some photos to make a "vision board" to help manifest it into reality. Whatever the hell that means, I really hope it works.

Turns out that whole job thing at Authentic Soul was not one of Lena's whims after all, and I fill out the application with Lena's moral support on FaceTime, which is followed swiftly by a heated discussion with Dad over dinner about taking a job *at such an important point in my academic career*, so it's gone 8 p.m. by the time I finally head upstairs to do my physio. But when I see Joel has sent me six messages – the final one being just a "?" – physio can wait.

Joel's face pops up on my screen after one ring, but he doesn't say anything.

"Hey," I say. "Sorry, been a mad one. You OK?"

"Fine."

I take a deep breath, hoping my explanation will thaw the obvious frostiness in his tone.

"Guess what!"

"What?" Joel's face doesn't change and his voice stays monotone.

"I've applied for a Saturday job."

Joel frowns. "Why?"

"Because I want one? And so I can save some money."

235

"What for?" His brows knit together further. I feel my enthusiasm being sucked out of me quicker than I can replace it.

"Lena, Demi and I are planning on going to Venice before uni."

More silence.

"I'm excited," I say, unable to bear it any more.

Joel huffs. "What about me, though?"

Stay calm. "What about you?"

"Would be nice if we could go on holiday together. Why can't I come?"

"It's just girls."

"I don't get this whole *just girls* thing. What difference does it make if I'm there or not?"

I smile and my cheeks ache from the effort. "You and I *can* go on holiday together. Where do you want to go?"

He ignores the question. "And a Saturday job? But you come here on Saturdays."

I'm determined to stay on the high road, but I'm dangerously close to the kerb. I take a deep breath and lose the smile but not my cool.

"We usually hang out in the evenings on Saturdays and I finish at five so I can still come to yours at six thirty. If we want to hang out in the day, we can do Sundays instead."

Joel's face softens. "OK, fine."

I hate how he says "fine" like I'm asking for his permission, but I can't be arsed to start anything. At least he's dropped the idea of coming on our girls' holiday. I take that as a win.

26

"Mum told me about your vag." Sammy kicks a stone down the gravel canal path as we make our way to our favourite coffee place – a canal boat called the *Golden Arnold*.

Mum and I agreed she could tell Sammy about the operation because I couldn't face doing it myself and we can't hide that I'm going in for surgery. I'm sure Mum's spoken at length with Dad about it already – how can she not have? But it's easier for me to pretend that he doesn't know the ins and outs of my failed sex life and it seems the feeling is mutual. In typical Dad style, he hasn't said a peep.

I look over my shoulder, but the only signs of life are the colourful canal boats docked end to end alongside us. All their windows and doors are closed and the only ears that could possibly be listening to our conversation belong to a chubby ginger cat rolling around on the roof of a banana-yellow wide beam.

"So delicately put," I say. "What did she tell you?"

"She said you were having difficulty being 'sexually intimate' with Joel and that a doctor has said you needed an op to fix it. I can't believe you've been going through this for months without telling me."

Our feet move in tandem over the grey stones. "I was embarrassed. What else did Mum say?" I keep my gaze down.

"You've had some pelvic-floor physio. What was that like? Only tell me if you want to."

I meet her eyes and pull a face.

"That bad?"

I nod. "The doctor was all up in there, hands, vibe, you name it." I lower my voice as we approach the floating cafe; the bitter but alluring smell of coffee greets us.

"Vibe, as in vibrator?"

"Shhhhhhhh," I hiss, keen not to put the two greying ladies sitting at a bench off their toasties.

We order two hot chocolates and brownies, paid for by Sammy.

"It's the least I can do," she says with a wink.

We settle on a bench as far into the trees as possible,

as I don't trust Sammy to keep her voice down. I sensed her fizzing beside me, like she was going to explode the whole time we were waiting for the drinks to be made, so I'm not surprised that the minute we sit down she bursts.

"Did *Mum* buy you a vibrator?"

"Yep." I sip my drink even though I know it'll burn my lips. This conversation is excruciating.

"That's not fair. Where's mine?"

"Don't you dare." I have visions of her asking Mum for one at the dinner table.

"I'm only joking. Sort of." She smirks. "Have you, you know … *used* it?"

"Sammy! No I haven't."

"You should."

"It doesn't seem right given that Mum bought it for me for medical reasons."

"Mum won't mind…"

"Buy one yourself if you're that desperate."

"I might just do that."

I shake my head, but can't stop my mouth turning up at the corners.

"All jokes aside, it sounds awful. I got my coil fitted last year and, don't get me wrong, I'm glad I did, but it felt … weird. Legs akimbo, someone poking about inside me." Sammy shudders.

"I know the feeling well."

"I know it's not the same, but I get it at least a little bit." Sammy licks the cream from the top of her luxury hot chocolate with the unselfconsciousness of a puppy – God love her.

"What was your first time like? If you don't mind me asking." It's something I've wanted to ask her for ages, but I didn't know how to bring it up. I may as well make the most of the conversation while it's well and truly in the sex territory.

"My first time was crap. Maybe not as bad as yours, but it wasn't great – nothing like the world had promised it would be."

"How was it bad?"

"It was awkward as hell and his mum came back halfway through. I didn't bleed and it went in, but it didn't feel nice. Bless Nicoli, he tried his best, pulling out all the moves he thought I'd like from all the porn he'd watched. It was a hot mess."

"You lost your V to Nicoli? I remember him. Really long hair and tanned, right? He was super handsome."

"He was a babe, but not even sexy Nicoli knew what he was doing at first. It ain't a one-size-fits-all box of tricks I'm afraid. You have to learn together. And we did, and it got better. Saying that, anything's better than an

241

impromptu threesome with his mum." Sammy looks into the trees behind me with a smile, like she's remembering a fond memory.

"I'm glad to hear it got better."

"It's still not always fireworks and unicorns, but I know what I like now and I'm more confident asking for it." Sammy slurps the final dregs of her drink and puts the cup on the table like she's just downed a shot.

I think for a moment. "You say it's not always fireworks and unicorns, and I get that – I've heard the same from enough people recently. But why is it so amazing for people like Reggie at school? She clearly loves sex. She wants it all the time and she's so confident."

Sammy shrugs. "Everyone's different. Maybe she had a positive first experience and it made her want to do it more. The flip side of that is true too. If your first experience is painful, violating or traumatic, then of course you're going to be more wary of it or even avoid it completely."

Would it be too dramatic to describe my experiences as *painful, violating or traumatic*? I'm not sure. Those words sound about right to me. I pull the lid off my hot chocolate and stare into my cup.

"Do you think there's also a possibility that it's not as great for Reggie as she makes out too?"

"That's also possible. You're not in the bedroom with

her so you don't know, and people often pretend it's better than it is… But also, in the same way it's not always fireworks and unicorns, it's also not always complicated for some people. So maybe it *is* amazing for her and she *does* love it."

"OK. I can't tell if that gives me hope that it can get better or makes me feel disgustingly jealous of Reggie."

"How about both?"

"True." I chew my lip. "So you think the operation will be worth it then?"

"Of course. It gives you options. You might love having a penis inside you or you might prefer other stuff." Sammy waggles her eyebrows. "But at least you'll have a choice."

"Choice would be nice."

A flustered-looking mum with a toddler and a baby sit at the table next to us.

"Let's talk about something more PG now," I say, twitching my head towards the newcomers.

"Sure. Let's talk about how *amazing* these brownies are." Sammy grins. "They're better than sex anyway." She takes a bite and closes her eyes; I'm grateful she doesn't moan.

27

Snuggled in Joel's bed and breathing in his musky scent has made me feel that everything is right in the world again. Over the past hour we've not argued once, instead reverting to our normal chit-chat, like whether Rory McFadden still makes strange breathing noises when he's working in silence (he does) and whether Lena has recovered from the time she farted during Dance (she hasn't).

"I missed this," he says, cupping my chin in his hand. Given that we've seen each other more than usual recently, I can only assume that what he's missed is *how* we are together, which confirms that he's well aware of the roller coaster we've been riding. It's nice to know that at least we've been riding it together.

I do feel a bit guilty that I keep turning Demi and Lena down to hang out with Joel, but I'm stuck between a rock and a hard place trying to balance seeing my friends, revising, my physio and keeping my relationship afloat. Oh, and potentially starting a new job. At least I'm able to message Lena, but I've noticed Demi is barely messaging me at all now. It feels shit and like a relief at the same time.

Joel's lips are warm and soft as they meet mine with a feather-light touch. I kiss him back, although I can't help but wonder if he wants this to lead to something more. Will his hands go wandering? Will he be pulling my knickers off in a few minutes? Ugh, why can't I just enjoy the moment without these stupid thoughts hanging over me?

But Joel's kisses stay tender and I finally let myself dissolve into his body and be held by his firm hands. His fingers tickle my scalp and stroke my neck, sending shivers to the tips of my toes, and I reciprocate, caressing his soft earlobes between my thumb and forefinger and running my hands through his ginger waves. This feels safe. I can relax and enjoy this territory as his hands stay comfortably above my hips.

We explore each other's mouths, necks and ears for what feels like an eternity and no time at all. He pulls back too soon, his breathing heavy and hair roughed up.

"This is killing me," he breathes before he pulls his top off. I'm OK with him taking his top off, but I don't mirror him. I need his lips back on mine. I pull him into my arms and relish the soft warmth of his back. The pads of his fingers find my skin below my clothes and draw delicate circles on my skin. They start on my shoulder blades before making their way down to the small of my back.

And then they go lower.

And lower.

Until they find the elastic of my waistband.

My whole body stiffens. The magic is gone.

Why does Joel want to ruin such a perfect moment? But then again, maybe I do owe him…

Owe him? What the hell am I thinking?

I pull back. His kisses are now too intense, invading my space and pushing against me even as I pull away.

He frowns. "Everything OK?"

"Yeah, all good."

"Do you not want to…?"

No, I don't want your greedy fingers anywhere near me. I think on my feet; there are only so many times I can use the excuse that I'm on my period.

"It's not that I don't want you to," I lie. "I just have another idea."

I sit up and shuffle to the bottom of the bed. I can see in his eyes that he knows what I'm about to do.

"Are you sure? You don't usually like doing tha—"

"I want to," I lie. Again.

Joel's face is contorted as if he's trying to work me out, but as soon as I reach for his belt buckle and tuck my hair behind my ears, any angst he has swiftly disappears.

It's official. I don't practise what I preach.

I've done the opposite of what I've been preaching to Holly and Skye. I've done something I didn't want to do, but I felt pressure to, just to make Joel happy.

When I get home and walk into the living room, Mum is there and I'm sure my flushed face makes it obvious what I've just done – like a branding mark that screams, *I just gave head, all the way to the end*. But there's a voice in my head too, a smug one, saying: *You're such a sexual goddess – you can satisfy your man as much as the next woman.*

After the conversation with Sammy at the *Golden Arnold*, I'm more confident talking to her about sex stuff, and I can't go to bed feeling as confused as I do right now. I edge into her room and flop on to her bed. With her Sammy senses, she can tell something is going on before I even say anything.

247

"What's up?" she says. She's sitting at her desk, but she turns to face me.

I drum my fingers on her pillow and look at my feet. "Have you ever, you know … *swallowed*?" I mouth the last word.

She narrows her eyes. "I have. Why? You don't have to whisper it, you know." She turns back to her laptop and starts typing something.

"I just did it." My stomach roils at saying it out loud. Even though I brushed my teeth when I got in, I still feel like I want to scrape my tongue.

The typing stops and Sammy shuts the laptop. "Congratulations?" She looks bemused.

"I didn't want to."

Sammy frowns. "So why did you?"

"I didn't want him to touch me."

"So why didn't you just say that? I know it's not easy." Sammy looks at me, her brow softening and genuine curiosity in her eyes.

How do you *just say that* without sounding like a bitch?

"I didn't want him to think I was rejecting him. He didn't make me do it or anything."

Sammy sighs. "I know. But you still felt forced. God, I hate that for you."

"That's on me. It's in my own head. I'm trying to keep him happy."

"While making yourself sad?" Sammy bites her lip.

"I'm not sad."

"What are you then?"

I don't reply and instead melt under the duvet and pull it over my head. I don't *know* what I am. Stuck? Desperate? Making a mountain out of a molehill?

Sammy pats the duvet, obviously thinking it's the top of my head when, in actual fact, she's just high-fived my eye.

"Owww."

"Sorry. Look, you owe Joel nothing." She yanks the duvet off me. "Sex is all about two people enjoying themselves, not one person feeling obligated to do something that they don't want to. If you keep doing that, you'll start to resent it *and* resent him. That's even worse for both of you. So next time you're in this situation I encourage you to open your mouth, but use it to express how you feel. OK?"

"OK," I say.

Although, at the moment, being honest doesn't seem to be getting any easier.

28

I got the job. Lena wanted to give me the good news in person and turned up on my doorstep sporting a party hat and blowing a party horn.

"Mummy Lola said that your application is exactly what they're looking for and you can start next Saturday."

"Your mum is too kind," I say, as we make our way up to my room. I can't believe I officially have a job and that I'm starting next week. It's exciting … and terrifying.

"My mum speaks the truth."

"Well, tell her I said thanks and I look forward to seeing her on Saturday."

"On the subject of things that speak the truth, look what I brought." She rummages around in the pocket of her daisy-embroidered flares and pulls out something that looks like a pointed crystal on the end of a chain.

I squint at it. "I'm going to need more information here."

"It's a pendulum. We can ask it questions and it will tell us the answer. It will swing one way for yes and another for no. Let me just work out which way is which." Lena goes silent as she holds the pendulum in front of her and stares at it. Then she nods. "Ready. Ask it a question."

"You go first."

"Will I get on to my course?" Lena lifts the pendulum up in front of her again and watches it intently. She beams. "Yep. Next. How about … will Demi be an influential figure in Parliament and not be crap like the dickheads we currently have?" The pendulum swings again. Lena nods. "Yep."

"That was an easy one! Of course she will."

"It's not me doing it! It's spirit. Your turn."

I roll my eyes. "Fine. Will Joel's penis ever find its way inside me?"

The crystal starts to swing, first in small circles and then in much more exaggerated ones. Lena's eyes widen before she stuffs it back in her pocket.

"What are you doing? What did it say?"

"The spirits don't want you to know the answer to that."

"The spirits don't want me to know? What does that mean?"

"We're better off not knowing some things."

"So we won't have sex then."

"No! It doesn't mean that. It means you'll find out when the time is right."

"That's useful."

Lena shrugs. "I don't make the rules. I'm just the messenger."

I huff. "If you say so."

For the rest of the evening the pendulum doesn't make a reappearance, and instead we swap looking into the future with prepping for it by studying. But, no matter how much I try to focus on my Biology notes, the thought that I might never have sex with Joel has taken up residence in my brain rent-free. Stupid spirits that I don't even believe in, why didn't you just tell me everything is going to be OK?

When Lena leaves, I type out a speedy message to Joel and send it. It simply says: Got the job 🍤 Though I bet a bit of him would be relieved if I hadn't because it would mean more time spent with him.

I put off checking my phone for as long as possible, and I'm in bed before I finally reach for it on my bedside table and flip it over so I can see the screen.

Joel: Well done x

I'd have liked more enthusiasm, but at least he's not being unkind. A little voice in my head asks if I have such low expectations of him that "not unkind" is the bar I've set, but I push it away.

Joel is typing

Hold that thought.

Joel: Just to let you know, I booked a lads' holiday with Tom. Magaluf. Hope that's OK x

I knew it! I knew he'd book something in retaliation for my holiday. And it's fine. *It's fine.* But despite it being *fine*, I send a screenshot of his message to Lena.

She replies instantly with a voice note, saying, "Don't worry about it – he's not the type of guy to do anything behind your back. Love you."

Am I being out of order? I'm going on holiday so why can't he? But everyone knows that Magaluf has its Shagaluf nickname for a reason. Sex. Lots of sex. If a teen boy actually made it through a holiday like that without so much as kissing someone, some might deem it a miracle.

Venice is absolutely not the same as Magaluf.

But Joel is Joel, wherever in the world he is, and I need to trust him not to cheat.

The problem is, it feels near impossible when I'm unable to meet all his sexual needs and when my vagina doesn't work and everyone else's does and…

Nope. Stop. Don't go there, Rose.

I send a thumbs up and nothing else. I can't be *that* girl.

29

On my first day of work, I wake up three hours earlier than necessary due to my internal anxiety alarm clock, with old friend Dread sitting in the pit of my stomach and long-time chum Panic weighing heavily on my chest. True to form, the what-ifs buzz around my head like trapped wasps the second I open my eyes. What if I'm absolutely useless at everything? What if I accidentally book a complete beginner called Martha on to an advanced hot yoga class? What if I answer the phone and forget the name of the centre and sit there in stunned silence?

At least there's one person who's confident in my ability to not totally balls things up.

Lena: GOOD LUCK, MY ROSEYCHEEKS! YOU'RE

GONNA SMASH IT. PS not seen you in the chat
recently – everything OK?

Rose: Thank you, my lovely Moongirl! Very nervous!
And yeah, fine, just busy x

I *have* been busy, but I also feel embarrassed going back to
the group after they were so excited about my decision to
become a counsellor. I don't want to admit I've just thrown
that all away.

By the time I arrive at Authentic Soul and walk past the
giant stone Buddha that greets me at the door, I've already
done three nervous poos and forgotten how to breathe, but
then Mummy Lola wafts round the corner in a cloud of
incense and serenity and everything feels a little less scary.

The first thing she does is show me her office, which is
exactly like her house – full of hanging plants that could
knock you out and little knick-knacks from her world
travels. On her desk are loads of framed photos of Lena
and River as babies and kids, both sporting mullets and
outfits that look like Lola dressed them up by covering
them in double-sided tape and rolling them through a load
of curtain offcuts.

After a tour around the centre, Mummy Lola takes

me into the staff barn to introduce me to my co-worker Omar, even though I've technically already met him. It's funny to see behind the scenes, and I feel like a VIP as we enter through the large oak double doors. The room has a kitchenette in one corner and some sofas, floor cushions and yoga mats in the other. Stained-glass effect stickers decorate the windows and bathe the room in a rainbow glow.

"Here's the main man." Mummy Lola weaves her way towards the sofa area where Omar is sitting on his phone. He stands as I approach, black curly hair bobbing. He tucks his hands and phone into his pocket and nods at me.

"Rose, Omar. Omar, Rose. I think you two will get on like a house on fire."

"Hey, Rose. I think we've met before. It will be nice to have someone else around to help out," he says with a small smile.

Mummy Lola puts her arm round him and squeezes. "Omar's currently doing the same job as you single-handedly. He's doing great, but we thought it would be nice for him to have some company on Saturdays, given that it's our busiest day."

"Cool," I say, returning his smile. "Looking forward to you showing me the ropes."

He chuckles and seems to relax, taking his hands out of his pockets and running them through his hair. I hope that didn't sound like I was flirting with him – he's not a bad-looking guy. But of course Joel's the only one for me.

Five o'clock rolls round so fast I can't believe that my first day of work is done already. I needn't have worried about Omar thinking I was flirting. I spent the rest of the day with him and he's super chill and doesn't take anything too seriously.

As I walk out of the main entrance of the centre and back past the stone Buddha, I'm dead on my arse. My feet throb with every step and I have a banging headache, but my brain is buzzing.

I'm in a bit of a daze, looking for Mum's car, when a voice startles me.

"'Ello, 'ello. Fancy seeing you here."

I spin round and it's Joel, all goofy smiles and glinting eyes.

"What are you doing here?" I say, shocked, but I throw my arms round him and lean into the kiss he plants softly on my cheek. I'm over the whole Magaluf thing now. Well, more like just trying not to think about it, because if I think too much about it, I get worried. He's gone out of his way to surprise me and I'm going to be happy about it.

Joel grins widely. "I thought it would be nice to meet you after your first day."

"Where's Mum?" I say. "I don't want her to come all this way and—"

"I texted her and sorted it. No sweat."

"Ah, thanks. I was worried for a second."

Joel chuckles. "When are you not?"

I playfully swat him. "This is a very cute thing for you to do. I need a shower, though. I smell."

Joel ducks down and starts sniffing me like a pig hunting truffles. "A bit stinky," he says, still tucked into my neck so it's muffled.

I squeal. "Get off, you weirdo."

The door to the centre behind me squeaks open and I spin round, hoping that whoever it is didn't just see Joel and me acting like idiots.

It's Omar, wearing a wide smile and jangling his car keys off his middle finger. He definitely saw us. FML.

"See you next week. Nice meeting you." He nods at me and then at Joel.

Joel nods back and then watches him walk all the way to his car. "Who's that?"

"Omar, he's the main person I'm working with. He does the same as me but more hours."

"Mm-hmm," Joel says. He jerks his chin up in a curt nod and looks towards Omar's car again.

"How did you get here?" I look around the car park.

"Mum gave me a lift. She wanted to see the centre."
Joel rolls his eyes and it's only now I spy Sonya's peroxide
bob and red Mini at the far end of the car park.

"How romantic," I tease.

I'm acutely aware that Omar's still sitting in his car with
the engine running. He must be on the phone or sorting
out some music or something.

"Come on," I say, turning to make my way to Sonya's
car, aware she's waiting, but Joel slides his arm round me
and pulls me to his waist. He presses his lips on mine,
which takes me by surprise, so I kiss him back quickly, but
resist his efforts to stick his tongue in my mouth. It feels
unprofessional to kiss in front of a colleague.

Joel doesn't notice my hesitation. "Come on, you, let's
get you back to mine," he says as he leans down and sweeps
me into a cradle carry. As if this isn't mortifying enough,
there's no way Omar can't not see us, because Joel chooses
to walk directly past Omar's windscreen. I can't deny that
it feels nice to be off my aching feet, but with the weight
of embarrassment I'm now carrying I'm surprised Joel's
even able to lift me.

In the back of the car, Joel's hand engulfs mine, my
small fingers at maximum stretch to accommodate his. I'm
noticing more and more how parts of us don't seem to fit
together like they should.

"The centre looks great – and it's such a beautiful spot, much nicer than the ones I go to in town." Sonya looks into the rear-view mirror and I catch her eyes framed by her heavy fringe.

"Yeah, it's lovely in there. You'll have to check it out some time," I say.

"I'll have a look at their timetable – I'm always up for trying new classes."

Sonya drives and we sit in comfortable silence for a few minutes before she breaks it.

"Who was that chap who left at the same time as you? He looked nice."

I much preferred the silence.

Joel's grip on my hand tightens.

"Omar?" I say. "He's my co-worker."

"Is it just you two or is there anyone else?" Joel asks.

Does he think he's being subtle? I look at him and squeeze his hand, hoping to convey he's got nothing to worry about.

"Just the two of us doing that specific job, but there are others like the chef and teachers. And Lola, of course."

Joel chews his lip. "Does he have a girlfriend?"

"I didn't ask him whether he's seeing anyone – girl or otherwise – I only just met him." I squeeze Joel's hand again, but he just looks out of the window.

"What a lovely place to work," Sonya says, oblivious to the jealous undercurrents – or should I say riptide – bouncing around the back seat.

I've not looked at my phone all day, so I slide it out of my pocket and use the ten-minute journey to catch up on messages. I let the family chat know I survived my first day at work, send a selfie of me with the caption *New job. Who dis?* and then mindlessly scroll through various social streams. Demi's posted something new again. My thumb taps it before I can stop it.

It's a video of her and Lena revising, pages of notes spread out in front of them and a side of two hot chocolates. I wouldn't have been able to go because I'm with Joel, but *they* wouldn't have known that. I didn't know myself until he turned up. Maybe Lena assumed I'd be too tired after work, but it would have been nice to be asked.

Truth be told, I'd rather be with the girls tonight. It's not that I'm not happy to see Joel, but recently it's been a bit … repetitive. Sonya feeds us and leaves for some meeting or exercise class. Joel and I go upstairs and he starts kissing me and, even if I'm not feeling it, I kiss him back and let him put his hands in my pants. I let him probe around for a few minutes before it feels unbearably like it does during physio. He doesn't try to put his finger inside me, but I hate how even just him touching there

262

now feels uncomfortable, so it doesn't last long until I pull his pants off and crouch at the other end of the bed. It's pretty unappealing, but less so than the thought of him continuing to touch me. I wouldn't say I've got used to it, but if you do something enough times you know where to drift off in your mind to avoid being fully present.

I expect tonight will be no different.

I'm sipping my tea as slowly as possible and trying to keep Sonya chatting. It would be perfect if I kept her chatting long enough that she'd lose track of time and end up missing Zumba. However, my fantasy is quashed when at six thirty on the dot she stands.

"Right," she says, slapping her hands on her thighs and standing with purpose. "I'm off. See you two later. Really pleased to hear work is going well and that you're surviving the revision." She smiles at me then heads out. The sound of keys jangling and the front door slamming confirm she's gone and Joel and I are alone.

To my relief, the minute she's gone Joel stands. "I'm putting a pizza in. I'm bloody starved," he says. He throws his phone on to the sofa beside me. "Find something for us to watch?"

I open his phone and click on the internet. He's the only person I know who doesn't have YouTube downloaded because he doesn't have any space on his phone. Oh, it looks like he's already started looking—

It takes a few seconds to register what I'm looking at. Rows upon rows of videos, but it sure as hell isn't YouTube. I can see boobs, arses and the word "fuck" more times than I can count.

I drop his phone on the sofa and hurry down the hallway. "Just going to the loo," I call.

"Enjoy," Joel calls back, oblivious.

I lock the door behind me and sit on the toilet lid. *It's just porn. It's not like he's cheated.* But, no matter how many times I say it to myself, I can't stop my eyes from pricking or my heart from hammering so hard my chest hurts. Would he be watching this stuff if we were having sex? Or if I was doing a better job of meeting his needs? It's one thing to assume your boyfriend might watch a bit of porn and another thing to know it. I don't want to *see* the women he masturbates to, because then I can compare.

Let it go. LET IT GO. You are not that girl. You are not a jealous, insecure bitch.

Then I remember that Joel had a go at me about my vibrator. What a hypocrite! Why is it OK for him to get moody about that sort of thing when he's sitting there actually getting off on other people that aren't me?

Ugh, I can't stay in here all night. I need to make a

choice – let it go or talk to him about it like an adult. Am I capable of doing either of those things? I don't know. I flush the toilet for show then stride out of the room before I can change my mind.

I don't look at Joel as I sit on the sofa beside him.

"And the winner for the *Guinness Book of World Records* longest poo goes to" – Joel drum-rolls – "Rose Summers."

I smile meekly. *Let it go.*

Joel shuffles up beside me and leans into my eyeline. "You OK? You're being weird."

I nod totally unconvincingly. He reaches for my knee. The warmth of his hand provokes a reaction in me that's more akin to being touched by a scalding rod. I stand up quickly, his hand sliding off. "Please don't."

OK, so letting it go isn't going to work. I've never been good at acting.

"What did I do?" Joel snaps his hand away from me like I've electric-shocked him.

"Nothing," I say, but it's pointless. My face is the opposite of poker and I'm actually shaking. Anger? Panic? Not sure.

"Bullshit. What have I done now?"

Words batter me from the inside, desperate to escape. Vile insecurity mixes with raging injustice and fizzes like a mint dropped in Coke, ready to explode.

And then I do.

"You have some nerve getting moody with me about my vibrator when you're the one looking at disgusting stuff online."

Joel's jaw clenches. "You snooped on my phone?"

"No! You left your tabs open."

"I don't believe you."

I position myself in front of him, hands on hips. "I'm not lying! Do you think I *wanted* to see that?"

"If you look for something to be annoyed at, you'll find it. Give me your phone."

I chuck my phone on to the sofa beside him. It bounces off his knee and I flinch. "Be my guest. You won't find anything and then you'll just look like an idiot."

Joel grabs it and starts scrolling.

I pace the room, unable to sit still.

"Why have you got his number?" Joel thrusts the phone at me. The screen blurs as I make sense of what I'm seeing. Omar's number.

"Omar? I've never messaged him before! Look. I've got nothing to hide." I thrust it back. "I have his number so we can sort shifts. Because we're *work colleagues*."

Joel crosses his arms. "Whatever. Point proven. You look, you find."

I'm back on my feet again. "For the last time I DIDN'T

LOOK." I'm shaking with rage. "You're worried that I'm texting a co-worker, when it's you who's going on a lads' holiday to Shagaluf." I know I said I wasn't going to bring it up, but the evening's ruined anyway.

Joel rolls his eyes at me. "Don't start. You're sounding really possessive, you know."

Is he serious? After all his needy calls and texts and making me hang out with him instead of my friends, he's calling *me* possessive?

"You are UNREAL – you know that, right? You must realize how ridiculous you're being. And I am not possessive. I'm *upset*. Why can't you just reassure me?" I'm not quite shouting. I'm angrier than that. It's more of a hiss.

"What do you want me to say?"

"Tell me I'm better than them. Tell me I'm enough for you. Although clearly I'm not." I sound desperate now.

Joel rolls his eyes. "All boys do it."

"Do they? Or is it just boys who aren't happy with their girlfriends?"

Joel shrugs. "You said it, not me."

My breath catches in my throat and my mouth falls open. "Do you mean that?" It comes out as a whisper.

He looks away from me. I don't recognize him the way he is now – his face contorted with anger.

I need to get away before I do something I regret. I need to remove myself from this situation. "I'm done with this conversation."

Sammy is on the driveway in less than fifteen minutes, though it still feels like a lifetime while I sit in silence replaying the last ten minutes over and over. Joel says nothing, just scrolls on his phone until I get up and head towards the door. He shouts a sarcastic *Bye then* just before I slam it behind me.

I miraculously manage to keep it together in the car because I know Sammy would go into protective big-sister mode if I told her what Joel had said and I don't want to get her involved. I just told her I needed to be back earlier than normal to finish off an assignment due for Monday that had slipped my mind. Instead, we speak about my first day, and seeing how proud of me she is makes it even harder to hold in my tears. By the time I'm in the safety of my room, it's all too much. I try to gulp in some air, but the strangled growls I suffocated in the car force their way out of me. I swear into my pillow. I wish I could scream, but I can't without someone hearing me.

The sound of my phone going off has me close to ripping my hair out. If it's Joel wanting to carry on the argument, I'm turning it off.

It bleeps again and then again.

"Oh my God, leave me alone," I say, but I open them anyway.

Joel: I'm so sorry. I love you so much and I don't want to lose you

Joel: I have a plan. All you need to do is turn up. Mine, Friday at 6 p.m. Argument-free zone. Only love allowed x

Joel: Please? For us x

My heart slows. Joel recognizes that we're slipping away from each other and he's trying to fix it. He wants this as much as I do.

30

"Can't wait for Friday," Demi says. "Shopping for prom after-party outfits. With my besties."

It's Tuesday and Demi's sipping hot chocolate from her usual perch on the radiator in the computer room while Lena and I sit at computers revising.

I'm so lost in DNA and RNA nucleotides that it takes me a minute to realize what she's said.

"Hang on a minute, Friday? I can't do Friday." I dread to think how Joel might react if I cancelled on his special plans. This Friday feels like it's make or break for us. Why is the universe conspiring against me having a happy relationship and keeping my best friends happy?

Demi rolls her eyes and doesn't even try to hide it. "What? We arranged this ages ago!"

We probably did, but I must have forgotten.

"Can't we go on Saturday instead? Or the Thursday before prom? It's over a week away…"

I've missed out on a hell of a lot recently and I draw the line at missing this. Our pre-prom shopping trip is something we've done for the last two years. Every year we order our actual dresses online because there's way more choice that way, but we always shop together for shoes, jewellery and the all-important after-party outfit to mark the occasion. And this is our last year before we all go our separate ways.

"I can't go on Saturday. I'm seeing my grandma in the morning because it would've been Grandad's birthday, and the Thursday before is leaving it way too late," says Demi.

"I can't go on Friday, though," I repeat.

"Why?" asks Lena.

I shoot her a death stare. "I'm seeing Joel, but—"

I see the whites of Demi's eyes again as they somersault in her sockets. "You see him all the time! Can't you choose us over him for a change?"

"This is important."

"So is this!" Demi folds her arms. "We ask you to do one thing and you choose him over us. Again and again."

Injustice stabs my gut. Or is it guilt? I'm not the only one in the wrong here, am I?

"Funny, you seem to pick and choose when you want to hang out with me and when you don't."

Demi snort-laughs. "Are you for real?"

"You two hang out without me all the time."

Lena coughs, reminding me she's here.

"Not that you aren't allowed to," I say. I don't want Lena to feel like I'm blaming her — this isn't about her; it's about Demi. "But I don't think it's fair to have a go at me."

"What's the point of us asking you to anything? You wouldn't come anyway. You're always with him."

"You know the days I see him." Why do I feel like I'm going to cry?

"I'm not going to plan my life around you."

"I'm not asking you to. Just some flexibility—"

"Some flexibility," Demi scoffs. "Yeah right."

"I've had a lot going on," I mutter.

"No more than the rest of us," snaps Demi.

That's it. I'm going to tell her. I need to get it all out. I need her to realize how awful things have been and that I'm not ditching them "just because". That if I don't choose Joel this time, there might not be a next time.

Where do I start? The failed sex attempt. The lie. The physio. I open my mouth, but Demi speaks first.

"Forget it. Lena and I will go on Friday. Enjoy your

night with Joel. Again." She raises her eyebrows at me, challenging me to keep battling.

"You're out of order," I say, pushing my chair back, grabbing my bag and storming out of the room.

Lena: You need to tell her

Rose: It's none of her business

Lena: She's your friend and she loves you

Rose: Does she?

Lena: Yes!

Rose: She has a funny way of showing it

Lena: So do you x

31

"This is amazing" is something I never thought I'd say about Joel's garage, yet here I am. Probably a mix of my ever-lowering standards and the fact that Joel's really put effort into making it look less shit. I know this is his way of apologizing for our bust-up on Saturday, so I'm willing myself to be as enthusiastic about the whole thing as he is.

The dingy, cluttered dumping ground is speckled with fairy lights and a modest-sized pottery wheel sits in the centre. The washer and dryer are still tucked into the corner at one end, but Joel's covered them with a blanket and turned them into a mock bar, with two glasses, a bottle of fizzy wine, two bar stools and a bowl of Doritos. When Joel first told me to meet him by the garage door, I hadn't known what to expect. But this slightly naff attempt at romance is absolutely perfect.

"Loving the bar," I say with a cheeky grin, prodding Joel under the ribs.

He scoots his waist away from me. "Oiiiiiiiiii!" He puts his hands on his hips to protect himself from further attack.

"You're so ticklish. I could fart on you and you'd take off."

Joel scrunches his nose. "Let's not test that theory."

We both laugh and his eyes crinkle at the corners. It's been so long since I've seen him express pure joy – time slows down and all the reasons I fell in love with him come flooding back. I wonder if he has similar moments of appreciation for me.

"So what's the plan, Stan?"

"I thought we'd start off our lovely romantic evening with two Rustler burgers à la microwave, followed by throwing on the wheel and then some after-dinner aperitifs," says Joel, pronouncing "aperitifs" in a dodgy French accent.

"Sounds perfect."

"Watch and learn," Joel says. "I'll show you the skills that got me into Sunderland."

"And I won't be far away," I say. I feel one hundred per cent confident in having Sunderland as my first choice for the first time in, well, for ever.

★

I'm not sure what I expected from a microwave burger, but, providing I don't end up spending all night on the toilet, it was all right. Joel and I could have been chewing on an old boot and it wouldn't have mattered. I've laughed to the point of choking on multiple occasions. I don't know if it's the novelty of the garage setting, but we've reverted back to childlike silliness, only heightened by the two glasses of wine we've sunk in the last couple of hours. We seem to have found each other again for the first time in months, like we've been transported back to a moment in our relationship before everything became so complicated.

"Who'd have thought you could have such an amazing time in a garage with some crisps and cheap wine?" My cheeks hurt from smiling.

"It's because it's us. We could be anywhere and still have a laugh," says Joel, his own goofy smile showing no signs of faltering.

"Yeah?" I say, not meaning for it to sound like a question.

It used to be true, but I'm not sure it is now. I remember one of our earlier dates to London, when we went on an open-top bus tour around the city, but no matter how many sights we drove past, all I saw was him. We stopped off for lunch in Regent's Park and I have a clear memory that I was on my period and Joel was pretending to do reiki on me by mimicking pulling out the cramps. He looked like a total maniac and we were both laughing so much the people around us probably thought we were on drugs. So much has changed – but maybe we can be like that again. Perhaps this can be the blank slate we need to start afresh.

"Clay time," Joel says, standing up and rubbing his hands together. "Would madam like to follow me?"

He hands me an apron that I put on, seeing as I made an effort today with my best skirt and a top I nicked from Sammy. He's equally as dapper, with a proper shirt on and his black jeans. I settle on to the dusty clay-spattered stool in front of the wheel and suddenly feel incredibly out of place. This is a big part of Joel's life that I know nothing about, aside from being the lucky receiver of many trinkets made by his talented hands.

Joel pulls his own stool beside me and places a lump of clay on the wheel with a splat.

"Here, I'll start it for you," he says. He dips his hands in a tub by our feet, causing the clear water to instantly cloud grey. "Let's make a little bowl. Watch how I do it."

"You're optimistic, thinking I'm going to be able to make anything you can give a name to."

"Aim high. You never know, you might be better than me."

"Unlikely," I snort.

I watch him expertly use his hands to form the clay,

first into a cone and then into a flat doughnut shape. The look in his eyes is of both pure focus and total peace. I *knew* how important sculpting and throwing was to him – it was obvious in the way he spoke about it and his ambition to study Ceramics. Now, though, I can *see* it and *feel* it. He's doing the right thing by following his dreams.

If only I could say the same for myself.

Not going there. I'm going to enjoy the moment.

Joel looks up from the wheel as it slowly stops spinning.

"See, easy," he says. He stands and washes his hands, wiping them on his smart shirt. "Your turn."

"I don't want to ruin it," I say, pulling a face. "I can just watch."

"Absolutely not. You have to have a go. I want you to enjoy it."

"All right, but I'll need your help."

"Sure. I've always wanted to recreate that scene from *Ghost*."

He laughs and comes back over. I haven't a clue what he's talking about, but I laugh anyway. I shuffle awkwardly on to Joel's stool, the seat still warm. He shifts the other stool directly behind mine with a scrape and settles into it, so I'm firmly wedged between his thighs. His weight presses into my back as he reaches round me and motions to wet my hands. I oblige, now highly aware of his breath on the nape of my neck. I turn to smile at him, our faces centimetres apart. I'm suddenly self-conscious.

"I'll do the pedal," he says. "Just do this with your hands." Joel holds his hands out in front of me and demonstrates a gesture that looks complicated and simple at the same time.

"OK, here I go…"

I try to replicate Joel's movements, but after a few minutes I've got something that looks more like the splodge we started with than anything else.

"I've ruined it," I say with a laugh. "It's really fun, though. I love how squishy it feels. I—"

"I love you so much," Joel breathes into my ear with an intensity that makes my head spin. My stomach leaps and my body responds with an overwhelming urge I don't know what to do with.

"I love you too," I whisper, and I lean my head back on to his shoulder, my neck an open invitation that Joel accepts both hungrily and tenderly. My hands are covered with clay but I don't care. I reach back round his neck and yield to the electrifying feeling of his lips on my skin. Minutes pass and his kisses become more urgent, as does the call in my body for more.

I part my legs a fraction. As with my neck, Joel follows my lead, his hands tentatively finding their way down to my hips and then lower. My skirt gives him easy access to my inner thigh, which he circles so gently with his finger I can barely feel him. The slow pace of his movements is a stark contrast to the hammering of his heart on my back, which mirrors my own. As Joel's finger traces a delicate path higher and higher and finds the satin of my knickers, the fluttering of my heart is now a pulse all over my body.

"Is this OK?" Joel whispers in my ear, his hot breath causing my already overstimulated body to melt.

I want this so much. But I'm scared.

I nod, wordless, and lie my head back on to his shoulders. I'm so glad he can't see my face, scared that I'll be wincing in pain or disgust.

Joel slips his hands into my knickers. Even though his stroke is light I battle with the involuntary reaction to snap my legs shut and withdraw. During physio, this is the moment when I must float away from my body, cut myself off at my neck and find solace in the numbing effect my thoughts can have when connecting to my body is unsafe. I'm sucked there as a reflex and the desperate urge for Joel begins to fade.

But I pull myself back into my body. This isn't physio; this is Joel. I'm safe here.

I lean into the sensations and try my hardest to stay in my body and make a conscious effort to not slip back into my mind. It's hard at first – I'm seeing a peek of Joel's ginger curls and inhaling the smell of his neck and then I'm thinking of revision notes and university applications. I'm in my body and then I'm out. In. Out. In. Out.

Until I'm more in than out.

And I'm finally able to surrender to the pleasurable sensations that take over my body and anchor me firmly within it.

I don't orgasm, but I don't need to. I felt *something*. Connection. Safety. Pleasure? It's more than enough for me, and more than I've felt in a long time.

Rose: Thank you so much for earlier. I had an amazing time

Joel: Me too. Like old times

Rose: Better than old times :P

Joel: Many more to come

Rose: I hope so

Joel: I know so. Love you so much x

My Joely, I've got him back. I've got *us* back. I can't express how good that feels.

32

Prom is finally here. The plates from the meal have been cleared and students are slowly trickling to the dance floor. Alcoholic drinks have been restricted to one per person over the age of eighteen, but it's clear from all the staggering around that most people went heavy on the pre-drinks.

"This is nice," says Lena, holding up her glass and beckoning Demi and me to do the same.

Demi raises hers. "The gang is back together again."

"Cheers to that," I say, and we clink our glasses.

We managed to put the argument about me ditching the shopping trip behind us and have made up. At least I think we have. I can't tell whether we're being really mature about it or just sweeping it under the carpet and pretending it didn't happen. Either way, it works for me. We've danced, we've laughed, and I've been floating on air since my and Joel's romantic evening last Friday.

Joel's meeting us at the after-party because only students from our school are invited to the actual prom. Lena, Demi and I got ready together like we have for the past two years. We cranked the music up, dumped out the contents of our make-up bags and sipped bubbly until our choice of transport – Lena's family camper van – took us to the far-from-glitzy-but-it-will-do Hilton Hotel.

"Love you guys. Let's promise to stay best friends once we all eff off to uni next year," I say, the reality of it all finally sinking in. Us going our separate ways is something I haven't allowed myself to think about.

"I'll try my best not to replace you both with cooler people." Demi winks.

"I'll try my best to replace *you* with someone a bit nicer." Lena winks back, and we all laugh.

It's fun just girls. I feel like I'm betraying Joel by saying that, but I'm allowed to enjoy the company of my two best friends for a change.

"I'm going to the toilet," I say, pushing my chair back and standing, bag clutched in hand.

"I'll come with," says Lena.

"Me too," says Demi, standing also.

We head to the loos, weaving between the tables and clusters of students. In the cubicle, I pull my phone out.

On the toilet, I do what I can only assume most people do – check my messages and scroll socials. A photo of a really pretty girl catches my eye. I'm pretty sure she's been on *Love Island* or something like that. I click on the thumbnail just to be nosy. I can't be the only person who likes to torture themselves by looking at people online who are one hundred times more attractive than themselves, right?

Joel64 likes this.

The cubicle spins around me and the sides close in. I should click off, but I can't; my fingers move all on their own. I scroll through the rest of her feed, taking in her figure and the way she can wear casual clothes and no make-up and still look perfect.

Joel64 likes this.

Joel64 likes this.

Joel64 likes this.

I count at least seven likes and I'm only back to March – a picture of her in just underwear, captioned *A little me time* with the horny emoji. I should stop, but I can't. I go to his profile and look at his activity. I click through his recent follows. They're all girls: random influencers wearing next to nothing.

Joel64 likes this.

Joel64 likes this.

Joel64 likes this.

My stomach roils when I spot he's recently followed Reggie. They aren't even friends, so what's he doing that for? I click on her page, despite knowing I'm asking for trouble. In Joel's words: you look, you find. There's a picture of her with a really low top on, red lipstick and a kiss emoji.

Joel64 likes this.

So he's just like every other guy at school then. It's one thing liking random people's photos, but how disrespectful is it that he's liking a photo of a girl I know? She will have seen that, knowing he's my boyfriend, and then what? *Poor Rose, her boyfriend fancies me and she doesn't have a clue.* What an absolute twat – how much of an idiot does that make me look?

I exit the app and see that Joel has texted me.

Joel: I'm here. How much longer till u arrive?

I smack the "lock" button and drop my phone into my bag with shaking hands.

Demi bangs on the door, causing it to shake at the hinges. "You dead in there?"

I pull my knickers up and open the door in a daze.

Lena eyes me suspiciously. "Everything OK?"

"Yeah, all good." I plaster on a wonky smile.

Just forget about it. It doesn't mean anything. Boys will be boys. Don't be a jealous bitch.

Demi looks like she's about to say something, but I run the hand dryer to end the conversation.

At the after-party, Joel's standing in Holly's garden on his own.

"Finally decided to arrive then. Didn't fancy replying to my texts?" he half laughs, half grunts.

"Our lift was late," I grunt back. "Maybe I'd have replied to your messages if you hadn't been such a snake lurking on girls' socials."

"What are you on about?" Joel has the audacity to look confused.

"You've been liking photos of half-naked women, no?"

"Are you serious?"

"Yes. You liked Reggie's, for fuck's sake. Do you not think how that makes me look? Like an absolute mug."

"I'm not having this conversation."

We stare at each other. I don't know what words I can say to communicate the storm of emotions battering me internally. How did we get here? And after last week's magical evening too.

"I don't know why you're being like this."

"I don't know why *you're* being like this," Joel replies almost in a whisper.

"Rose." Demi's voice pulls my gaze away from Joel and causes me to jump. Where did she come from?

"Come with me a sec," she says, not giving me a chance to think before she links my arm and steers me away. I look back at Joel, but he's looking up at the stars.

Demi drags me down the side gate to join Lena, who's standing on the driveway shifting from one foot to another and continuously looking over her shoulder. She smiles a small smile, but then looks at the ground.

"You OK?" Lena says to my feet.

"Yeah. Why?" I say. Why are they being so weird?

Lena looks towards Demi.

I squint at them both. "What?"

"Lena and I are heading to Monica's now for a bit," says Demi. She's trying to look me straight in the eye, but is leaning on Lena and swaying, so I know she's had a glass of wine too many. I can see Monica and her pink hair over Demi's shoulder, with a random guy by a bashed-up black Fiat.

"But you've only been here for ten minutes. Please don't ditch me." I don't plan for the desperation to be so audible in my voice, but there's a quiver that I have to swallow down.

"Why can you ditch us all the time, but when we do it we're shit friends?" Demi's arms are crossed.

I should have known. Of course she hasn't forgiven me that easily.

"I never said you were shit friends!" My voice is loud and high, but Demi doesn't flinch.

"Why should we stick around? You've got Joel and I'm sure you won't leave his side. Plus it's not just about tonight. You know that."

"That's not fair. Life's been busy." I falter when I say this last part. How can I defend myself with any conviction when she's right? I change tack. "Since when were you besties with Monica? Does Holly know she's having her own party?"

Lena puts a hand on my arm. "It's not a party, just five of us for some quiet drinks. It's already getting messy here…"

Demi huffs. "Enough of this. Do you want to tell her or shall I?" She raises her eyebrows at Lena.

There's a long silence as the two of them share a look with each other that I couldn't decode even if I tried. I'm no longer part of their unspoken language.

"It's your news," Lena says quietly.

"Fine." Demi turns and waves at Monica, gesturing her over.

Demi holds her hand out and pulls Monica close to her.

She kisses her tenderly on the lips. Their eyes linger on each other and there's a softness in Demi's eyes that I've not seen before. "Yet another thing you've missed while you've been busy wedging your head up Joel's arse. Monica and I aren't *besties*, Rose."

It takes me a few seconds to comprehend what she's saying.

"You and Monica are…?"

"Yeah. I was going to tell you. I tried, lots of times – like on the bus, remember? But you've been so busy with Joel that you clearly weren't interested in anything that wasn't to do with yourself or him."

On the bus? That was ages ago. And Monica messaging me about her secret crush… That was about Demi! I look at Lena, who's staring at the floor and drawing circles in the gravel with her sandals. "You knew about this?" I ask.

Demi speaks again. "Of course she does. We're best friends."

"So are we," I say. That's all I can say without breaking.

"I don't know any more. We've been drifting apart for a while."

"I know. I'm sorry," I whisper.

"Is that all you've got to say?"

I shrug, defeated. If I say what I want to say, I'll lose it, and I can't say it in front of Monica anyway. I wish she'd stop watching the whole thing like some sort of soap opera.

"No 'I'm so happy for you, Demi' or 'how was it telling your parents, Demi?'? Nothing?" Demi's voice breaks and turns into a whisper. "You missed me introducing Monica to my parents, Rose. You know how much that meant to me. The first person I've ever brought home."

I squeeze my eyes shut to stop the tears. I can't believe I missed this. I can't believe I wasn't there for her.

A long drip of mascara traces Demi's cheek and runs down her neck. She wipes it away fiercely and shakes her head. "We're leaving. Come on, Lena."

But Lena doesn't move. She looks between us and then shakes her head. "You know what, screw this," she says in a voice I've never heard from her before. She turns and starts walking off down the road.

Demi and I snap our heads towards each other, eyes wide. Demi crying and Lena shouting? What is going on tonight?

"Lena," I call. "Wait, where are you going?" I hurry after her, followed quickly by Demi and Monica.

"Don't go home! It's prom night – you can't!" Demi grabs Lena's arm, but she pulls away.

"I'm not feeling it any more. I've already texted River. He's picking me up any second now."

I look at her in her flowy gown with flowers in her hair,

all dressed up for a night to remember, and guilt wallops me so hard I feel sick. I've let her down too.

"Please stay," I beg.

"Do you both not realize how awful it's been for me? Having to run between the two of you. Keeping secrets. Knowing that, whatever I do, one of you will be upset or angry at me for 'taking sides'."

"Secrets?" Demi looks at me.

"I'm done." Lena shakes her head again. "Enjoy, both of you."

As she says this, River's crappy Vauxhall Corsa pulls up behind her, the pungent smell of weed wafting through its open windows. She pulls open the passenger door and climbs in, not looking at either of us. The door slams and she's gone with the screech of wheels and the crunch of dodgy gears.

Silence.

"Poor Lena." I watch as the car's lights disappear from view.

Demi looks at me. "Whatever. Go and talk to Joel about it."

"I—"

"Come on, Monica. Let's go." She totters off, dragging Monica behind her, who looks at me and shrugs apologetically.

My mind is a blur of everything that's just happened. Every word that was said, every word that was not. I can't believe how lost in my own stuff I've been. Lost in my lies. How did one tiny lie snowball into such a big horrendous mess?

I make my way back to the garden on shaky legs, but Joel isn't where I left him. I head further down the garden.

It's almost pitch-black the further down the path I go. The only light visible is the glowing phone screens of the people congregating in huddles on the dampening grass. The atmosphere is thick with the fug of cold night air, vape and cigarette smoke.

"Heeyyyy, Rooooose," a voice slurs from the bottom of the garden.

The swaying silhouette of a person makes its way towards me.

It's Holly. She's looking a bit worse for wear; her hair is ruffled and her skirt is rising with each wobbly step. She falls into me and hugs me, all knees and elbows. I can't hug her back as I'm too busy holding her up and pulling her skirt down.

"Come for a wee with me," she says, and giggles.

I glance around, but Joel's nowhere to be seen.

"Sure," I say. I grab Holly's clammy hand as we slalom past merry students and handsy couples before finally making it to the bathroom upstairs.

Holly starts pulling her dress up before I've even shut the door. She falls on to the toilet and rests her head in her hands. "Where are Demi and Lena?" she mumbles.

I look at myself in the mirror and rub away the black smudges beneath my eyes. "Demi went to Monica's and Lena went home." I try to seem casual by pretending to fiddle with my hair and touch up my lipstick.

"Horny bitches." Holly attempts to wink, but just looks like she's got something in her eye.

Hold up. She knows too?

"So they finally told you then?" Holly goes to grab the toilet roll, but knocks it to the floor.

I kick it back within her reach. I'm trying to stay cool, but my body betrays me and I have to clear my throat in order to get two paltry words out. "Yeah, course."

"Phew, I'm not good at keeping secrets." Holly staggers as she hoicks up her lacy black knickers. "Are you pissed off they ditched you?"

"No," I snap. "We aren't attached at the hip, you know."

"Sure." Holly attempts to flatten down her flyaway hair with water at the sink.

I stand by the door and tap my foot impatiently. I need to find Joel so we can go home and sort things out. "I have to go—"

I'm interrupted by a stifled snort and look up to see

Holly's face crumpling in her reflection. "I feel sad," she squeaks.

I rush over and hold her up. She's even floppier now as I survey the room and work out where's best to put her. I slam the toilet lid shut with my heel and lower her on to it, just as she bursts into tears. We seem to be making a habit of this.

I crouch in front of her. "What's happened?" I unravel copious amounts of toilet roll and press it into her shaking hand. She sniffs and wipes her eyes, causing mascara to smudge into her temples. "Rob's not broken up with you again, has he?"

Holly snorts. "Can you break up with someone you aren't even publicly going out with?"

Good point. I shrug, not sure what to say.

"Am I sexy?"

I stare at her. Of all the things she could have said, I wasn't expecting that.

"Very. I'm jealous of your confidence. And your flirting game is on point."

"I don't believe you. I'm obviously not or … or …" Holly breaks down again.

"Or what? You're beautiful! What's this about?"

"I make Robert soft."

I assume we aren't talking about making him sensitive because that prick is about as soft as a cactus.

"Soft as in…"

"He keeps losing his boner. Like, all the time."

"But I thought you had loads of sex?"

"We did when we were together the first time. But since I've gone back it's changed. He goes soft every time before we can get it in. He said it was the condom at first."

"What a load of crap."

"Well, when we were on our 'break' he had sex with two girls without one and said it felt better – but even when we tried without, it kept happening."

"You tried without?" My mind flashes back to the safe-sex talk we had in year eight, where we were taken through a slideshow of STDs that put me off my lunch (and the idea of sex) for a good few months afterwards. Not forgetting pregnancy.

"I'm on the pill. He asked me to go on it. I said I didn't want to because it gave me headaches, but he said it was the only way we'd be able to do it. One time he blamed it on the fact I hadn't shaved that day. And there's something else too…"

"What?"

"You can't tell anyone."

"I swear," I say, and I mean it. I might not be planning to study Psychology any more, but one thing I am good at is keeping secrets or, in therapy speak, *confidentiality*.

"He said I looked *weird* down there. He used to joke it looked like a kebab, but he didn't mind because 'kebabs are his favourite'. He also said that when he's earning lots of 'moolah' – again, his words – he'll 'treat me to a designer vagina'." Holly's voice cracks and she's crying again.

I shake my head, unable to hide my disgust. I count to five and try to unclench my fists. "He's clearly not seen as many real women's vulvas as he claims to if he thinks they all look like bloody Barbie."

Holly tries to laugh, but her cheeks are red and covered in mascara. "What if he's right, though – that there really is something weird about mine? He might like it, but if we split up for good, what if the next person thinks it's disgusting?"

"What he's doing is not OK. You know that, right? He's making you feel bad about yourself, destroying your confidence. And I'm going to send you a really good website where you can see loads of normal vulvas and you'll realize that there is nothing wrong with you in any way. Whatever is going on with Robert in the erection department has *nothing* to do with you. He needs to take responsibility for it."

"I mentioned a doctor, but he just got mad. He makes me feel stupid, like some sort of dumb bimbo."

"Don't tell me he called you that." And I thought Joel could be bad sometimes with his occasional man moods.

"Not in those words, but he always comments about how I should go to uni because all successful people go. Plus I'm the first in my family to go straight to work from school. And I *do* feel stupid compared to you guys, especially Demi."

"Demi makes Stephen Hawking look average," I say, and Holly lets out a small giggle.

"True."

"Firstly, Robert is a narcissistic twat. I know you love him, but I'd be a rubbish friend if I didn't tell you I think you should cut him off for good." I have the urge to apologize for saying it, but I stop myself. It's the truth and I've waited long enough. "Secondly, I thought you didn't care about uni. You were so happy to get on your training."

"I don't want to go to uni, but I feel like I *should*. I feel like I've let Mum down." Holly's looking watery-eyed again.

"Props to you for choosing your own path and not just doing what your mum wanted for you, or what your dickhead of a sort of ex thinks you should do. You are a strong independent woman."

And I am not. The irony is not lost on me. Perhaps I shouldn't have let Joel talk me into going to Sunderland... Why is it so easy to give advice to other people and then do the complete opposite when it comes to yourself?

"You really think I'm a strong independent woman?" Holly smiles weakly at me.

"I do."

"Rose, you are the best. Come with me to get another drink?"

I should find Joel, but I'm not going to leave Holly. I've been enough of a crap friend recently and it's time to change that. Better late than never. With any luck, we'll bump into Joel anyway.

Holly attempts to teeter past me in her ridiculously high heels.

I take hold of her wrist gently. "Hang on a sec, let's sort out your face first. You're a bit smudgy." A polite way of saying, *You look like you've been given a makeover by your three-year-old niece.*

When Holly's mascara massacre is fixed, we head downstairs, me wincing with every wobble until she's safely in the kitchen. My eyes are on stalks looking for Joel in every crevice of the house.

"Isn't this the best party ever?" Holly says, head inside a cupboard, doing her usual thing of going back to being totally normal as if our bathroom chat never happened.

"Yeah, it's OK." I can hardly say it's been utterly shit.

"Just OK? You defo need a drink." She waves two plastic cups and bumps into me on her way to the breakfast bar.

"Sure," I say.

Any alcohol I drank was hours ago and has fully worn off. Maybe I'll have a better time if I drink – I'll be Rose 2.0 who's ready to party the night away no matter what. If the night when your boyfriend's done a disappearing act and your two best friends hate you isn't a good time to get sloshed, then I don't know when is.

Holly surveys the various bottles strewn across the tabletop. She plucks a full-looking pink bottle from the centre, narrowly missing a glass of vodka with her elbow.

"Ooooohhh, rosé for Rose." She splashes the cups full of the cheap wine. "Here." She passes one to me. "Drink up."

I gulp it down, swallowing manically so as not to gag on the sharpness of it as it hits the back of my throat.

Rose 2.0 can stay.

It's like I'm watching myself from outside my body; I can hear myself talk and I'm saying things I only usually say in my head. I also no longer give a flying fart that Demi and Lena aren't here. And I'll find Joel eventually to clear the air. I've been on the hunt for him this whole time, which is hard when people are just blurs and I'm floating from room to room with no concept of time or space. Literally – I seem to have misplaced my phone and people keep bumping into me.

I need a wee again.

Skye and two girls I don't recognize follow me into the bathroom, but I'm so desperate I don't care. I plonk myself on the cold toilet seat and wee while they reapply their lipstick and brush their hair. I'll just add them to the list of People Who've Seen My Vag.

"Skyeeeeee! How's it going?"

"Rose! It's going well," she slurs, being jostled by her two mates as they decide they're going to climb into the empty bath. She lowers her voice. "I spoke to Tegan. Told them that I'm not ready. And guess what!" She giggles.

"What?"

"They're fine with it. Just like you said."

"Knew it. I—"

"Skye, Rachel, get in the picture," says a girl called Jodie – I think that's what her mate called her anyway.

Skye grabs me and I wrestle my knickers up with one hand as she drags me towards the bath.

"Yes, join us, Rachel," says the other girl, who's propped up against the grey tiles like the Leaning Tower of Pisa.

"Rose, not Rachel," I say as I'm heaved into the bath by manicured hands. A bright flash goes off in my face.

Someone is leaning on me to hold them up. I'm leaning on someone else. It's slippery underfoot and it smells like beer.

"Ahhhhhhhh!" My foot slides and I grab for whoever I can. We all scream and collapse in a heap on top of each other, a pile of bare legs and sticky skin. We snort uncontrollably.

"Owwwwwwwww!"

"You're squashing meeeee!"

The other girls manage to pull themselves up and over the edge of the bath.

A foot smacks me in the cheek and I laugh again. I barely feel it.

"You coming with?" says Skye, holding out a hand towards me.

I try to move, but I can't. Gravity holds me firmly to the base of the bath.

"Noooooo, go on without me. I need to find someone in a minute."

The girls totter out and the bathroom is empty and silent. The plughole by my bare feet spins.

"Joel," I call out weakly. The thumping bass of the music makes the bath feel like it has a heartbeat. "Jooooel, where are you?" I call again, struggling to get any volume, and I lie back down in the bath again.

"Rose?"

I look over the rim of the bath and see legs that I recognize, but they aren't Joel's.

"Omar?"

Omar walks into the room and crosses his arms. Am I flashing? My bum cheeks feel suspiciously stuck to the metal of the bath. I shimmy my dress down.

"What the hell are you doing in there?" His laughter echoes in the tiled room.

"Resting." I blink at him and smile. "Give me a hand." I reach in his general direction. He grabs me, his skin warm against the clamminess of my own.

"Ready?"

"Ready."

My arm strains and I find my feet, cold on the hard base of the tub. I topple sideways.

"Almost," says Omar. "Come here." He reaches for my other hand and bears my whole weight as I wobble my way out, one foot at a time.

"Thank youuuuuuuuuu, I owe you one." I punch him on the arm, weak fingers meeting hard muscle. "You didn't tell me you were coming. What about work tomorrow?"

He chuckles quietly. "I didn't know I was until half an hour ago. I'm not drinking so work will be fine. I'm a pro at doing shifts on no sleep." His smile turns into a frown. "Why are you in here on your own?"

"I…"

"She isn't."

I spin so quickly I topple again and feel Omar's hands on my shoulders.

Joel's blurry figure looms in the doorway. He glares at Omar.

"I'll leave you to it." Omar squints at me. "You OK?"

I nod.

"See you next weekend," Omar says, looking once more at Joel and then me, before he leaves.

I sit on the edge of the bath, fold my arms across my chest and look away.

"What's wrong with you?" Joel snaps. "And what the hell are you doing with him?"

"Nothing. He just helped me out of the bath. And don't make me out to be the bad guy. You're the one liking girls' pictures."

"Chill out – it doesn't mean anything."

"If it doesn't mean anything, then why do it?"

"I'm allowed to think someone else is hot."

"I know you are, but why do you have to do it so publicly? Have some respect for me. How do you think it feels for me to see that?"

"I didn't think you'd see it."

"So you were hiding it from me."

"Clearly not very well." Joel rolls his eyes.

"S'pose you want to shag Reggie then." I know I've gone too far, but I can't stop. The words flow out of me in all their jealous glory. Rose 2.0 doesn't know when to keep her trap shut.

"You're being ridiculous, do you know that?"

"I'm *upset*. Why can't you wrap your head round that? When I see these things, it makes me feel like I'm not *enough* for you."

Joel sighs and says nothing.

I need to hear him say I'm enough for him. Instead, he walks past me and perches on the edge of the bath. He begins to pick and bite his nails as he sits in silence.

I'm trying desperately to feel steady, but the room around me spins.

Joel breaks the silence. "Something's not right between us, is it?"

The floor shifts beneath my feet and the foundations of my existence begin to shake.

What have I done? Damage control. I need to backtrack. Say sorry.

I nuzzle my head into his neck, desperate to regain some stability, but he stiffens. "It's normal for people to argue," I say. "I'm sorry. I don't know why I'm like this."

"It's not you; it's us. People argue but not this much. We're making each other miserable."

Miserable? The wine in my stomach churns. It's not been perfect, but I still love him. I can't imagine my life without him.

"You don't make me miserable," I whisper, but even as I say it I know it's been a long time since he made me happy in the way he used to.

Joel shakes his head. "I don't know why, but I feel so angry all the time. And I'm clearly not making you happy."

"We can work it out together. We're already getting back on track. Last Friday was amazing. Remember you said we'd one hundred per cent get through this? Life's been stressful recently, but everything is going to be OK. I know it. I—"

"Do you not feel like something's changed between us?"

The words whip the air out of my already struggling lungs. He said it out loud. He's not willing to keep denying it any more.

"But … I love you," I croak.

"I love you too, so much. But all we do is argue now, Rose. And I don't know why, and I don't know how to fix it." Joel sniffs and wipes his eyes with the back of his hand.

He's talking like he's given up. Like we're beyond repair.

My breath comes too fast. In, out, in, out.

"We can fix it… Nothing's broken." My voice cracks.

"You can't say you haven't felt it too…"

His face is in sharp focus, blurring everything around him. I no longer feel tipsy, but I'm dizzy. I'm losing him.

I lunge towards him and find his warm neck beneath my lips.

"Come here," I whisper desperately.

I reach for his waistband.

Love me. Love me. Love me. Please.

Joel throws his head back and takes a deep breath, gently sliding out of my grip and standing up. "That's not the answer." His eyes flick towards me, pleading, then he looks away.

I've lost him.

Tears are falling thick and fast down his cheeks. He wipes them away aggressively with the crook of his arm.

"I know I can't have sex with you right now, but I'm working on it," I say. "The operation will be soon; we won't have to wait much longer—"

"It's not that."

"What is it then? Tell me!" I'm shouting now, but I don't care.

"I don't know what it is!" He raises his voice to match mine, then turns away, breathing hard.

"That's the only thing that's changed," I shout again.

"Fine! If that's what you want to hear! Maybe it has made a difference. Not because we haven't done it yet, but because how could it not? You wouldn't let me touch you towards the end…"

"The end? This is the end now, is it?" I try to shout, but my words come out as barely a whisper.

Joel finally turns to look at me. His eyes are rimmed red and sparkling wet. "I can't do this any more," he croaks.

He can't… What? He didn't just say that. Not after promising me we'd always be OK. Not after saying that one day he would marry me. Not after us agreeing to move to university together. No. He wouldn't…

He opens the door and is swallowed by the darkness of the hall.

I try to put one leg in front of the other, but they aren't working. I stagger after him, already losing sight of him in the blurry crowd of bodies.

At the bottom of the stairs, my legs buckle. The force I hit the wooden floor with should hurt, but I'm not in my body enough to feel it. The rosy filter of the wine has vanished; the scene in front of me is a tragic mess. Two random people are slumped asleep on the bottom stair as I stumble over them. The splashes of sticky alcohol covering the wooden floor glint in the moonlight coming through the back door as I see a flash of ginger hair disappear through it. I can smell weed and alcohol and sick and BO all mixed together, and I can hear a girl howling. She's making the sound of someone who's either totally hammered or who's just been told that someone they love has died.

And then I realize that the person howling is me.

33

It's been three days since Joel and I broke up and it's all my fault. If only I hadn't been so needy or jealous. If only my body hadn't betrayed me and stopped us from having sex. If only I could have just been normal, then perhaps I'd not be sitting here with my heart in a million pieces.

I'm technically on study leave, but I can't concentrate. I'm sitting at the kitchen table, staring down at my revision notes, words blurring before my eyes. Heartbreak is so much worse than I ever imagined – it has ripped through my past, present and future and left them all in tatters. It's like being forced to live without an essential part of my soul. Something is missing – gone for ever. I still can't wrap my head around the fact that to feel like this is "normal". Like death, heartbreak is an inevitable part of life, and it baffles me how the world isn't full of people collapsing into a heap on a daily basis. Or maybe it is and other people are better at hiding it than I am? Is Mum going to sit me down – like she did when she told me Santa wasn't real – and tell me that life really is *that bad*?

This morning I cried about a fart. A FART. Sammy let one rip and it took me back to Joel's first fart in front of me. It made me laugh so much I farted too, and instead of almost dying from embarrassment, we both almost died from a lack of oxygen from hysterically laughing. That memory, although stupid, rammed home even more that what Joel and I had was rare. I don't think I'll ever find it with anyone else.

Sammy said I was grieving. Sure, Joel's not dead, but he isn't a part of my life any more.

I wake up, I cry.

I brush my teeth, I cry.

Like I said, I'm supposed to be on study leave, but unsurprisingly there's been minimal studying. I'm home alone on weekdays, which is good in one way because I can cry as much as I like, but also rubbish because I can't escape my thoughts. It's hard to focus on anything when my mind is a sea of what-ifs and my eyes are a blurry barrier between me and my revision notes.

I can't even message the chat for support because it's

Lena's group and I no longer feel welcome. She and Demi are totally blanking me. If I was at school, there'd be no hiding from them. I guess as far as they know Joel and I are still together. Joel's socials are ghostly quiet and I'm not deleting a single trace of us from mine, so, on the surface, nothing's changed. I want to keep it that way. I'm not ready for anyone else to know yet. I can't face the sympathy slapped across people's faces or the whispers behind my back when they find out.

But I've never needed my girls more than I do right now. I need ice cream and hugs and Lena's tarot cards and Demi's convincing way with words. I need them to realize how bad things have been so maybe they can forgive me for being such a rubbish friend. But they've never felt so far away, and I don't have the words or energy to work out how to bring them closer.

I snatch up the tear-stained page from the table and force it into a crumpled ball just as the metal clang of the letter box sounds. I chuck the scrunched paper at the wall and make my way to the hall, grateful for any distraction.

Most of the post looks like bills or junk mail, but as I flick through there's one addressed to me. My stomach tightens. It couldn't possibly be… No. Surely life wouldn't be so cruel? I chuck the rest of the post on the dining table and make my way up to my room.

I stare at the white envelope for a moment, trying to bring myself to open it. I savour the last few seconds of denial, then I tear it open.

I skim through the formalities, eyes on stalks, zoning in on the important part.

Scheduled procedure: 6th June.

My stomach lurches. The date is there in black and white. My operation is in three weeks' time. Do I want to cry or be sick? Both?

I read it again, but before I reach the end the inked letters become a smudge of black slugs and the paper begins to tremble in my hands.

Here come the tears again – this time full-body wracking sobs.

It's official. On 6th June I'll have a working vagina, but no one to use it with. I'd be lying if I said I wasn't having second thoughts about going through with the operation entirely.

The irony of the situation is not lost on me. I haven't thought about sex since Joel broke up with me and my Shame Sack has sat untouched in my drawer – a painful reminder of a journey that now feels pointless. Maybe I'll want to have sex with someone else in the future, but the urgency has totally gone now.

The minute Mum got home from work last night, I flapped the referral letter in her face. She didn't even need to read it to know what it was given the state I was in. She said we'd talk about it today when I was able to think straight. I'm not sure I'm quite there yet, but if we want to cancel, we only have a few days to do it. I've finally managed an hour without crying so there's not going to be a better time than now to sidle into my parents' bedroom.

Dad's downstairs and Mum's just got out of the bath. She's lying on the bed with one towel wrapped round her hair and one barely covering the rest of her. As she likes to do after her baths, she's watching *Pointless* on TV. She mutes it when she sees me and pats the space beside her. I get under the duvet, the mattress warm where Mum's been sitting. I trace the damask-patterned cover – the more I do to keep myself busy, the less focus I can give to the sadness sitting precariously close to the surface.

"I don't know if I'm ready to talk about this," I say heavily.

"I understand that," she says. "Listen, would it help if I told you my news?"

I lift my head. "Yeah? Not pregnant are you?"

"God, could you imagine?" Mum shakes her head. "No,

not pregnant, but I have applied to an Open University course in English Literature."

"No way! That's amazing." This time my mouth manages to form a smile. "Maybe one day you'll write a book and you can recommend it to people at the library."

"Maybe." Mum smiles shyly, cheeks pink. "Ready to talk about the op now?"

"No," I say meekly. "But I'm going to." I scratch at the remainder of my pink nail polish left from prom.

"So we've got a decision to make. Ultimately, it's up to you."

I whimper. "I don't want to choose. Look where that's got me before."

Mum's eyebrows rise, but she doesn't say the dreaded *I told you so* about me accepting Sunderland. If I want to change my firm and insurance choices, I need to start the process ASAP as the final deadline for all things UCAS is speedily approaching. But I can't face that on top of the op and my A levels. Also, I can't bring myself to close that door just yet.

"Well, you don't need to make this decision on your own. Let's talk about the pros and cons of doing the op now versus in the future."

I screw my face up. Why does this have to be my real life?

Mum continues. "You'll be away at uni for the next

314

three years and then looking for a job or doing further training. So now could be the best time to do this."

"True. But I'm single now. Feels pointless."

"This is about you, not Joel."

I wince at the mention of his name. It's starting to feel alien already and I'm not at all prepared for that.

Mum goes on. "And I know it's hard to imagine right now, but you might meet someone else at uni."

"I *can't* imagine it, but I suppose you're right." There's a slim chance that I might meet someone else and I don't want to have to go through all this again.

Mum looks at me, her face soft and open. "Whether you wait three years or three weeks, it's going to be a scary thing, you know? That won't change. It might feel better for you to get it over with so you can move forward without it lingering like one of your dad's Sunday roast farts." She smiles.

I shift to lie down and bury my head in the pillow. I chuckle and softly wail at the same time. Three weeks. All this could be over by the end of my exams.

I emerge from the pillow. "It would be amazing to close the door on this chapter for good."

"So what you thinking?" Mum reaches down and starts to play with my hair. Her support and presence fills me with a courage I didn't know I had.

"I'll do it," I say with as much certainty as I can muster. "I need to. For me, not for anyone else."

I'm about to do a stupid thing. I should stop myself from doing the stupid thing, but I have no control over my hands. I'm typing a message to Joel to tell him I'm having the op. It doesn't feel right that he doesn't know.

I've been thinking… (Dangerous? Maybe.) The operation *should* have changed everything. Joel would've had more of a reason to stick around and the parts of our relationship that were on wobbly ground could have been built back up on a solid bed of mind-blowing sex and the intimacy that comes with it. I *was* thinking it was too late. Joel's gone and that ship has sailed.

But what if the ship hasn't sailed yet?

What if the ship is still docked? Or at least close enough to the shore that I can throw myself aboard and the two of us can sail off into the sunset? It's not been long – there's still a glimmer of hope. The operation and the physical change it brings could save us. Why else would the universe or God or whoever the hell is out there have ordered things in such a way that my operation is happening RIGHT NOW? If everything in life is supposed to happen for a reason, as Lena constantly barks on about, then perhaps this is a test. A test that

Joel and I are meant to surmount, coming out the other end stronger.

As these thoughts splash through my mind, I scrabble to type them down, not wanting to miss out on imparting a single part of this divine wisdom to Joel himself.

I might be delusional, but the good thing about being delusional is that you don't care. I believe enough in the goodness of the world that life cannot possibly be this cruel.

I press "send".

34

Sammy has made me promise not to message Joel again and has made her feelings about him very clear.

"Joel's a twat and doesn't deserve you or your sacred fanny," she states, sitting across from me in the living room, having just handed me a hot chocolate with cream and marshmallows. I can't smell its sickly sugariness because my nose is permanently full of snot at the moment. I know Mum and Dad are in the next room, but I don't have the energy to care if they can hear her.

I barely flick my eyes in Sammy's direction before they find the floor again.

"Think about all the guys you'll meet at uni," Sammy continues. "You don't know how lucky you are not having someone tying you down. And you'll be able to have sex then, if you want to obviously."

"The thought of meeting someone else horrifies me," I say, swallowing the lump in my throat. Why the hell did I put Sunderland as my firm choice? "No one will ever compare to Joel. I was lucky to have ever met him." How can I meet someone else and start all over again? How could they possibly understand me and everything that's happened this past year?

"That's the biggest load of shite I've heard in a long time. *He* was lucky to have *you*. You feel like that now because you're heartbroken, but with time you'll realize that there's someone else out there for you and they'll be an even better fit for you than him."

"I doubt that." I choose not to point out the obvious pun in what she's said.

"I'd literally bet my entire life savings on it."

"What? Thirty quid?" I hear what she's trying to say, but she doesn't know Joel like I do. "He was the one." My voice cracks and I'm crying again, snuffling into my hands and frozen in a shaking, sobbing ball.

Sammy shuffles closer and squeezes me into a hug so tight I can barely breathe.

"He *was* the one," she whispers in my ear. "You've

learnt a lot from the relationship and now it's time to move on." She strokes my hair.

"I … don't … want … to," I manage between sniffs.

Sammy lets go and looks me directly in the eyes. She reaches for my hands and grips them tightly in my lap. "Well, you have no choice. Don't, whatever you do, go crawling back. Got it?"

I take a deep breath and nod.

"And I don't want to push it, but you might want to think about the whole Sunderland thing."

I lose whatever self-control I had grappled back. "It's too soon to think about that," I whisper. Pulling my application feels so final. It symbolizes truly letting Joel go.

"Just think about it. We don't want to lose future Rose's hopes and dreams in the midst of present Rose's grief."

"You sound like Lena." I'm crying again.

"Right, I think it's time to drink hot chocolate and snuggle on the sofa. Just one last thing from me. This time next year, you'll be wanting to give Joel a pat on the back and a massive thank you for setting you free and putting you on the right path for your actual soulmate," she says. "Mark my words."

35

It's now been almost a week since I messaged Joel and all I've got is two blue ticks to show me that he's read it and couldn't be arsed to reply. He's also blocked me on every social media platform imaginable.

I suppose that's a good thing as I don't want to see his face pop up all over the place, but it makes everything feel so final. To rub salt into the wound, I received a text from Holly last night.

> I've done it. Cut him off completely. Thanks for sending that website btw. You're right. Rob's clearly not seen many if he thinks there's anything wrong with mine!!! Dickhead. He tried crawling back the other day and it was hard but I blocked him. Every

time I want to text him, I text a friend instead or do
something for me

I am beyond proud of her, but part of me feels extra
pathetic that I'm not able to do the same with Joel. I've
also still not heard a peep from Lena or Demi. Demi I'm
not surprised about, given her stubbornness, but it hurts
that Lena still hasn't reached out. I guess she reached her
breaking point, and it's not like I've messaged her either.
Sammy said she'd sit down and help me write a message,
but I don't think a message will do justice to what needs
to be said, so instead I put it off.

The good news is I'm now only crying every couple of
days and I've been able to get my head down and do some
revision. It's helped to have something to focus on. I don't
want to make the hat-trick of being dumped, doing a uni
course I hate AND failing my exams; I'll stick with the
first two if I can help it. If someone had told me this time
last year I'd be grateful for the distraction of revision, I'd
have laughed in their face. Then again, I never thought
I'd basically have been fingered by a middle-aged lady,
so I can say with confidence that stranger things have
happened.

As with my revision, work has been a welcome
distraction from my spiralling thoughts. I messaged Omar

the night before my first shift back after being dumped to tell him Joel and I broke up and that I didn't want to talk about it. He's been a real babe since then, ignoring my make-up-free puffy red eyes and giving me the jobs that require the least face-to-face interaction with customers. He's not mentioned it once, which might explain how I've managed to not shed a single tear at work. It also helps that the centre is not somewhere I associate with Joel. At the centre I've only ever been Rose, not Joel and Rose like everywhere else.

I'm working today, and I feel a little better, buoyed by the knowledge that I've managed to get through two shifts post-break-up.

"Today is the last day that I'm going to take advantage of your kindness, promise," I say to Omar, as I place a freshly brewed cup of tea on the reception desk where he's sitting. He's done all the reception shifts for me and I am very grateful.

"You know I don't mind. I like sitting down and being lazy," he says, taking a loud slurp of tea. "Thanks for that. Perfect cuppa as always." He lifts the cup like he's doing a toast.

"I'm happy to share the reception shifts next week, though."

Omar shrugs. "Only if you're ready."

"I am." I glance at the clock over his shoulder – 1.45 p.m. "Right, I'd better go and sort out the barn for the two o'clock class."

I head to the equipment room where I pack up seven mats, yoga blocks and lightweight blankets into a wheeled basket. I head across the courtyard in the direction of the exercise barn. The sun reflects off the glass windows surrounding me on all sides and glimmers on the wind-touched surface of the koi pond. The trickling sound of the water feature fills me with a tranquillity I've not felt in a long time. I stop and take a deep breath, closing my eyes to feel the warmth of the sun on my eyelids and allowing myself to bask in this rare flicker of peace.

"Sorry, excuse me." A voice from behind startles me.

I snap open my eyes. "Sorry, I … uh…"

It's Sonya.

The moment of recognition. She looks as horrified as me. "Rose, I didn't realize—"

"It's OK, sorry," I mumble again. I'm shaking. I can hear it in my voice. It's not been long, but it's like looking at a stranger. I force a smile as my eyes prick hot.

"Are you here for the two o'clock?" I hear my professional customer voice say.

Sonya looks surprised at the sudden formality. "Yes, I

usually go to the leisure centre, but had to skip this week…
I didn't think… I forgot…"

Did she really forget I worked here?

"It's fine, nice to see you," I say, but it comes out as a mere squeak. "Excuse me a minute." I spin on my heels and stride as fast as I can in the opposite direction, leaving the basket of exercise materials and a helpless Sonya behind me.

I don't know where I'm heading. The bathroom? Reception? Staffroom?

Out of the front door.

I make it to the car park on trembling legs as pressure squeezes my chest. My surroundings blur in a smudge of colour as darkness creeps at the edge of my vision.

"Rose?"

It's Mummy Lola. Her arms are round me and I lean into her soft but stable form as I finally take in a breath big enough to keep me standing.

I'm sipping a sugary tea in the safety of the staffroom, empty except for Lola and me. I'm feeling better, but still wobbly.

I was just about keeping it together with everything separate and boxed. At work I worked, at home I cried. Seeing Sonya messed all that up.

"Why didn't you tell anyone?" Lola's eyes are kind and wide and her brow furrows with confusion.

"I told Omar. I didn't want anyone asking about it."

Lola nods and bites her lip in the same way as Lena does. "Lena didn't say—"

"She doesn't know."

Lola fails to hide her shock. "Why not?"

"Life's been a bit weird recently," I say, hoping she won't ask me to go into any more detail.

She frowns. "It has been a while since we've seen you at the house."

I nod. Think. Open my mouth. "Can you call her for me, please?" The words fall out before I'm able to stop them.

"Of course, my lovely. Back in two." Lola floats out of the room, a vision of colourful beads and tassels.

Lena and I are walking around the Daisy Fields, a park just down the road from the centre. There's no one here apart from an older man and his dog at the other end of the field. Lola insisted I finish early today, and I wasn't going to argue.

"I'm so sorry," I tell her. "For everything. I should never have treated you like I have. I was so caught up in my own stuff I didn't even think how it made you feel having to go between me and Demi. And, God, what a complete arse I've been to her too. I have a lot of grovelling to do."

She squeezes my hand. "It takes two to tango. I should have stuck up for myself more. I absolutely need to work on my boundaries and not be so nice all the time. Nice and kind are very different things, I've come to realize. And as for Demi … I know she's not always the most agreeable, but she always comes from a loving place."

"Apart from that time you dyed your hair blue and she said you looked like a troll."

"She wasn't wrong, though, was she?"

"She never is."

"Let's sit. Tree. Grounding. You know the drill." Lena gestures to the large oak we're under and drops into a cross-legged position. She pats the grass and I sit next to her.

"I can't believe you didn't tell me he broke up with you." Lena tears a clump of grass and then sprinkles it back on to the ground absent-mindedly.

"I thought you hated me."

"I've never hated you. And just because you were a right willy doesn't mean you weren't worthy of my unconditional love. I just needed some space."

God, I've missed her.

We sit in silence with only the sound of us breathing and the tuneful melody of a robin filling the air.

Lena shifts then frowns. "Hold on a minute. The sex thing better not be why he broke up with you."

"I dunno. He did say it made a difference..." Here come the tears again.

Lena pulls me tightly towards her. Her hair smells like lemons and her clothes smell like incense and she's warm and cuddly and I love her SO MUCH. How did I almost lose her?

"I get it hasn't been easy for either of you, but I didn't realize it had got that bad."

"How could you realize when I didn't tell you everything?"

Lena releases me and I wipe my eyes and nose with the back of my sleeve.

"Screw him. Well, don't actually."

I snort. "I wish. Wished."

There's a beat of silence. I need to tell her about my surgery. I don't want to say it out loud because that makes it real. But I need to get over that because it will be happening, whether I like it or not.

"My op is on the sixth."

"Of June? As in next week?" Lena looks close to tears.

All I can do is nod, unable to cope with her pity.

"Fuck."

"Indeed." I chuckle at that.

Lena sighs. "Do you want me to tell Demi?"

How much easier it would be to let Lena do the explaining, to not have to relive the past few months. But I owe it to Demi to talk to her directly.

I shake my head. "I'll do it when I get home. I mean it this time. Wish me luck."

"You'll be OK," says Lena. And for once a tiny part of me believes it.

My stomach churns as I navigate to Demi's name and tap video call. I know the sooner I do it the better. Our friendship deserves this second chance.

"Hey," I say quietly, taking in the blurry image of her lying on her back on her bed with her hair in a messy bun. It feels familiar and alien at the same time.

"Long time no speak," she says. She's trying to sound confident, but there's no denying the awkwardness.

"Just a bit." I manage a smile. "How're things with you?"

"Fine. Great, in fact. Things are going really well with Monica…" She trails off, her eyes not looking into her camera and instead off to the corner.

"I'm glad. You deserve it, and more."

Silence.

"Why did you call?"

That's a big question.

"To apologize. And to explain why I've been such a poo friend."

Demi's face softens and hardens at the same time. "I knew something was up with you. OK, hit me with it," she says. "I promise I won't judge you. Much. Sorry, that was a joke. I'm not good at this."

I take a deep breath. Here goes nothing.

Demi makes all the right noises at all the right times, gasping at the horrors of the physio and mouth agape at the prescription vibrator. Most of the time she looks like she doesn't know whether to laugh or cry.

"God. I'm so sorry to hear what's been going on for you. I feel like a right bitch. I—"

"You are *not* a bitch. I was so busy with my own stuff I forgot how to be a decent human being. I was selfish. I'm sorry."

"You weren't selfish." Demi goes silent. "I get it must have been hard for you to tell me, but I'm sad that you didn't feel like you could. I thought our friendship was a space where we could be honest with each other, and I'm sorry if I made you feel otherwise."

I shake my head emphatically. "I was scared to share, but that wasn't your fault. It was my crap, not yours."

330

"Well, for the record, I'd be more than happy to have made it *our* crap."

"I wish I had."

"Me too."

More silence.

"So we're both sorry. Let's put this behind us and promise to communicate properly in the future. I've missed having you in my life. A Rose-shaped hole is hard to fill."

"You're telling me."

It takes Demi a few seconds. Then her eyes go wide and she gasps, hand over her mouth. "I didn't mean that – it slipped out!"

"I'd rather it slipped in, then we wouldn't be in this mess," I joke. "It's fine. Both you and Lena have now had a severe foot-in-mouth situation. It's good to laugh about it."

And it's true. Chatting about this stuff with Demi feels like a weight off my shoulders.

I'm keen not to make this entire conversation about me, aware of how much of her life I've already missed. "So, Monica…"

I can see in Demi's face she's unsure how to proceed. I can't imagine she wouldn't want to talk about it – I know how the beginning of a new relationship feels and you want to scream about it at the top of your lungs. But she's probably hyper-aware of how sad I am about Joel. I want to reassure her.

"Tell me *everything*. I promise I want to hear about it. It will be a good distraction from Joel."

Demi still looks wary. "Really? You sure?"

"Never been more sure."

"Well then, who am I to deprive you?" Demi pulls her naughty face and rubs her hands together.

I lean closer to the camera and adjust the volume. I have a feeling I won't want anyone else in the house hearing what she has to say.

"I'm ready," I say with a grin so massive my cheeks twitch.

Demi's eyes twinkle. "Well, when people say women know what they're doing *down there*, they aren't lying…"

"Amazing."

"Monica's amazing." Demi goes quiet and chews her lip. "But I'll be upfront with you. I've been feeling like I haven't got the foggiest what I'm doing in that department. I know we have the same bits as each other, but it doesn't mean everything works the same. She's had way more experience than me too."

"Oh, you'd think in some ways it would be easier with another woman."

"I know, right! But it's *absolutely* not. What works for

me does not work when I try it on her. I can tell it's not hitting the right spot because she starts smiling and being all polite."

"Oh dear. What are you going to do?"

"Google it maybe or watch some videos?"

"Hate to say it like I have a clue what I'm talking about, but I'm not sure googling it will help. Those people still won't be Monica and still won't work in the same way… Controversial, but you could *ask* her what she likes."

"Ugh, you're right. I don't know why I don't want to. I think I'm worried that stopping to ask will ruin the mood?"

"Surely she'd rather you asked her if it meant you could pleasure her better."

Demi laughs. "*Pleasure her better.* What do you sound like?"

"I know, get me acting like I know how to pleasure anything other than one nob out of all the genitals in the entire world. I can't even add myself to that list."

"Well, you pleasure my brain and heart just by existing. So."

"Aw, thanks. I don't deserve you."

"You deserve the world."

"Thanks, babes."

"You are very welcome."

I hang up the call feeling, for the first time in ages, like one part of my life is back on track. Yes, I sabotaged my future *and* Joel doesn't love me any more, but I've got my girls back and I'm never letting them go.

I also decide to finally message the VW group chat.

Roseycheeks_x: I'm sorry I totally fell off the face of the earth. Things have been hard. I've got my op in five days, and my boyfriend and I broke up

Endo2005: I'm so sorry to hear that 🙁

Anon_69: Here if you need to talk xxxx

It_hurtttsssssss: Thinking of you. Let us know how it goes

Even just those few messages make me feel a tiny bit better about everything. It's nice to think that there are random people across the world who are in my corner, cheering me on when I need it and reminding me that, no matter what happens and how it might feel sometimes, I'm not in this alone.

36

I thought I was nervous before attempting to have sex for the first time. I thought I was nervous before all the appointments where I had to get my vag out for strangers, and I know I was bricking it before each and every one of my mock exams. I'm internally laughing (crying) at that now. None of these things compares to how I'm feeling right this minute as I walk to the hospital ward for my op.

My sweaty hand slips in Mum's grip as we move across the car park towards the doors. I hope Mum's in less of a daze than I am because one of us needs to stop us getting hit by a car.

We walk through the double doors to reception. They're the kind of double doors you only get in hospitals because they're big enough for very ill people to be wheeled through them with multiple people on either side.

The receptionist says something that goes in one ear and out the other and I find myself being pulled through the doors. Mum's arm is linked through mine, solid and present.

My nose is assaulted by the sudden change in smell as I enter this sealed box of antiseptic. The grey floor, scuffed below my sandalled feet, is visible for a second before a misty veil of tears blinds me. I refuse to look up.

My legs have long surpassed being unsteady and I can no longer feel them, grateful to Mum whose momentum seems to miraculously be getting me from A to B.

"Here's your bed," a nurse tells me – I've no idea when she arrived. "The chair on the right and the set of drawers are yours. Just ask any one of us if you need anything. The anaesthetist and surgeon will be over soon to introduce themselves and answer any questions you have. Your mum can stay until then."

I nod and stare at the bed in front of me. Is it a bed at all, or is this actually a gurney masquerading as one, with its thin-looking sheet and sagging pillow?

"I won't be far away. If you need me, just call or text." Mum balances herself on the edge of the bed and empties out the carrier bag that she's had hooked over her wrist.

Magazines, paper, pens, a phone charger and even an iPad land on the bed.

"To keep your mind busy while you wait. Oh." Mum fumbles in her bag and pulls out an envelope. "Open this when you wake up." She puts it in the drawer of the bedside table and pats the top.

"What if I don't wake up?" I whisper, throat hoarse.

"Oh, Rose. It's a minor operation, love. You'll be just fine."

I nod, my lungs unable to draw breath.

Mum's warm arms wrap round me, guiding me to the chair beside the bed.

"I'm … scared," I say with a sniff, followed by a strangled squeaking noise.

"I know." Mum squeezes my shoulder. "But I promise this is very safe. We wouldn't be here otherwise. Just think, by teatime everything will be all done and we never have to do this again."

I desperately want to close this chapter of my life, but the next few hours seem like a hurdle so high I can't even see the top, let alone jump over it. Why am I putting myself through this just to have sex? It'd better be worth it.

The next three hours pass in a blur, watching people being wheeled past my bed and through the double doors at the end of the room. I avert my eyes to preserve their privacy and my own sanity. At one point a nurse even requests for me to do a pregnancy test – standard procedure apparently. The irony is not lost on me. I tell her the reason I'm here is because I can't have sex, but she insists anyway. I'm sure I'll laugh about it one day.

I move from the chair to the bed and back to the chair again, my magazine open on my lap but unread. The lights above me are so blinding they burn my eyes and I have a headache so huge I'm surprised my brain hasn't started leaking from my ears. My phone charges on the bedside table, recovering from the two hours I spent scrolling earlier not engaging anything other than my thumb.

Then I'm told it's almost time.

I fumble out of my own familiar clothes and into the cold, scratchy material of the hospital-provided garments – a gown that looks like it's lacking either a back or a front, stockings like my nan used to wear and a pair of "knickers" that could actually be made of paper. I guess at least I get to wear underwear, although something tells me they won't be staying on for long. I put the gown on back to front and sheepishly poke my head out from the curtain to call a nurse to help. By the time I settle back into the bed, the gown has already ridden up and I feel like even the smallest fart might rip a hole through the knickers. I wasn't comfortable before, but now there's more chance of hell freezing over than me being able to do anything but sit in paralysed fear until it's my turn to be wheeled in.

I see another patient from two beds over be rolled back to their bay and deduct I must be next. One in, one out. I tap a rushed text message to the family WhatsApp group and the malevolent voice of my anxiety hounds me with the thought: *This might be your last opportunity to tell them that you love them.* Both Dad and Sammy hugged me earlier when I left the house. Sammy calmly and confidently told me I would be absolutely fine, but I could see the worry in her eyes, and Dad squeezed me tighter than usual and held on to me a little longer too.

The second I press "send", a nurse walks over to my bed.

Her mouth moves and she and another nurse move round my bed and start to push it. My chest rises and falls quicker than a hummingbird's wings. My heart is no longer beating but fluttering.

It's happening. Now.

Through the doors we go, my surroundings merely a smudge of grey and white as my eyes stop working.

We halt. Brown eyes on a blurry face find mine. A hand on my hand. A disembodied voice.

"I'll be with you the whole time. OK?"

"The mask will go over your mouth and you will count back from ten. OK?"

I gasp a strangled breath. Shake my head. "I can't..."

"If you want this surgery, then we have to."

A wail. I can't go in, but I can't not go in. I've come this far. And Mum would be furious.

A reassuring smile. "You'll be OK."

Lots of sniffing and gasping.

"OK."

I lie down. A mask is lowered on to my nose and mouth. It smells like plasticky rubber and its rim pokes my eyeballs, making me squint. The brown eyes are reassuring but far away.

"Count back from ten."

Ten.

I nod and blink.

Nine.

I fight the urge to throw the mask off.

Eight.

I feel tense.

Seven.

Not any more. Loose.

Six...

This is it.

I'm alive. The room around me is bright and silent apart from a steady hum and rhythmic beep. I blink a few times. A nurse looms in my vision. "It's all gone well, Rose. You can rest now," she says.

I smile at her so wide my whole face hurts. I've not felt this calm in yonks.

I drift in and out of sleep for the remainder of the day. I attempt to sit up a few times but I'm not up long before a wave of nausea and dizziness hits me and then I'm lying back down again. I'm hot. I'm cold. I'm hot again. My paper knickers have vanished.

After some time, a nurse comes over and says I can go home with Mum as soon as I've managed to successfully go to the toilet. She assists me on wobbly legs and I leave the door open a crack in case I faint. Back at my bed, I remember the envelope in the drawer. I sit and although I'm weak it's not painful so the meds must be doing a cracking job. I pull open the envelope with shaking hands. It's a card with a crudely drawn sketch of a vulva with a face. I think it's supposed to be smiling, but it looks more like it might kill me in my sleep. My shaky body warms.

Congrats on your new vag!!
Hope she heals quickly.
We love you loads,
D and L xx

I smile before another wave of nausea hits me and I have to lie back down, clutching the card to my chest.

37

It's been eleven days since the op and I no longer wince every time I move or dread going for a poo. I'm also past the risk of infection and the stitches have all dissolved, thank God. An infection would have been the cherry on top of this cherryless cake. I'm still a bit sore, but nothing like how it was at the beginning.

In some ways it's been easier to get my head down to revise, seeing as I have nowhere to go and little to distract me. Lena and Demi are frequent visitors via video call to see how I'm doing and spot-test me on types of conformity for the Psychology exam, but I've not been anywhere other than the petrol station with Dad to get a takeaway coffee.

This prompted an awkward conversation, where Dad asked me how things were and I for some reason answered honestly with the word "sore". Then there was an awful lot of silence for the rest of the drive, until Dad climbed back into the car with what seemed like the entirety of the chocolate shelf – his endearing way of letting me know he cares without subjecting me to the horror of a father-and-daughter "birds and the bees" chat.

The girls in the VW chat are also keeping me sane, and it's nice to be part of the group again. They all celebrated with me when I let them know the op was done and we've laughed at some of the funny messages I sent in a drugged-up haze just after I came out. It's especially good to see Anon_69's most recent "Little Wins This Week" post.

> **Anon_69**: Today, with help from my therapist, I deleted ALL the accounts on my social feeds that make me feel shit about myself. I've not yet been able to look at myself in my undies in the mirror, but I did manage to take some pictures of myself wearing a dress that I don't hate. Baby steps.

> **Roseycheeks_x**: 😦 <3 Couldn't be happier for you xx

I feel guilty for totally ghosting them for a while, but my head just wasn't in the right place to deal with anything more than trying (and failing) to keep my relationship and friendships afloat, and trying (and failing) to not totally mess up my future. I'm still interested in the idea of being a counsellor. I suppose there's nothing stopping me from training after my degree. I just have to be a little more patient.

Speaking of future, I've got my first A level English exam at 10.30 a.m. today. Thankfully, I'm no longer taking codeine – a strong painkiller that does such wonders for the pain that five minutes after I take it I'm so dead to the world I wouldn't be able to feel it if someone sawed me in half – so I'll at least be able to stay awake at my desk.

However, much to both my horror and relief, Mum contacted the exams officer citing "gynae issues" and made arrangements for me to sit in a different room to the majority of students. I also – get this – have the option to bring a pillow to sit on. A PILLOW. So, on top of the fear of walking out a complete failure, I must also choose between a stinging vag *without* a pillow or burning embarrassment *with* one.

How I'm going to sneak a pillow in without the rest of the school noticing is still something I'm panicking about ten minutes before I'm set to leave. The best thing I can do is shove it in my trusty bag for life, because although that's weird in itself, it's better to be known as the girl who bought a bag for life into her exam than the one who has something wrong with her bum. I say "bum" because, unless I wear a shirt saying "I have a sore vulva", I bet the assumption would be that I have piles or some other anus-related issue.

Wish me luck.

I needn't have worried about anyone else clocking me with my pillow. Everyone's crowding outside the main exam hall sporting panic-stricken faces, unwashed hair and revision notes as permanent accessories. They're too in their own worlds of pre-exam panic to notice me and my bright orange bag waddle past on the other side of the quad as I head to the temporary classroom I'll be sitting my exam in.

I knock on the door to the little grey hut and let myself in. Thank you, Universe – the exam invigilator is a woman. I want to do a happy dance, but then I spy the exam paper on a desk and remember where I am. This is no time for dancing. I'm sitting my REAL-LIFE A level exams.

"Rose Summers?" she says, looking me up and down over the rim of her tortoiseshell glasses.

"Yep." If I say much more, I may be sick. My shame surrounding the pillow has been a good distraction from the fact that the next three hours have the potential to balls up my entire life.

"Set up and make yourself comfortable; we're starting in five minutes. Please make sure all phones are off and in your bag."

I pull my phone out of my pocket to double-check for the tenth time that it is turned off. I crouch down by my bag for life and pretend to look for something. Do I say anything about the pillow or do I just act like it's totally normal? Maybe the invigilator knows I'm in here for a gynae issue and therefore we have a mutual understanding of the pillow. Maybe she doesn't have a clue and will ask me about it. What do I say then? Maybe I'll just leave it in the bag. But then I might be in pain and then I'll fail my exam…

"Everything OK?" The invigilator snaps me from my spiral.

"Yes. Sorry."

The invigilator goes to the front and starts to write the exam start and finish times on the board. Three minutes to go. I grab my pillow and three pens and hurry to my desk.

I can do this. I think.

Monica was sitting the English exam too, so she, me, Lena and Demi have arranged to meet at the park for a little picnic and debrief afterwards. Monica and I are currently mooching our way across the back field towards the lane that leads to the village.

"How'd the cushion go down?" says Monica, gesturing at the unsubtle bag for life slung over my shoulder.

"Invigilator didn't question it. She must have been briefed."

"That's a relief. Demi told me you were a bit worried about someone clocking it. If it's any help, I didn't even see you arrive. Sleep deprivation's a bitch."

I gave Demi permission to tell Monica and Holly about my problem as long as Holly swore on her dog's life that she wouldn't tell ANYONE. She rang me up the minute Demi told her and was super kind about it.

"I know, I swear I haven't even found the time to wash my hair for the last five days because I've felt guilty doing anything that's not revision."

"Preach."

We walk in tandem in comfortable silence for a few minutes before Monica clears her throat.

"I was wondering ... has Demi said anything about us?"

"What do you mean? Are you guys OK?"

"Oh yeah. I'm just worried that she's, I don't know, feeling a bit ... weird about my past. That I have a bit more experience."

My heartbeat quickens. I don't want to dob Demi in

because what she told me was in confidence, but I also don't want to lie to Monica. I guess I can look at it like two counselling clients – respect both their *confidentiality* and offer them both a *non-judgemental space*. Might be the only opportunity I get to give it a whirl anyway.

"What makes you think that?" Yes, that was very counsellory – from what I've seen on YouTube videos anyway.

"She seems a bit, I don't know, self-conscious maybe?"

"And you think it's your past that's causing her to feel that way?" *Reflecting back what she's just said*. Look at me go, living my therapist fantasy…

"Well, yeah. I've been with a man and a woman before. And I'm her first. I know she comes across as super confident—"

I laugh. "That she does."

"But I don't want her feeling anything other than comfortable and safe with me."

Ugh, Demi and Monica are literally perfect for each other, and even they are having their own mini wobbles when it comes to sex.

"Do *you* feel OK about your past?"

"Hmm. That's a good question. I *did* before Demi, but I guess I do feel a bit guilty now."

"It's not wrong that you had a history before Demi,

349

so there's no need to feel guilty. Maybe what's going on for you both is not about the past but about your present? Like how you both feel *now*." Wow, where did I pull that from? Is this what Lena means when she says the universe is speaking through her?

"That makes a lot of sense. I'm going to talk to her."

Bingo.

"Absolutely the best idea. I know she can act tough, but if she can be vulnerable with anyone, it's you."

"Thanks. That's really helpful." Monica smiles. "Speak of the devil."

I look up and see Demi and Lena chilling on a picnic blanket under the shade of the same large oak Lena and I sat below the other day. The picnic was Lena's idea. She insisted that we all needed Mother Earth's healing after the trauma of our exams.

Monica scoots down beside Demi and they kiss, eyes lingering on each other like they're the only two people here. It's weird to see Demi so loved up. I never thought she'd be the lovey-dovey type, but Monica brings out a softer side to her and I'm so here for it. I have no doubt their overdue conversation will go swimmingly.

"How was the exam?" Demi asks.

"Fuck knows," says Monica.

I laugh. "I *think* it went well. Let's hope my luck is

changing." The three-hour exam flew by, and by the end of it I had a banging headache and cramp in my hand, but I'm confident I've managed to scrape at least a C.

I pull my pillow out of my bag and drop it on to the ground next to Lena. "May as well use this damn pillow while it's here," I say as I kick my sandals off and settle on to it cross-legged.

"Ooh, speaking of pillows – I humped one the other day," says Lena.

"And?" I say.

"Couldn't feel a thing."

Demi shakes her head. "Shame."

"On the plus side, despite not finding my way to an orgasm or the meaning of life, yet, I have decided on my next step after uni. I'm going to train as a transpersonal coach. Think life coach meets spirit."

Seems like trusting the universe has worked out for Lena after all.

"You're going to be the absolute best at that," I say.

Lena beams. "The stars have truly aligned."

I pull my phone from my pocket to take a picture of the adorable little hamper Lena has brought, but the notification blinking at me makes my stomach somersault. It's a name I've not seen on my screen for a long time, however much I've wished for it.

Joel.

I blink, frozen.

"Everything OK?" Lena looks at me, eyes squinting with concern.

"Mmm. Just having a brain fart." I smile and shove my phone into my bag.

The topic of conversation moves quickly from the trauma of our exams to the excitement of university next year, and although I try hard to be part of the conversation whirling around me, I'm somewhere else entirely.

"Have you pulled your application to Sunderland yet?" Lena says, bringing me back to the present. She's threading two daisies together to form a chain to match the one she's balancing precariously on her head.

Demi stares at me. "You have, right?"

And here I am again, at a crossroads. What I say next has the potential to open up that gulf between us once more.

"I haven't yet."

Lena drops one end of the daisy chain and frowns. Demi looks at Monica.

"What do you mean, you haven't yet?"

"Ahhh," I wail. "It just feels so final, you know? I don't feel ready to let it all go just yet." I pause. "And there's something else too."

"What?"

"Tell us."

"Rose!"

"OK! Joel just texted me, like, two minutes ago." I tear at a clump of grass to fill the shocked silence that greets my admission.

"What?" Demi looks furious. "He broke your heart – why is he sliding back into your DMs now? Convenient it's when you're all healed!"

Lena steps in. "What did he say?"

"I haven't opened it yet."

"Open it now. Let's see what the prick has to say for himself." Demi sits forward, but Monica puts her hand on her shoulder gently.

"She doesn't have to if she doesn't want to," she says.

"It's OK. I'll open it. I'd rather do it now with you guys here."

I reach into my bag and pull out my phone with shaking hands. I tap on the message and read it.

Joel: Hey. I hope everything is OK with you? Fancy a Nando's and a catch-up? X

He wants to see me again. I do mean something to him. My heart continues to hammer. Am I going to pass out?

"What does it say?"

"Put us out of our misery then!"

I hand my phone to Lena, who then reads it aloud.

Demi huffs, Monica hmms and Lena says nothing.

"I don't trust him," Demi says. "What if he wants to use and then dump you again? I highly advise you against going back there."

I know she's only trying to protect me, but I need to think about this for myself.

"Maybe I want to use him. I thought you were all about female empowerment?"

Demi blinks. "You can do what you like. But you've been through a lot to get here so make sure whatever you do is actually what you want."

Lena nods emphatically. "Don't lose sight of your worth."

"I won't. I'm not stupid," I say. "I'll be sure to set some ground rules before meeting up with him."

Demi's still scowling, but it's not up to her. For the first time in a long time the next decision I make is up to me and me alone. I'd be lying if I said that doesn't feel a little bit good.

"What sort of rules are you thinking?" asks Monica as she massages Demi's shoulders.

"Well, if we're going to be friends, then we need to be honest with each other. If there's anyone else on the scene, for instance, we need to be open about that." That's what mature adults do, isn't it? Set boundaries. Although the thought of other people being on Joel's scene makes me feel sick.

Monica nods. "Sounds like a solid plan."

But Demi purses her lips. "I'm still not sure about it, but I trust you know what you're doing." She leans back into Monica's legs.

"Yeah, and keep us in the loop this time," says Lena. "Here, give me your wrist." She proceeds to slide her finished daisy chain over my hand. "Beautiful bracelet for a beautiful woman."

To my relief, the conversation moves away from Joel and back to how LSE, in Demi's words, has a *banging debating society*. As the initial wave of adrenaline I had when I saw his name in my inbox dissipates, I start to wonder am I just kidding myself? Yes, I want to see Joel again – on my terms. But am I really the one in control here?

38

I'm sitting opposite Joel sharing a Fanta and chatting over peri-peri spiced chips. Nando's music is the same as it's always been, and Joel's still unconsciously nodding his head to the rhythm. It's like the old times, sort of. Like the old times, but with a gigantic elephant in the room that isn't welcome at the table because I won't let it get too close. It can keep its massive swinging trunk away from me – too-large trunks are what got us into this mess in the first place. Jokes aside, I've been through too much to deny myself this one last chance at a happy-ever-after. I've not told Sammy, which feels naughty, but Demi and Lena know I'm here. They're not happy about it.

The minute we sat down we slipped quickly back into our old selves, pretending like we haven't just spent the last month ignoring each other's existence. The only sign of that being we have more stuff to talk about.

Joel plucks a chip from my plate after scarfing all his own. "Work still going well?" he says, eyes looking greener than ever.

"Work's good. They're keeping me on the rota for when I'm back during uni holidays and stuff."

Joel smiles and nods. We sit quietly for a bit and I busy myself with eating. Things don't feel comfortable any more and it's weird to feel awkward in the presence of someone who's seen me naked. Thankfully, Joel breaks the silence.

"I suppose I'd better stop skirting the subject and ask about your situation." Joel nods towards my lap.

A chip catches in my throat. Is he really asking me about my op before saying sorry about the other *situation*? The one where he ghosted me for ages and broke my heart? I compose myself, but it might be too late to hide the shock plastered on my face. *Keep it casual, Rose. Don't let him see you as weak or needy.*

"You don't beat around the bush, do you?" I laugh. "Some things don't change."

Was that aloof enough?

"So…?" Joel pushes chicken bones around his plate.

I can see he's desperate to know more, curiosity

outweighing his attempt to play it cool. It wouldn't be the worst thing in the world to share some details about the operation, would it? I wouldn't mind a bit of sympathy and for him to acknowledge what I've been through. It feels quite nice to be in control of the conversation for once.

"What do you want to know?" I rein back my desire to dump the whole story on him. I want to keep the power in my court and make him work for it.

Joel shrugged. "Is it, you know, working? Fixed?"

Is that it? That's all he wants to know?

"Don't you want to ask me how it went?" My voice wavers, betraying me. "It was really scary, being put under and all that. I wasn't sure I was going to wake up." My stomach constricts as I remember that moment then I shove it away.

Joel grins. "Some things never change, you little drama queen." His playfulness does nothing to stop it from feeling like he's just smacked me in the face. The voice in my head is screaming now. *DON'T LET HIM SEE YOU AS WEAK OR NEEDY*, it bellows.

I take a deep breath. "I'm not being dramatic. Going under general anaesthetic always carries some risks and I'm a worrier." There's an edge to my voice that wasn't there before.

"Yeah, but it's hardly open-heart surgery, is it?"

"Well, no. And I'm grateful for that, but it doesn't mean it wasn't a hard time for me."

"Yeah." Joel nods. "S'pose so."

Not exactly the gushing sympathy I'd hoped for, but maybe I'm expecting way too much from someone who couldn't possibly understand what it was like.

"So how is it? How long does it take for these things to heal?"

"A few weeks." I take a slurp of Fanta in the hope of drowning out any more questions. "Anyway, less about me. How's your mum?"

"So you've almost healed then. Bet you're relieved about that."

"Mmmmm. I'm glad it's over, yeah. How did your exams go?"

Joel squints at me and cocks his head. He sighs. Finally he takes the hint.

"Yeah, fine. Pretty much done now, so not much to say."

"Cool."

"Cool."

Joel picks up his fork and spins it in his hand. He taps it on the table a few times with a tinny clang. "You grumpy now?"

My chips churn in my stomach – they haven't even had time to digest and Joel is already going back there again. Doesn't he want this to work as much as I do? Why can't he see that we can't keep doing the same thing and expect different results? It's up to me now. If I don't handle this in a certain way, then everything will be ruined.

Breathe.

"Grumpy? No, why would you say that?"

Swallow the anger down.

"You just seem a bit funny with me asking about your op." Joel takes a slurp of Coke and the glass smacks the wood as he puts it down.

"I'm not being funny with you." I smile and frown at the same time, hoping my face is clearly saying: *Nope, you've got it all wrong!*

"*I'm not being funny with you*," Joel echoes in a high-pitched mocking voice.

"I'm really not." I roll my eyes, shake my head and lose the deranged smile. I'm done trying to be cool. It takes two mature people to have a mature conversation. What more can I do?

The waiter chooses a good time to come and see if our food is OK, and Joel and I put on our happy faces and nod effusively until the guy leaves.

I chase the remainder of my rice around my plate for

360

what feels like for ever, waiting for Joel to say something. He looks at the ceiling, then at the floor, then at me. He smiles awkwardly. I mirror him, but my thin smile wobbles and I shake my head, blinking. I will not cry. *Please, God, or whoever is out there, send me a miracle.*

And for once my prayers are answered.

"I'm sorry." Joel's funny fake smile is replaced with a look of genuine sorrow. My body and soul collapse with relief. The old Joel is still there, lurking under this overconfident banter and mask of *I'm fine; everything's great with me.* He reaches for my hand. I should snatch it away, but the warmth of his touch muddles my head and I can't think straight. "Come here. I'm only messing. Sorry, I'm really nervous about this."

I didn't think he had it in him to be nervous, not about this anyway. I say as much.

"How could I not be nervous?" he says. "I've missed you so, so much. Life hasn't been the same without you."

"Really?" If he missed me that much, why did he ignore my text? Why didn't he reach out? "You could have messaged."

Joel's thumb rubs mine. Has he been using hand cream?

"I know. I kept writing a reply, but I couldn't say everything I needed to and just ended up deleting it and chickening out. I blocked you on socials because I didn't

361

want to see what you were up to without me. It was shitty, I know."

The thought that Joel was also desperately fiddling with his phone, writing messages that he'd never send, hadn't crossed my mind. I guess people deal with break-ups differently, but would it have been that hard to send me *something*?

"I didn't need much." My grip on Joel's hand tightens. "Anything to know you cared."

"Well, I did, didn't I? We wouldn't be sitting here otherwise."

He made me wait almost six weeks in painful purgatory, but I suppose he did reach out eventually. The glimpse of the Joel I love shifts something in me and I find myself feeling a bit more confident. There are a few things I need to say in order for this to be OK. I take my hand back and cross my arms in front of me.

"That's true. I'm going to need some reassurance from you if you want to do this again." I gesture at the two of us. For a moment I hesitate. Should I backtrack? I've finally got him back opposite me; the last thing I want to do is push him away by being too demanding…

But he just nods again. "That sounds fair."

It does? I try not to let my relief show and start picking at my napkin.

Joel stares at me, eyes genuine and full of remorse. "I want to do whatever I can to reassure you that I'm not going to be a dick again."

"I just need to know that you're as committed to this as much as I am." The words fall out of my mouth and hang in the air between us.

"I'm committed to whatever this is."

Joel makes a good point. What is *this*?

I keep speaking without really thinking about what I'm saying. "And we can take things slowly, as friends to start?" Is that even what I want? I don't know. I just know it's what people say. I look at my napkin, now torn to shreds on the table in front of me.

"Of course."

Well, that's that then. I have some sort of commitment, although to what I don't know. But, even though I don't know, it feels good.

"I'm so glad we're here together." Joel reaches for my hand again and grips it hard. He cocks his head and bites his lip.

"Me too." I squeeze his hand despite myself.

We look at each other, neither of us loosening our grip on the other. I wonder if Joel can feel me shaking. I don't know about him, but I never want to let go.

39

It really is a case of use it or lose it, I'm afraid. Words said by Doctor Andrews that will haunt me for the rest of my life.

I've just seen her for the last time and I've officially been discharged. So why then am I sitting here with my knickers off and Promises in my hand? Well, before discharging me, she informed me that my new vagina requires regular upkeep – news to me.

I waited for her to laugh at her joke, but she didn't.

Mum coughed. "What does that mean?" she said, alarm noticeable in her voice.

"It's important to keep up with the vibrator or dilators until Rose is having frequent penetrative sex. It's highly unlikely to go back to how it was; however, with some of these skin conditions, there is the possibility of recurrence.

As Rose doesn't have an active case of the condition, it should be fine, but it doesn't hurt to keep everything in working order."

So, although I *should* be fine, I'm taking no chances. The plan is to test it out quickly and get back to my revision. But can it really be that simple?

If I was still with Joel, I'd no doubt have checked things out sooner. But I've been putting it off because, deep down, I'm worried the operation hasn't worked.

Out comes the Shame Sack and I get into my usual position. I close my eyes and take a deep breath.

I push Promises in a tiny bit, waiting for it to hurt. It doesn't. I keep my breath steady, making sure I'm relaxing as much as I can. I push some more, and then some more. My heart hammers as I watch Promises disappear into me a centimetre at a time. I'm not breathing as I continue to push slowly. What is happening?

It's in. It's actually in.

It doesn't feel pleasurable and it's tight and uncomfortable, but it doesn't hurt, and my sheets are still fresh white with no crimson stain to mark a failure.

I pull Promises out and focus on steadying my breath. I want to dance and scream and cry and laugh, all at once.

It worked. *I* work. Now what?

40

Joel and I are at the bowling alley and arcade, pretty confident that no one we know above the age of sixteen is sad enough to hang out here any more. Joel asked me to meet up again because, in his words, he was bored. I told myself he said that because he didn't want to look too keen, but I still wish I wasn't so weak when it comes to him. I said yes as soon as his message hit my inbox. It's pathetic, but I love how in the few hours we've spent together recently the heaviness that's hung over me since the day he left feels so much lighter that I can almost forget it's there. Now I get why Holly found it so hard to let Robert go.

We play on the dance mat, fail to win a teddy on a claw machine, and I obliterate Joel in a game of air hockey. It's nice to just have fun – we definitely lost that towards the end of our relationship.

After all that excitement, Joel offers to get us some drinks from the cafe.

"Lemonade, please. Just going for a quick wee," I say, still struggling to catch my breath from the overzealous air-hockeying.

"You look like you need a cold shower after that." Joel salutes me as he moves towards the bar. I head to the loos, but turn round to glance at him one more time. He's had the same idea because I catch his eye and he blows me a kiss, causing butterflies to assault my stomach.

After I'm done in the loo, I do a quick phone check. I definitely felt it vibrate a few times when I was with Joel.

Lena: WHO THE CHUFF IS THIS?

She's attached a photo clearly taken at a party, of a couple grinning, arms wrapped round each other. I don't know who the girl is, but I know who's with her.

Joel.

My hands shake as I zoom in. Her chocolate-coloured hair with face-framing layers is perfection – the sort of hair I'd take to my hairdresser as inspiration, knowing I'd never get my own flat hair to do anything of the sort. Her lips are plump and her eyes are that sexy feline shape, paired perfectly with a tiny chin that's both sharp and soft at the same time.

Who is she and how does Joel know her?

Rose: Where did you get that?

Lena: Holly screenshotted it from Tom's story the other night. Wasn't sure if she should say anything so I said I'd ask you. Her name is Hannah but her profile is private :(

It makes me feel sick, but I zoom back in again to take a look at her body and the way Joel's arm snakes round her waist. My mouth is dry, but no amount of swallowing makes any difference.

I need to ask him who the hell she is, but I also need to stay rational. If I act jealous (again), he'll leave (again). I need to tame this jealous monster, wrap it in heavy chains and drop it into the deepest part of the ocean.

I walk to the bar in a daze, almost toppling over a child in the process.

At the table I act normal. Sip my drink. Say thank you. Work out how the hell I can ask him who Hannah is without seeming like a stalker.

"What's up? You seem weird again," Joel says, head cocked.

Deep breath. "I'm fine. I just saw you in a photo with someone called Hannah. Who is she?" I try to say it casually.

Joel wrinkles his nose, a massive cheesy grin plastering itself across his face. "You been stalking me again?"

A hot and cold chill of shame engulfs me. "Don't flatter yourself. Lena sent me it."

Joel looks bemused. "So *she's* stalking me?"

"Stop! I'm just curious."

"OK," replies Joel in an *if you say so* way. "We met at a party a few weeks back."

I nod and bite my lip.

Joel still has a glint in his eye and an annoying twitch at the corners of his mouth. "Don't be like that – we aren't together, remember? 'Just friends'."

Using my own words against me feels like a rogue bowling ball to the stomach. He's the one who blew me a kiss less than five minutes ago.

My head goes straight to the place I've been desperately trying to avoid – what if Joel has done stuff with other girls in those weeks when we had no contact? What if he's had sex with someone? He could've done whatever he wanted and I wouldn't have a leg to stand on – he was well and truly single. So much for commitment. I knew I should have made it clearer what I meant by that.

I stammer a reply. "I-I know that we aren't together…"

Joel's eyes soften. "Please don't get upset again."

I look up at the ceiling and blink manically. I want to be

this fun, refreshed version of myself, not the one who still cries every time we are together. Why do I have to be so goddamn fragile?

"I'm fine," I say when I manage to compose myself. Not a single tear falls from my eyes. "It's just hard." My voice wobbles but doesn't crack. Perhaps my shell is hardening after all.

"If it makes you feel better, she's a friend. There's not been anyone else since you."

Relief floods me. My heartbeat retreats from my ears and finds its way back into my chest. It's what every cell in my body wanted to hear, but I couldn't let myself believe it until I heard it from him.

"Same for me. No one else but you." I smile.

As the evening progresses, I try to hold on to Joel's words. *There's not been anyone else since you.* But I can't stop picturing Hannah's sharp chin and catlike eyes. I can't let go of the thought that my style is nowhere near as fashionable as hers or that she could be much more skilled in the sex department than I am. The worst part is the voice that whispers: *Hurry up or she'll get there first...*

41

Things between Joel and I are going swimmingly – and not just a leisurely breaststroke but a full-pelt front crawl. We've been messaging like crazy and things have got way more flirty. We're not expressing our love to each other, but he turns most conversations into chats about sex and I've been entertaining it. At one point he was even playing with himself while he asked me very rude questions.

I don't know how I feel about it. As seems to be my general state of being now, I have two conflicting voices battling to be heard – the classic Angel and the Devil. This is how the debate goes in my head:

Devil: *He wants you. He could have anyone else and he's still chosen you. He could've got with Hannah but* didn't. You're special to him. If you weren't, he wouldn't be here.

Angel: *He just wants to get his rocks off and you're the easiest option. He knows you still love him and he's using you.*

Devil: *But it makes you feel good. You deserve this after everything you've been through.*

Angel: *You don't like it; it makes you feel dirty and used. You deserve better after everything you've been through.*

Devil: *You want Joel, don't you? Now you've got him. Why can't you use him? #feminism*

Angel: *You haven't got him. You might feel close to him in these moments, but is it real? What about everything he's done that wasn't OK? The Devil wouldn't know feminism if it smacked him in the face.*

Devil: *He still loves you. This is the way to his heart; you just need to give it time.*

Angel: *After everything he's put you through, do you really want him back? You're so close to letting him go — do you really want to go through all that heartbreak again?*

Me (when I finally find my voice): *I DON'T KNOW. Shut up, I beg you.*

Angel and Devil: *The power is in your hands.*

At least they agree on something.

★

Joel and I are sitting on the grass in the park with my bare feet on his lap while he massages my toes. It's fairly PG, but for some reason it doesn't feel it. We've just been for a walk and we ended up holding hands. It felt so natural it wasn't until twenty minutes in that I realized maybe we shouldn't have been doing it – unless we've now crossed the threshold from friends to more than friends through habit rather than a conscious decision. I take my feet off his lap, put some space between us and look over to the entrance of the park. Imagine if Sammy appeared out of nowhere and saw us? She'd kill me if she found out. It doesn't make for a very relaxing experience.

"You're so sexy, do you know that?" Joel shuffles over and closes the gap I just put between us.

My stomach flips. "Really?" I say, not knowing how to respond. Do I want him to think I'm sexy? Is it too soon to go back *there*? I smile and grimace at the same time. "Thanks?"

Our eyes meet and I don't have time to think before his lips meet mine and his tongue is in my mouth. My arms hang limply in Joel's lap as one of his hands reaches round to the nape of my neck. Is this what I want? I don't know. It feels like Joel is having no such doubts. I continue to kiss him back, going through the motions. I don't want to ruin what we've built back up, despite his tongue feeling like a lukewarm slug in my mouth.

He pulls away, grinning. "Let's go back to mine. Mum's not in."

My heart stops and then suddenly starts beating again at double speed. An empty house. We both know what that means.

"I don't know. It's getting late." I'm not mentally prepared for this to happen right now.

Joel's smile falters.

"All right, just for half an hour. Otherwise Sammy will get suspicious."

I don't know why that slipped out, but Joel's smiling again. The entire walk back to his I can't think straight. What am I doing? This is it, the thing I've been working towards for so long. There's nothing stopping me from having sex with him. No fear of pain; no fear of the unknown because nothing can possibly be worse than everything I've already been through. And that's terrifying. If I have sex with Joel, I can never take it back. But if I don't have sex with him, he'll have sex with someone else, and that scares me just as much.

We're on Joel's bed before I've even had a chance to ask for a glass of water.

My mouth is dry despite the fact I'm swallowing continuously and I switch to performance mode, fuelled by adrenaline.

I move on top of him, kissing and caressing him, showing him what he's been missing. His skin is softer than I remember beneath my stroke, which is more urgent than I remember too. Urgent or desperate? No time to work it out.

Off comes Joel's top, joined swiftly by his jeans. How is it possible that the sight of his freckled chest and that mole on his collarbone feels alien *and* familiar? Why does this feel so right and so wrong?

My top is off now and Joel's tugging at my skirt. It slips off my legs and in a blink I'm beneath Joel, his body looming over mine.

"Do you want to, you know?" Joel says into the crook of my neck.

Do I? Yes. No. Don't know.

I need more time.

"I'm still a bit sore down there," I whisper, as Joel nuzzles his nose in the space beneath my ear.

He pulls back. "Oh, OK." Something flickers across his eyes but it's gone before I can work out what it means.

"Soon," I say, going back to hungrily kissing his shoulder blade. Hopefully showing some willing is enough to convince him I'm telling the truth, not just buying time.

Joel moans beneath my kisses, his skin warm beneath the damp of my lips.

"How about at Holly's end-of-exams party?" he says, kissing my collarbone in the space between the words.

"Perfect," I hear myself saying. That's three days away.

"Mmmmmm, can't wait."

"Me neither," I say in a voice that isn't mine.

From the moment I made my promise, it was textbook fooling around, exactly as we would've done before. I made all the right noises and did what I could to make him feel good and to make me feel good enough.

A part of me enjoyed feeling his skin on mine. He kissed me and cuddled me and held me and looked at me in the way he used to. I loved how easy it was to make him feel good, and I loved how, for those moments, he was mine and only mine.

But a bigger part of me didn't love how he smelt different and wore a different brand of boxer shorts. I didn't love how he closed his eyes when I went down on him in case he was imagining I was someone else. And I didn't love how, even though all the motions were the same, the energy between us felt dead, or at least in the final throes of dying.

42

I don't want to go to Holly's end-of-exams party, but I also don't *not* want to go. If I go, I'll have sex with Joel. If I don't go, Joel and I will be truly over – for real this time – and he'll have sex with someone else. I don't like the sound of either.

Having sex with him *should* be everything I've wanted this whole time. It means we can lose our virginity to each other and things will be as they were supposed to be all those months ago. It will symbolize the end of all the rubbish we've been through and the start of a new phase of our relationship. Even Doctor Andrews said use it or lose it – so why don't I feel like celebrating?

For a start, I know how Lena, Demi and Sammy would feel if I did have sex with Joel. As much as I want to say balls to what other people think, I do care. If I was channelling Lena, I'd say that the universe clearly doesn't want us to do it and it was never meant to be. If I was channelling Demi, I'd say Joel's an arsehole and that I'm better off alone than with someone who doesn't recognize my worth.

So what if I channel Rose? It seems that, no matter what choice I make, there's always the risk of regret. Regret for having sex with Joel or regret for not having sex with Joel. Go figure.

Getting ready to leave for the party with Lena and Demi, I can barely sit still. Demi is faffing with her hair and Lena is topping up my glass, but all I can do is pace back and forth from Lena's room to the bathroom and back again, under the guise of taking photos and touching up my make-up. The amount of adrenaline fizzing through my veins makes sitting still impossible.

"Come on, the party started an hour ago."

Demi's brow furrows. "You don't usually mind being fashionably late."

"I'm just bored waiting," I say.

Demi thrusts my drink towards me. "Down that and you won't be bored."

Maybe if I drink enough, it will calm me down. I gulp the wine, gagging at its sharp aftertaste.

Lena is frowning at me. "Is Joel going tonight by any chance?"

"I think so," I say, even though I know for sure he is.

Lena continues to frown.

"What are you worried about? Other people judging you for being mates with him?" says Demi, finally turning the curlers off with a flourish.

I hadn't even considered what other people might think about seeing Joel and me being friendly. I'll add that to the list of reasons to panic. It certainly sits below number one – agreeing to have sex with him.

I did debate telling Lena and Demi about my and Joel's agreement, but I want to wait until I'm sure it's even a thing. I can't face telling them and him not turning up, and I want to make this decision for me, not for anyone else. If I do go ahead with it, they will be the first to know – I'm not holding on to any more secrets – but whether I'm having sex with him or not, I want the choice to be mine.

Lena squints. "You do seem a bit nervy."

I wish she wasn't so perceptive. Time for the half-truth.

"I thought I was hiding it well. I'm feeling anxious, yeah. It's weird, isn't it? Seeing Joel in a big group. The dynamics are obviously going to be different to when we were together and when it's just us." Why do my eyes feel hot when I say that? I busy myself with pulling my heels on.

"That's understandable. Stick with us and we'll look after you." Lena's hand is warm and gentle on the small of my back.

I spin to her and smile. Don't cry.

"Yeah, if he acts like a dickhead, we'll sort him out," says Demi.

I feel like a fraud. The girls think I'm this strong woman, totally in control of the decisions I'm making, when actually I feel the complete opposite. I have no idea what I'm doing or what I want – all I know is that I still love Joel, despite the fact that he hurt me. And it seems easier to ride this roller coaster of confusion *with* Joel than live the rest of my life *without* him. Forever is such a long time.

"He's acting like a bit of an arsehole, isn't he? Why hasn't he come over to say hi yet?" Demi's arms are crossed and she's tapping her foot, surveying Joel who turned up fifteen minutes ago and is currently swanning from one group of people to another. He's also managing to expertly avoid the corner of the living room where Lena, Demi and I are hovering.

"Maybe he's just feeling nervous like me?" I say, aware

that my stomach's been doing flips since the second he arrived. But knowing what we did a few days ago and how lovey-dovey he acted, he should at least acknowledge my existence.

"Maybe," says Lena, scrunching her nose.

"Also, since when has he ever been this loud and obnoxious?" Just as Demi says this, Joel guffaws with laughter and then gestures to Tom to go outside for a vape.

"He is being a bit loud." I'm glad it's not just me that's noticed his apparent total personality change from the person who would quietly mingle to this guy who vapes like a nobhead and works the room like he's God's gift.

There's a loud rap at the window, making all three of us girls jump – clearly no one can hear the doorbell over the music and most people are outside or in the kitchen, not hiding in the corner, desperately trying to avoid seeing their peacocking ex-boyfriend.

Demi rolls her eyes. "I suppose I'd better get that, seeing as no one else is."

She trots out of the room and I hear her open the door and the sound of heels clacking on the laminate floor. A group of girls teeter into the living room, a pungent cloud of perfume and biscuity tan marking their entrance. They make their way to the open patio doors at the far end with

Demi following close behind them, pulling a face and mouthing, "Who the hell are they?"

It takes me a second to work out why the girl striding confidently at the centre of the gaggle looks so familiar.

"Is that who I think it is?" says Lena, confirming I'm not seeing things.

It's Hannah. At the same party as my sort-of-single ex-boyfriend, looking absolutely drop-dead gorgeous. She's wearing jeans and a skimpy top and her hair is bouncy and voluptuous yet effortless at the same time. My body-hugging satin mini-dress seems disgustingly try-hard in comparison. What was I thinking?

"Oh," says Demi as the penny drops. "Joel had better not have invited her. Are you OK?" She reaches for my wrist and squeezes it.

I force a smile. "Fine. Yeah. He'd have told me if he had." I try to sound cool but my voice wavers.

I'm very close to purging the rosé from earlier as it sits dangerously high in my throat. It's done nothing to make me feel drunk and carefree — all it's done is make me feel sick. I can't just sit here and let Joel and Hannah bond and then fall in love. It's now or never.

Rose 2.0 is back. Ish. I don't think I'm quite as tipsy as at prom, but it's enough to give me the confidence I need to mingle outrageously with everyone here and ensure I am noticed by Joel. There's no way he can miss me now. I'm parading around in front of him every chance I get. Take that, Hannah. I might not be sure whether I want to have sex with him, but I don't want you to get there before I've decided. I've been through too much to have this yanked from my grasp.

In the garden, Holly is outrageously flirting with a guy I vaguely recognize.

I reach for her hand. "Hollyyyyy! Come. Please," I say.

"I'm all yours." She grins, before glancing back at said guy. "I'll be back."

"All right, Arnold Schwarzenegger." I lead her to a quieter corner. "How are you doing?" Rob's here but she's not looked once in his direction. That might mean nothing – Joel and I haven't either – but I have a feeling that Holly has let go of Robert for good now. Still, I'm keen to check in.

"Honestly couldn't be better."

"And Rob…?"

"Who?" Holly laughs, but it's not one of those laugh-or-you'll-cry ones; it's totally genuine. "Binned him off, totally. Never going back there. I mean it. Thank you for everything; it must have been like watching a car crash in slow motion, trying to counsel me through that shitshow."

She's pretty spot on, but I don't say so. "Always happy to be of service. Now I shall let you get back to that fitty over there."

Holly pulls me into a hug and squeezes my hand as she walks away.

I rejoin Lena and Demi at the bottom of the garden and survey my surroundings. Joel and Tom are standing with a few other guys and Hannah's crew are way too close to them for comfort. I shift from one foot to the other.

"I'm going to talk to him. Screw all this game-playing." My ankle rolls. Grass and heels aren't the easiest things to navigate, especially after a few glasses.

Demi grabs my wrist, but has to hold on to the tree beside her to stop herself from falling too. "Strong independent woman not taking any shit." She punches the air with her fist and topples.

"You are amazingggggg." Lena pats me on the head with the base of her Coke glass.

"Thankssss, my lil Moony-G," I say.

Am I being a strong independent woman going to him and not waiting for him to come to me? Or am I just being desperate? Whatever it is, I can't wait any longer.

"Want backup?" says Demi as she squints at her phone. She looks fierce in the light from its screen. I'm not sure I should subject Joel to her wrath, and anyway, if we're going to … you know … I can't make that decision under the judging eyes of my beautifully outspoken friend.

"I'll be OK. Thanks, though." I surprise myself by saying it in a way that says, *I'm confident – I've got this*, and not *OMG, am I about to make a really terrible decision?*

Demi shrugs. "If you're sure. Monica just texted saying she's stuck at the end of the garden with a guy who's decided he could turn her 'fully straight'. Dickhead. I'm going to kill him… Coming?" She looks at Lena.

Lena nods emphatically. "Er, definootley."

"Good luck," I say.

"I think you need it more."

I stride up to Joel and the girls in Hannah's group turn to look at me. *Don't fall over, look confident.*

"Long time no see." I say it so boldly I'm surprised I don't follow it up with a wink.

Joel looks taken aback, his eyes wide and dazed. Bet he didn't think I'd have the balls to approach him in front of Hannah. Just as quick as shock flicks across his face, it goes and is replaced with a cheesy grin. "'Ello, 'ello."

"Don't I get a hug?" I say, holding my arms out to him.

He hugs me quickly, but it's long enough for me to get a whiff of the new scent he's wearing. It's so strong I hold back a cough.

"Hi, Tom." I hug him too, not wanting to be rude.

"All right," he says, looking at me and then at Joel. "I'll leave you both to it?"

A look passes between them; I wonder whether Tom knows about our plan. What if he says something to Lena and Demi?

Joel smiles awkwardly. "Want a drink?"

"Always," I say, although I'm not sure another one is a good idea. I do, however, really need a wee and want to remove myself from Hannah and her friend's prying eyes.

I follow Joel up the garden path back to the house. Once inside he pours me another glass of wine and opens another beer for himself.

"I thought I'd never get you alone," he whispers, despite the fact that the kitchen is totally empty.

"You didn't try that hard."

Joel looks hurt. "I didn't want to embarrass you. Wasn't sure if your friends knew you were seeing me again."

"Are you sure it's not because *you* were embarrassed? About me?"

What if he didn't want Hannah to see him messing around with his ex? Perhaps I'm being harsh. *Be cool.*

"Pretend I didn't say that. Lena and Demi know; it's all good."

Joel audibly sighs and steps towards me, pulling me into his chest. It feels weird and perfect at the same time.

"Let's go to the bathroom; it's more private," he whispers in my ear.

Before I let myself think about what that means, I allow my hand to be engulfed in his and I'm led out of the door and up the stairs. I gulp my wine and it's gone by the time we reach the landing.

Joel locks the door behind us.

"I need a wee," I state before he can say anything else. It buys me just a bit more time. I need to be sure about whether I want this or not. I need to know I'm doing it for the right reasons, and also I read somewhere about not having sex with a full bladder. Oh my God, am I going to have sex?

Joel chuckles and then leans on the door with his hands in his pockets, watching me. "Go for it."

"Turn round."

"I'll close my eyes."

I shimmy out of my specially chosen lacy knickers and do the biggest wee I've ever done in my life. I'm not embarrassed, though – why should I be? Joel's witnessed plenty of cringe moments during Operation Penetration. Anyway, I'm too preoccupied with the thoughts in my head. Do I want to have sex with Joel? And do I want to do it right now?

The room spins around me as the wine I've just downed hits me.

I pull my knickers back up, gripping the side of the bath to stop myself from staggering sideways. I wash my hands, my reflection fuzzy in the mirror as I try to focus. Here I am again, staring existentially into a mirror. The last time I did this I had the overwhelming sense that everything was going to change – and it did, just not how I thought it would. How am I back here again – a virgin staring back at me, with that same overwhelming sense that everything is about to change once more?

Everything I've been through in the last eight months floods my brain, threatening to drown me. Suffering not just physical pain but humiliation too. The doctor's appointments and the physio. Promises and the operation. Being dumped in this very room. I've endured so much to be able to have this moment that I need to know for sure it's what I want, but I can't make that choice a) drunk and b) in Holly's toilet.

"Nice pants." Joel's comment sucks me back to the room.

I spin round and lean my bum on the sink. I cross my arms and frown at him. "You said you wouldn't look."

"Sorry, I couldn't help it. You're too sexy." He takes a step towards me. The air is ripped out of my lungs.

"Gross. There's nothing sexy about doing a wee." I frown some more. Keep him talking, stop this from escalating. I cross my ankles too.

"Everything is sexy when you do it."

Joel's right in front of me now, nuzzling his lips into my neck. I'm tense as I shuffle to stop myself from slipping off the sink.

"Relax, I've got you." Joel slides his body between my legs and his hands find my hips, holding me firmly into him. I wiggle again, the ceramic is cold on my thighs and juts uncomfortably into me.

My breath quickens as Joel starts to kiss me roughly and press his hardening crotch against my legs. I'm limp now, unsure of what to do with my arms or lips. I feel far away.

Joel's thrusts get more frequent as he pants in my ears.

"Are you ready?" Joel's thumbs stroke my inner thighs so hard I'm surprised he doesn't cause a friction burn.

Can I say no? Is it too late?

"I don't have a condom," I whisper. My head is heavy, lost in the crook of his neck.

"I do."

Joel shifts to fumble in his jean pocket and pulls out his wallet. The room continues to spin around me. I need to sit down before I fall down. I smack the lid of the toilet seat down and drop on to it.

Joel rips open the condom packet with his teeth. "Come here. I want you so bad."

I don't move.

"Do you really want to do it here?"

Joel moves quickly towards me and kneels at my feet. He's centimetres away from my face quicker than I can blink. "We deserve to have this moment together. It was always meant to be you and me. Us." His breath is hot on my face and smells of stale beer.

Us. Sounds nice, but what does it mean?

Joel reaches up and strokes my cheek. "I can't imagine doing it with anyone else but you," he says. It's everything I want to hear, but surely I at least deserve a bed? Maybe even a candle, even if it has been poached from the bathroom five minutes before?

"Not here, not in a toilet," I whisper.

Joel's face scrunches. "What about that time when you said that you didn't care where it was, as long as it was with me?"

I remember that and him saying something about the alley behind McDonald's. But so much has changed. *Too* much has changed. I was kidding myself thinking we could start over; this is no blank canvas that we can excitedly cover in colourful memories and beautiful moments. We've already been there, done that and our canvas is smeared with shit.

"I thought we were going to take it slowly, work the trust back up, find us again. I—"

Joel takes a step back. He's sort of laughing, but something tells me he's not finding this funny. "How slow do you want to go? We've been waiting for months now."

I grip the toilet as I try to steady myself.

He's not wrong. I've had long enough to decide whether this is right for me, and here we are, over seven months after our failed attempt, and I'm still having doubts. Maybe I'm more sure than I realized. Sure that this *isn't* what I want.

That voice has been there the whole time, but I haven't wanted to listen to it. It's been easy to ignore because it's not been shouting or nagging. It's eloquent and measured. It's consistent and persistent, always there, even when I let my head run round in circles. It's saying, *This isn't what you want.*

"You're right," I say, not quite believing the words coming out of my mouth. "We're over. We've been over for a long time now. I know it and you know it."

Joel shakes his head, running his hands through his hair and looking taken aback. "I didn't mean to be pushy. I just thought it would be nice for us to lose it to each other. Feels like that's the way it should have been. Before uni too."

"I thought I wanted that too for a long time. But not any more." It takes all my strength not to crumble, but I hold it together.

Joel nods slowly. "Fine. If that's what you want," he says with no discernible emotion.

I take a breath. Compose myself. "If it makes you feel better pretending you don't care, be my guest. But I know you well enough to know you're hurting too, even if you have an emotionally constipated way of showing it." My bottom lip quivers but I manage not to cry.

Joel exhales. "I'm fine. It is what it is."

"Yeah, but what it is, is very sad." My voice wobbles again.

Our watery eyes meet.

Joel bites his lip and looks at the ceiling. Tears roll down his cheeks despite his attempt to stop them. "See, totally fine over here." This time he manages a defeated chuckle.

"Do you want a hug?" I squeak.

Joel sniffs. "Go on then – bring it in."

I nestle my face into his neck like I've done a thousand times before, our skin warm and sticky with tears. His pulse beats a million per minute against my lips.

"I'm sorry we couldn't make it work," he whispers softly into my hair as I try to stop myself from completely dissolving.

My whole life I've thought that love was enough. If you love someone, you can weather anything. But that's not true. Two people who love each other aren't always going to be compatible. It doesn't mean we should cling on when we can no longer make each other happy.

Joel coughs and laughs. "I think one of your tears just slid down my top and tickled my nipple."

I pull back, a laugh forcing its way out, all snotty and snuffly. "Nice." I look into his green eyes – speckled with hazel flecks and rimmed red. Is this really what I want? To walk away and let him go?

Want? Don't know.

Need? Yes. I love him, way too much to make sense, but I love myself more.

"If it's OK, I think it's probably best we don't stay friends – at least not for a bit. Murky lines and all that," he says.

"Fair. Look where that got us before."

"Don't be offended if I unfollow you on socials again too. Makes it easier."

"Good idea." My voice breaks.

This is it now. One hundred per cent final.

"Don't – you'll set me off again." Joel shakes his head and turns away.

I love how he's still smiling, even now. I reach out for

his hand and squeeze it one last time. I can't find any words so offer him a painful smile.

Joel nods once, twice, three times and then lets go. "Guess this is it then. Good luck next year, wherever you end up. Assuming I won't bump into you around Sunderland any more."

"Not unless I get disgustingly lost."

"I wouldn't put it past you."

We both chuckle again.

"Me neither." I move to the door, feeling like I'm floating and that none of this is real. The tears are coming again.

"Thank you. For everything," I whisper.

Joel's eyes meet mine. "Right back at ya."

43

"Well done, proud of you." Sammy squeezes my arm as I officially withdraw my application to Sunderland. "Now you can email Winchester about the Psychology course. We got there in the end—"

"Yes, I get it. Lesson learnt," I say. "But there's no guarantee they'll have me now."

Sammy beams. "You won't know if you don't ask, and you can always go through clearing for a counselling-related course – that's what it's for, right?"

I wish Sammy's optimism was contagious.

"You think I have a chance?"

"I think it's likely there'll be one course with a space. And, if not, there will be another way."

"I hope so."

"Me too."

Sammy shifts to lie on her stomach and settles her head on to a massive teddy that I pulled out from beneath my bed last night when I was desperate for something to cuddle.

"You know, I think way too much focus is put on the idea of virginity. Who cares if you were each other's firsts or not?"

"Yeah?" I frown at her. "Tell me more."

Sammy nods. "I read something last night that really got me thinking. It questioned whether virginity was even a real thing."

"What do you mean?" I shut my laptop and lie next to her, wriggling under the covers.

"They said it was a 'social construct' that can't be physically proven and means something different to everyone."

"Fancy words."

"Yeah, but would you say that Demi is a virgin until she's had a penis inside her?" Sammy's eyebrows are raised inquisitively.

I've never thought about it like that before. If Demi is only ever with someone who has a vagina, does that mean she will always be a virgin? That really doesn't seem right. That makes nobs seem *far* too important.

"I don't think so. I'd have to ask her, I suppose."

"Exactly. It's up to her. Do you get it?" Sammy sits up. "Also, and this is the bit I'm especially fond of – if virginity isn't a real, tangible thing, that means that it can't be given, lost or taken."

I'm quiet for a moment. "I see what you're getting at. I like the idea that it can't be taken and that people can choose for themselves what it means."

"That's it. Choice. You've got it spot on. Anyway, have a think – it might help." Sammy walks the teddy bear up my legs and makes him pat me on the head. "I'm choosing to say that I had sex for the first time with Nicoli, but he didn't *take* anything from me, nor did I take anything from him – apart from about ten of his comfiest jumpers…"

"Mmm. It still makes me feel weird knowing Joel will lose his virginity—"

"Have penetrative sex for the first time with," Sammy corrects me.

"I think after everything I've been through, whether it's a social construct or not, the first time does feel like something special."

Sammy sighs. "I'm not saying it's not important, but it's certainly *not* simple or straightforward, is it?"

"Nope. I appreciate you trying to make me feel better."

"That's what sisters are for," says Sammy, before pulling back the covers and tucking the teddy in beside me. "In other news, I have been officially roped into reading Mum's first creative-writing piece. She's actually really good, if a little heavy on the semicolons. And, speaking of uni, I'm well jel about you having it all to look forward to. I'll be visiting as often as I can. Relive my youth."

"You are twenty-three, not an OAP. And I'm actually buzzing about uni now." Yes I'm sad, I miss Joel and I still sometimes worry that I made the wrong choice, but the idea of uni next year – wherever that might be – actually makes me feel excited and free. It only took my life falling apart before I realized it.

"And I'm gutted that my baby sis has had her first heartbreak, but I don't think it could have come at a better time. You get to do you and no one else."

"Well…"

"Yes, Rose!"

"Kidding. I can't even think about that yet. But, yeah, it's nice to know that next year will be on my terms, and it will be easier to get over Joel if I'm somewhere new, surrounded by loads of new people."

"One hundred per cent. Freshers you'll be drunk, hungover or busy socializing and then the rest of the year you'll be too busy cramming for exams or pulling all-nighters to even remember he exists."

I pull a face. "All-nighters? No thanks."

"It's fun! Our department once stayed in the building all night, ordered pizzas and had a hilarious game of hide-and-seek in the spooky corridors. We left just as people were coming in for their morning lectures." Sammy cackles.

"Maybe if you spent less time eating pizza and playing hide-and-seek, you wouldn't have to pull all-nighters."

"Oh, my dear Rose, you have a lot to learn." Sammy shakes her head and smiles. "And you have *a lot* to look forward to."

44

Roseycheeks_x: Little Wins This Week – withdrew my application to Sunderland and am hoping Winchester might take me. If not, I'm looking at other options and feeling hopeful.

Anon_69: Woop woop!!!

It_hurtttssssss: OMG, I've missed so much! Sorry I'm so late to the party on all this **@Roseycheeks_x**!!! Been busy with my uni coursework. So the op is all done? It can't have been easy but now you know everything is working (sorry, can't think of a better word!), do you think you'll have sex soon?

Roseycheeks_x: It's OK, I literally ghosted for ages when Joel and I broke up (the first time LMAO). Honestly, no to sex soon. I'm not going out of my way to meet anyone, but who knows … maybe at uni.

It_hurtttsssssss: That's so exciting!! Oh, and I think it's time I change my username. I'm thinking LubeQueen has a good ring to it.

Moongirlxoxo: It's perfect! I'll forever be Moongirl 🌝. Any more contributions to Little Wins This Week?

Endo2005: My lil contribution … sex can still be painful – fuck endometriosis 😔 – BUUUTTTT I have talked to my bf about how I feel and he's been so lovely. We've agreed to take penetration off the menu for a bit 🤸 and are just focusing on what feels good. I'll be happy if I get to a point where I don't flinch or panic when he tries to touch me.

Moongirlxoxo: That sounds positive to me. You've got this!!!

Roseycheeks_x: Love that. "Off the menu" 🤸🤸🤸🤸🤸

Anon_69: ✋ I've actually decided that I'm pretty happy not having sex … ever? For now anyway. I know things might change, but if they don't I'm fine with that too. Shout out to my therapist for helping me work that one out!!

Endo2005: Your therapist sounds fab but you are fabbier. (Is that a word?!)

TK_1000: My turn. Soz if I've been a bit of a lurker! Nothing momentous here, but I have realized that the people who call me horrible names for enjoying sex are the ones with the problem, NOT ME! Says more about them and what's going on in their own heads than what I'm choosing to do with my body 🔥

Roseycheeks_x: Think we're all smashing it tbh. RIGHTTTT I'm off to Ikea now for a uni shopping trip with my one and only **@Moongirlxoxo**. Never been more excited in my life to buy my own bog brush. Catch up later and love ya all xx

45

"Better late than never," says Demi, munching on Chinese takeaway. We're in my bedroom and we've just paid the remaining balance for our trip to Venice, booked for the week I turn eighteen, and although I'm £300 lighter I've got something to look forward to – pizza and pasta on the balcony and midnight gelato after one too many alfresco Aperol spritzes being a few of them.

"And we can consider this a joint celebration, marking Demi's LSE offer and" – Lena does a drum roll on her lap – "the Yonic Mission experiencing its first take-off."

Demi stops midway through dumping an entire pot of chicken chow mein on her plate. Her mouth drops open. "Did you orgasm?"

"Did you?" I look at Lena expectantly, ready to explode.

Lena grins from ear to ear. "Honestly, I don't know if it was an orgasm or what. What I do know is that it transcended merely physical pleasure. I'm talking body. I'm talking brain. I'm talking spirit. I'm talking *the entire universe*. It was. Amazing." Lena closes her eyes and shivers. "Big thanks to Rose for sending me that stuff on anorgasmia."

"I've got goosebumps," I say. Is this energy thing contagious?

"Will you teach me?" says Demi.

"Of course. Just come with a mind as open as your legs." Lena winks.

"That can be arranged, as long as there are no aliens involved," I say.

"No aliens," Lena wiggles her fingertips like a magician who's about to pull a rabbit out of their hat. "But it will be out of this world."

"Things always are with you," says Demi. "Speaking of, Monica and I had a really good chat the other day. Things are much better in the sex department."

"I can't tell you how happy I am for you. And well done for talking about it – it's not always easy, talking as the queen of shit communicating."

"*Ex* queen. And thank you, my lovely Rose. We have you to thank for that – future therapist in the making!"

"I'm blushing," I say.

"There's another thing too. We also invested in a bullet vibrator. Gamechanger. In the words of Shakespeare, *Though she be but little, she is fierce.*"

Lena shakes her head. "Only you could bring Shakespeare into a conversation about sex toys."

I laugh. "You minx!"

Hearing Demi talk about her new purchase and all this talk about pleasure is making me think that now it's safe for me to try Promises properly. Like, for real, on my own with no one watching – out with Operation Penetration and in with Operation Orgasm.

"Rose," says Lena. "Have you blocked Joel on your socials yet?" She pops a spring roll into her mouth and chews loudly.

"Yeah, although that only works if Holly doesn't keep messaging the group about every single post he makes."

"The pottery thing? I've had a word with her about that." Demi shakes her head.

"He's such a dick. I bought him that!"

Hannah posted a picture and tagged Joel in it of them doing the "pottery experience for two" I gave him for Christmas. That hurt a lot. I think they waited all of ten days before making it "official". Do I believe what he said at bowling about them being just friends? I do, but what difference does it make now anyway? Even if Hannah was waiting in the wings, I made my choice and that means both Joel and I are free to do whatever we want. I can't even think about being with another person yet, but everyone deals with things differently.

I often imagine Joel and Hannah walking around holding hands and saying "I love you", and I picture Hannah sitting at my place at the dinner table. I wonder whether Sonya likes her as much as she liked me and whether the happy couple argues at all or whether their relationship is perfect. I also can't shake the thought that their sex life is way more fun and adventurous than ours was and that I was doing it wrong the whole time. But I know that's not a helpful voice talking. Whenever I go there, I try to calm myself down and step into counsellor mode, this time for myself. It's working a treat and, to use Lena lingo, I reckon I've had a real spiritual awakening recently. I guess going through a shitty time sort of forces that on you.

My time in the VagWarriors chat, being an accidental confidante to various people and muddling through my own struggles has taught me that there's so much more to sex than what's going on physically. It can be part of sex, but not for everyone and it's not the only part. The mind is important. So is how we talk to ourselves. Over the past nine months, I've told myself all sorts of rubbish – like I owe Joel or that having sex with him would make me more worthy of his love. Yet I've been the total opposite with my friends, talking to them with a kindness and a compassion that for some reason I could not extend to myself. But I'm finally ready to cut myself some slack, starting now. Better late than never, right?

Being nice to yourself is not easy in a world where we're constantly battling against what others are saying and doing, and telling us how we should or shouldn't be. We're fighting low confidence, social pressure, the feeling that we're inadequate or weird or different. No wonder we feel like we need fixing. But that would imply that we're broken, which we're not. The only thing that needs fixing here is the nasty voice that tells us we aren't good enough just as we are. I can say for certain that voice is chatting absolute shit.

Demi rips me from my Barbie-esque internal monologue by bouncing a chicken ball off my head. It's hot and sticky and a bit of sauce drips down my cheek.

"That's a waste of a good ball," Lena says incredulously.

"What was that for?"

"You were thinking about him. I could tell."

I can't help but laugh. "You're right. BUT I've been thinking about something else too."

Demi puts her fork down on her plate and looks at me. "I'm listening."

"OMG, it's not Omar, is it?" Lena's eyes twinkle.

"No! What makes you say that?"

Lena shrugs. "Just a Spidey sense."

"I'm not interested in meeting anyone else. Lovely though he is."

"Maybe after uni? If it's meant to be…"

I'm not against the idea … one day. I definitely want to do uni first, but I'll keep in touch with Omar because I'm planning to keep working at Authentic Soul in the holidays.

"So what *were* you thinking about then?" says Demi.

"I'm going to the GP to ask for a referral for some therapy," I say. "I spoke to Mum and, well, I think I might need it."

Demi nods. "Good idea. You've gone through a lot. It won't necessarily go away, even if you do your best to package it up nicely into a little box and pretend it's not there."

"Preach." Lena reaches her arm round me and squeezes me into a sideways hug. "You are a brave queen and I love you."

"And don't you think it's about time you chuck that clay dick he made you?" Demi nods at the ring holder on my bedside table.

I look at it: it's the last physical piece of Joel and me. "I've only kept it this long because I use it."

"Go on! It's an eclipse tonight. A good time to let go. I'll get you another one. Or you could just glue one of your dilators to a jam lid?" Lena cackles at her own joke.

"Ha ha."

I lean over to pick it up and tip my rings on to my bedside table. They clatter as they land in a heap. It's nothing but a reminder of what is no more.

"This is it." I spin it round in my hands.

"You can do it." Lena moves her plate of food to the floor and leans forward to watch me.

I exert force on the phallic sausage of clay and snap it off. "Mmmmm, now that *was* satisfying."

"Yessssssssss!" Lena claps.

"Bye-bye, clay willy. You won't be missed." I chuck it into the bin with a clang and wait for the inevitable tears to prick the backs of my eyes.

They don't come. All right, so they might at some point in the near future, but that's OK. Because pretty soon I'll spill my last Joel-related tear, and I cannot tell you how good that feels.

Roseycheeks_x: **@MyVagVicki** Just want to say a quick thank you for sharing your journey. Without it I'd never have found my VagWarriors tribe, even when one of them was literally under my nose! You're so brave for being open about everything and although we don't have the same diagnosis I could really relate to all your content (apart from your excitement at physio 🤣) SO THANK YOU. I WISH YOU AND YOUR VAGINA ALL THE BEST <3

Acknowledgements

Big thanks to my author friends who have helped birth this book in some way: Gina Blaxill (my Day One), Louise Finch, Daisy Jervis, Zoe Fitzgibbon and Sophie Jo. You are all babes and I couldn't have stayed (relatively) sane without you.

A massive 'ta' is owed to my family. My Twinny Heather – my other half and favouritest person ever. Please forgive me for squashing you in the womb and not dedicating this book to you (you can have the next one). Ma and Pa – the best parents in the world: Pa for staying a comfortable distance from my teenage shenanigans, and Mum for being on the frontline with me and braving that shopping trip to Ann Summers on my behalf. There are no words.

Big up to my main man Liam (@Guiglit) and his red pen, who supports (most) of my (sometimes crazy) endeavours. Without your unconditional support, I wouldn't have the time or mental capacity to do all the things that I do. The guardian of my solitude. Wub wub.

My agent, Sara O'Keeffe, is everything I could ever want and need in an agent. Thank you for being brave enough to take the risk on a book with the word "flaps" in the first line, and for seeing the potential where others ran for the hills. I can always trust your feedback and wise words – whether that be to squash the doubts or take out some of the fart jokes. You're always right, and IN SARA WE TRUST.

Everyone at Scholastic, you have made the whole publishing process feel like a dream. Julia, THANK YOU SO MUCH for championing this book and for loving it as much as I do. And a huge thanks to everyone else behind the scenes. You are amazing.

The Albany lot – Carrie, Aileen, Twig, Nee, Jed and Bhav. I appreciate your support very, very much. Bhav, get your chinos out – it's time to party!

Other special people I want to name but am running out of space(!): Ellie, Steph, Bree, Kat, Emily, Victoria, Lucy, Tash and Harrie. What did I do in a past life to deserve such wonderful pals?

My counsellor Jacqui. I look forward to conducting our future (life-changing) sessions in the comfort of my own swimming pool.

And my guinea pigs: Arnold, Arthur (RIP), Rodney, Mac, Smidge and Bertie. Without your cuddles and the joy you bring to my life, I would be an overwhelmed puddle on the floor.